COME OVER, RED ROVER

COME OVER, RED ROVER

A NOVEL OF SUSPENSE

by Stephen Marlowe

THE MACMILLAN COMPANY, NEW YORK

c.3

The Macmillan Company, New York
Collier-Macmillan Canada Ltd., Toronto, Ontario
PRINTED IN THE UNITED STATES OF AMERICA

TO MY FATHER

Contents

PART ONE

The Oberland

Top USIA official Bradley Frazer, flew to Switzerland to visit his hospitalized young daughter. She said her injuries were from skiing, but he learns that she was brutally beaten.

ONE

When he drove out of the shadow of the pines at the top of the pass, the snow-reflected sunlight was so bright that it hurt his eyes.

He saw a chalet to the left of the road, the great overhanging roof heavy with snow, a wisp of smoke rising from the chimney, a man and a woman coming out of the door, carrying skis. Then they were gone, the road plunged, and a blue and white Swiss highway sign said: *Saanen, 13 km.* Saanen was the village beyond Gstaad here in the Bernese Oberland. The hospital was in Saanen.

There was a Sunday morning emptiness to the road. He had passed no one since beginning the climb to the pass at Aigle. Suddenly he saw a village below him, a huddle of chalets and a big white church with its wooden belfry. That would be Gsteig. He knew this valley well, ever since he had first skied it, years ago, with Cindy's mother. The church bells pealed in the cold crisp air, as he drove through the single street of town. A few early skiers went by in stretch pants and parkas, their faces heavily oiled against the strong March sun, their skis clipped together and slung over their shoulders like rifles.

Then he left the village behind. The road ran straight across the valley after that, and he floored the gas pedal, punishing the little rented car. He saw cattle fences and snow fences and above them the high white mountains.

They had called him long distance in Madrid, reaching him, finally, at a party in the American embassy. They had spoken French. Mr. Frazer? Mr. Bradley Pickett Frazer? He had been dancing with the daughter of the Canadian military attaché.

3

She was young and pretty, and she had been flirting with him harmlessly. She had come to the phone with him, impressed that he had been reached, at midnight in the embassy, by a long-distance call from Switzerland.

The connection had not been clear. You are the father of Miss Cindy Frazer? The voice read off a passport number. He had no idea what the number on Cindy's passport was. What is it? he asked, cutting off the voice. Bad news. An accident. Serious? he asked. Not grave physically, the voice had assured him. But emotionally . . . he had missed the next few words. She needs you, monsieur. At the hospital in Saanen. You will come?

He flew Swissair's night flight out of Madrid and was in Cointrin Airport, Geneva, at five in the morning. He had thrown some things into a suitcase. He was still wearing his dinner jacket. He called Saanen from the airport. Two cracked ribs and contusions about the neck and face, they said. Something about a night fondue party at the top of a mountain, and a fall on skis. You will hurry, monsieur?

The Hertz office at the airport opened at seven. He waited, chain-smoking and drinking coffee at the all-night buffet. Finally a sleepy girl in a stewardess's uniform gave him a Volkswagen.

Not grave physically, he thought, driving across the valley. But emotionally the girl needs you. That was what they had said. Please let me be able to help her, he thought. Let me be able to help her this time. She's only nineteen and she's had a rotten life. I've bounced around too much. A succession of boarding schools were home for her. She's a wild kid, they tell me. But she's whip smart and pretty, and there's a warmth to her. She got that from her mother. Looks like her mother, too; the same small, fine-boned face, the same high cheekbones and big grave eyes ready to crinkle with laughter.

Please, I've got to be able to help her this time.

The hospital in Saanen was an out-sized chalet not far from the small airport. Had he been able to charter a plane in

Geneva so early in the morning, it would have cut hours off his traveling time. But no pilot had been available.

Once under the roof, the overhanging eaves and the muraled walls out of sight, it was like any other hospital—the antiseptic smell, the soft squeak of rubber-soled shoes on linoleum, the nurses hurrying past poker-faced, a bell tinkling somewhere, and a Herr Doktor Herrmann being called to surgery in Schwyzerdutsch.

They were expecting him. It was a room on the first floor. There was a nurse on duty in the corridor, the receptionist said. She raised an eyebrow at his dinner jacket. He'd forgotten his coat in Madrid. He thought he'd packed a parka in his suitcase, but wasn't sure. The white carnation in his lapel was wilted.

He took the stairs two at a time and hurried along the dim hallway. At the far end a nurse was seated at a desk with a small lamp shining on the slick paper magazine she was reading.

"I'm Frazer."

The nurse was gaunt and elderly. She wore a pince nez with a black silk ribbon dangling from the left side of the frame. "Yes, of course." She spoke English with no accent. "The doctor is inside with her now."

"How is she?"

The doctor came out. He was young and his eyes were bloodshot.

"This is the next of kin, Doctor. The father."

The doctor looked at the tall, raw-boned man—broad of shoulder in his rumpled dinner jacket—who seemed surprisingly young to be the father of the girl inside.

"How is my daughter?"

The doctor shrugged. He spoke in a soft voice. "Her injuries are not serious. The ribs will give her some pain for a time. Her face will not be pretty to look at, for a week, two weeks, perhaps. You will see."

Frazer started to move past him. The doctor grasped his elbow. "Has she been under some strain lately, your daughter?"

"I don't know," Frazer admitted. "She's pretty high-strung."

"High-strung. Yes, I see." The doctor seemed troubled by something. "The accident," he said. "She claims it was a fall on skis." The smile was tired and a little cynical. "But we are possibly the world's experts on skiing accidents here in this hospital. You understand, hundreds of patients every season?"

"Yes," Frazer said impatiently. He wanted to go inside to Cindy.

"A fall on skis, hard enough to crack two ribs, with no injury to the legs? I won't say it is impossible, but . . . and then of course there are the contusions about the face and neck."

"What are you trying to say?"

"It does not seem to me to resemble a skiing accident. I would have said your daughter was beaten."

The doctor stepped aside, letting the one unexpected word, beaten, hang between them. Bradley Pickett Frazer went into his daughter's room.

He saw the overhead light, bright on the pale green of the walls, the window, shut and fogged over, the head of the high bed cranked up, and Cindy, sitting there, watching him enter, looking very small.

"Hello, Daddy."

Frazer leaned down and kissed the top of her head. Her dark hair was long and fine.

"That's some shiner you've got."

"Going to turn all kinds of interesting shades of purple and yellow, the nurse says." Cindy smiled up at him. Her cheek was swollen and discolored too, and covered with a thick, greasy ointment.

"You didn't have to come, Daddy. I'm all right. You must have been worried sick flying here." Cindy winced.

"What's the matter?"

"Darn ribs. A sticking pain when I breathe too hard. I must remember to breathe with just the top of my lungs, the nurse says. Did you ever try to breathe with just the top of your lungs?"

Cindy smiled again. Her bruised lips began to tremble. Abruptly she was crying.

"Hey, Cindy, Cindy, come on now, what is it?" He stroked her hair awkwardly.

"Leave me alone."

He jerked his hand back.

"I'm sorry, Daddy. I didn't mean that. I don't know why I'm crying. Don't mind me."

She blew her nose and winced again at the pain in her ribs.

"See any bullfights?"

"The season doesn't start till next month."

"That's right, I forgot."

"Cindy, how did it happen?"

"What? Oh, skiing." Her one good eye widened and stared directly into his eyes, and he knew she was going to lie. "There was this fondue party at the top of Wasserngrat last night," she said quickly, "and we took the chairlift up, and I guess I had a little too much wine at the party or something. We skied down with torches, and I missed a turn and almost went right up a tree."

"Who's we?" Frazer asked.

"What? Oh, me and this boy I know." Cindy was still staring at him that way.

"What's his name?"

Cindy laughed nervously. "You sound like you're cross-examining me, Daddy."

"Sorry. I didn't mean to." Frazer waited.

"His name is Tommy Grayling. How long are you staying, Daddy?"

"A few days anyway. I thought we could drive down to Geneva together after you're out of here. Can we phone the university for some homework?"

"Don't have to. I'll make it up when I get back. Daddy? You

don't have to stay. I mean, if you're busy down in Spain or anything."

She was almost urging him to leave, he realized. "What's this Tommy Grayling like?" he asked.

"I told you he's just a boy I know."

"Going steady or anything like that?"

"Tommy?" Cindy laughed. "He's just a . . . child. He couldn't be more than, oh, maybe twenty-three."

"And you're a grandmotherly type of nineteen," Frazer said with a grin.

"I guess I mean it's his attitudes. He's positively the most politically naive . . . but I shouldn't be saying that to you, Daddy."

"Tommy's attitudes, I take it, are something like mine?" Frazer asked lightly.

"They're almost exactly like yours. I mean, they're all right in an older man who works for the government and all, but if Tommy's like that when he's twenty-three, what will he be like when . . . what's so funny, Daddy? I don't mean you're old. Forty-one isn't old. None of my girl friends have fathers as young as you. But you're settled in your ideas, and so is Tommy, and he's not much more than half your age. Let's not talk about it. Tell me about Spain, okay?"

He told her about Spain, as he had written her about Spain. They had flown over late last summer—Cindy to spend the Sarah Lawrence junior year in Geneva, Frazer to take over his new post as chief of the United States Information Agency in Madrid. They hadn't seen each other since Christmas, when Cindy had flown down to Madrid for two weeks. She had seemed happy then. There was no mention of Tommy Grayling or any other special boy in her life, but it was a lack that hadn't seemed to bother her.

Now, in the hospital room in Saanen, with Cindy settled back against her pillows, and Frazer telling her what it was like to be USIA chief in Franco's capital, he knew he was going about this all wrong. Cindy had lied to him, and she had cried for no apparent reason, and the young doctor's disturbing words came back: I would have said your daughter was beaten. Accuse her, Frazer thought, make her angry if you have to, but get to the bottom of this. Don't just sit here on the edge of her bed, re-counting the trivia of your daily life in Spain.

But that was all he did. He was afraid to lose the little rapport they had left. Whatever really happened, he rationalized finally, when she's ready to tell me, she will. I'll be here. I'm not going anywhere for a while.

In a few minutes the nurse appeared at the door. "You have another visitor, Miss Frazer," she said.

"Who is it?"

"A Mr. Grayling?"

Cindy looked at her father anxiously. "I don't want to see him now. I'm tired."

"Would you tell him to wait then?" Frazer asked the nurse. "I'd like to meet him."

"Daddy, I wish you wouldn't," Cindy said.

"Why on earth not?"

"I just wish you wouldn't, that's all."

"I promise not to let your Mr. Grayling know we're political blood brothers."

"It isn't that. Please, Daddy?"

"Well," Frazer said, "I ought to drive over to the Küblis' any-way and let them know I'm here. That's where you were stay-ing, isn't it?"

"Most weekends," Cindy said, giving him that direct, wide-eyed look again.

"Most weekends? I don't get it."

"I have this friend at school," Cindy said quickly. "Her par-ents rented a chalet in Gstaad for the season. Didn't I write you about it?"

"No," Frazer said, wondering with a feeling of helplessness what this particular lie meant.

"Well, anyway, sometimes I stay with them."

"Who were you staying with this weekend?"

"The Küblis," Cindy said, relieved.

"What's your girl friend's name?"

"Daddy, you sound like you're cross-examining me again. Her name is Tina."

She didn't supply a last name, and Frazer was unwilling to push it. He stood up and leaned down to kiss her. She offered him her cheek and kept staring at the nurse, as though surprised she was still there.

"You'll get goo all over you. Daddy, about Tommy, I still wish . . ."

"I'll see you later, honey," Frazer said.

"I love you, Daddy."

"Love you too, honey."

He followed the nurse out.

Tommy Grayling was waiting near the reception desk. He was just shorter than middle height. He had a dark crewcut and was wearing a black quilted parka, black ski pants, and heavy ski boots.

"Mr. Grayling?" Frazer said.

Grayling clomped across the floor self-consciously, looking down at his boots through dark glasses. He cleared his throat and removed the sunglasses the way you remove a hat in a public place. His eyes were gray.

"I'm Bradley Frazer—Cindy's father."

"Oh," Grayling said. They shook hands.

"Cindy's a little tired right now, Mr. Grayling. She doesn't want to see anyone."

Grayling looked disappointed and concerned. "How is she? What happened anyway? Frau Kübli said she was here in the hospital. I took the bus right over."

"Don't you know what happened?"

"Me? I don't know anything. Some kind of accident, Frau Kübli said."

"I got the impression you were with her last night. At the fondue party?"

"I was there. After the party you ski down by torchlight," Tommy Grayling said, shuffling his feet in the big boots and looking self-conscious again.

"You took Cindy?"

"Is that what she said?"

"That's what I'm asking, Mr. Grayling."

"Oh. I see."

"I don't see," Frazer said. "Did you take her, or didn't you?"

"Hey, don't bite my head off, Mr. Frazer," Tommy Grayling said. "I guess I better say I took her."

"But did you?"

Grayling shrugged. He seemed uncomfortable. He looked out the window, and Frazer followed his gaze. The sky was a brilliant blue, the valley and the mountains dazzling in the sunlight. A small, single-engined plane lifted off at the airport and flew toward a cut between two steep hills. The drone of its engine came through the window, faintly.

"Well, I guess I'll get going," Grayling said.

"Gstaad? Need a lift?"

Grayling studied him for a moment, making up his mind. "It's only three kilometers," he said, "but thanks. Might as well save my energy for skiing, Mr. Frazer. Do you ski? Sure you do. Cindy said you taught her."

In the rented Volkswagen Frazer said: "Boy friend or just friends or what?"

"Or is it too much to ask right off the bat?" Grayling suggested. "Hell, I don't mind. You want to know the truth, Mr. Frazer, I can't get to first base with that daughter of yours. Not that I haven't tried."

"What are you doing in Gstaad?"

Grayling looked at him levelly before answering. They had just pulled out of the hospital parking lot. There was something odd about the boy, Frazer realized. He seemed to be two different people. Just when you thought you could get to know him, a pleasant and shy American kid, somewhat wet behind the ears, he shot you a calculating look like that and you weren't sure you could get to know him at all.

"Oh," Grayling said finally, "I'm engaged in my second favorite occupation."

"What's that?"

"Skiing. I saved up a little dough, severance pay from the Army. This is my year to be a ski bum."

"What's the other one?"

"The other one what?"

"Your first favorite occupation."

Grayling grinned boyishly. "Well, if you're sure you won't get sore."

"No, go ahead."

"Trying to make out with girls like Cindy," Grayling said matter-of-factly. "Don't haul off and slug me one, Mr. Frazer. I already said I couldn't get to first base with her."

Frazer laughed. "At least you're frank. I appreciate that."

Grayling took off his sunglasses, squinted, and put them back on. He sighed. "Please pull over," he said slowly.

Frazer, surprised, pulled off the road near a barn which had been abandoned for the winter.

"This may take a while," Grayling said. "Got the heater going? You'll freeze in that monkey suit of yours. The sun can fool you."

Frazer waited, having no idea what was coming.

"Can you prove you're Cindy's father?"

Without a word Frazer took out his passport.

Grayling flipped through it. *"Salida* Madrid airport last night. That figures," he said, returning the little blue book. "Where was Cindy born?" he asked.

"Williamsburg, Virginia."

"What did you teach down there at William and Mary?"

"I didn't," Frazer said. "I ran the publicity office awhile and coached the football team."

"Where'd you win your own letter?"

"Same place. William and Mary. I went on the GI Bill. That's when Cindy was born."

"What position'd you play?"

"Tailback."

"Tailback?" Grayling chuckled. "That's before my time."

"We had a single wing."

"What year'd you make All-American?"

"It wasn't All-American. It was All-Southern. In forty-nine."

"When W and M played in what bowl?"

"We didn't. Our last bowl game was in forty-seven. We lost to Arkansas."

"Okay," Tommy Grayling said. "You're Bradley Pickett Frazer, I guess."

"Thanks for telling me," Frazer said dryly.

"Cindy stood me up last night," Grayling said. "Mr. Frazer, I'm going to take a chance on you. I'm in a jam, and I need your help."

"Is Cindy in a jam too?"

"I'll get to that. I work for the government, same as you, only I wear a uniform. And if you tell that to anyone here in Switzerland, I'll be out on my rear end and probably serving in a line company in Viet Nam before you could fly back to Madrid. I'd deserve it too. I'm here on assignment for CIC, and I blew it. Brother," said Tommy Grayling, "did I ever."

He took off his sunglasses and shut his eyes against the fierce glare. "Cindy write you often?"

"About once a week."

"Did she ever mention a guy named Curtis Severing?"

The name meant nothing to Frazer. He said: "Look, Tommy, if Cindy's in a jam I want to know what it is. Maybe this is just an assignment to you, but she's my daughter."

"It started out just an assignment," Grayling said flatly. "I told you I blew it."

Frazer said nothing.

"Let me off at the Olden, will you, Mr. Frazer? I want to get my skis. I need some time to sort a few things out, and skiing usually helps. You can meet me at the restaurant on top of Wasserngrat any time you say, and then we'll talk. All right?"

"I asked you if Cindy was in trouble."

"Give me a couple of hours, okay? I shouldn't be opening up to you at all." Grayling shook his head ruefully. "It's not anything they teach you in Counter Intelligence school at Fort Holabird but the best way to keep your eye on a girl is to date her." Once again Grayling sounded like a pleasantly shy kid, wet behind the ears. "I guess I did that part of my job too damn well."

Frazer started driving. It was just a short way to the ornate façade of the Olden Hotel in the middle of town.

"Make it one o'clock, Tommy. Top of Wasserngrat. You be there."

"I'll be there."

"What did you mean, you did that part of your job too well?"

Grayling got out of the car, holding the door open for a moment. "I guess I kind of fell in love with Cindy," he said, and then he was gone.

TWO

Frazer made a right turn just before the narrow, rushing torrent of the Turbach and drove up the hill, the Volkswagen fighting for traction in the rutted snow. Two switchback turns brought him to the top of the hill. Across the valley he could see the stands of pine and the ski trails, skiers like tiny black commas sliding down, and further off the high thrusting crag of Wasserngrat.

He parked a couple of hundred meters up the narrow road. Snowbanks were piled on either side as high as the roof of the car. He got out and went down the path to the Küblis' chalet, a two-story timber building with four feet of snow crowning the large, overhanging roof. The chalet, the view past it down the hill and over the stacked wood of the lumberyard and across the river and the long valley to the high Oberland mountains, the clarity of the air and the incredible blue of the sky—all of it was just as Frazer remembered. It was like coming home. More than that: the view was a way of life, at once serene and exciting, that the uncertain flow of time was powerless to touch. Frau Kübli, who rarely left the valley, had once asked Frazer and Cindy's mother, shortly after they had first come here, when Cindy was an infant: "If you have all this, why bother to go anywhere else?"

It was a question that Frazer had never been able to answer to his own satisfaction.

He heard music inside the chalet, and Gottfried Kübli's booming laughter. Memories came flooding back. Unlike most of their neighbors, the Küblis were not church-goers. Sunday morning was a time for a slow, enormous breakfast, platters of

deep red *bundnerfleisch* and the winy cheese casseroles, and
Mozart or Beethoven on the phonograph. "You had better remove the little Cindy from this unwholesome environment,"
Frau Kübli had said once, her face flushed from the heart of the
stove, her eyes twinkling, her big hands depositing the steaming
casseroles on the table, "or she will come to the conclusion that
Mozart is God." Then Gottfried Kübli had boomed his laughter, and the big breakfast had been finished, and Frazer, with
Cindy's mother, had gone off to ski while the Kübli children, all
of them grown now, and at least two of them married, had
amused Cindy.

Frazer knocked at the door. The volume of the music was
lowered at once, and he heard footsteps inside the chalet. The
door was flung open and Frau Kübli stood there, blinking
against the sunlight. She had put on weight in a comfortable,
rosy-cheeked, Alpine way, which was becoming. A great smile
split her face.

"Herr Bradley," she cried. *Gruetzi, gruetzi!"* She called over
her shoulder in Schwyzerdutsch: "It is Herr Bradley come to
visit us, and just in time for Sunday breakfast. He still needs
fattening up. *Ach,* these outlanders, what can you do with
them?"

Gottfried Kübli, more reserved, in a flannel shirt and cor-
duroy pants with wide suspenders, his hairline well back on the
crown of his head now, his small eyes almost shut with smiling,
came out. He shook Frazer's hand solemnly. Though he and
Frau Kübli were about the same height, she seemed to tower
over him massively. He still looked like a middle-aged little
boy.

"And now we eat," Frau Kübli said. It was a command.

They ate, and they listened to Ansermet and L'Orchestre de
la Suisse Romande playing Mozart, and Frau Kübli talked—at
the stove, en route from the stove to the table, at the table—in
that strange mixture of French and Schwyzerdutsch that she
employed for Frazer and all foreigners. Erica was married and
living with her husband in Geneva. A city man, she said, but

good, good. A dentist. Frieda, still unmarried, was an instruc-
tress at the Skischule. Ruedi had married the girl at the dairy,
the one who used to be all skin and bones and a hank of blond
hair, and now was a strapping matron with twin sons. *Ach,* we
are grandparents, can you believe it, Ruedi has taken over from
his father at the *sporthaus,* Gottfried is all but retired. Little
Gottfried is studying architecture in Zürich. You will have more
käseschnitte, Herr Bradley?

But he pushed back from the table, saying in English that he
was stuffed to the gills and then trying to translate that into
French. They had coffee in the living room, Frazer facing the
window and the view down the length of the valley. There was
a momentary silence. Frau Kübli looked at her husband un-
easily. He pursed his lips and nodded.

"You have seen the little Cindy?" Frau Kübli asked.

"I just came from there."

"How is she?"

He told them that Cindy's injuries were not serious. Again
Frau Kübli cast an uneasy glance in her husband's direction.

"We will visit her this afternoon," she told Frazer. "You spoke
to Herr Doktor Matti?"

"The doctor taking care of her? Yes, we spoke."

"We don't wish to meddle," Gottfried Kübli said, and cleared
his throat. "But Herr Doktor Matti is a friend of ours."

"Such a thing to happen," Frau Kübli said. "Your Cindy
could ski almost as soon as she could walk." She refilled their
coffee mugs. "Doktor Matti does not think it was a skiing accident, Herr Bradley."

"Not that anyone wishes to call the child a liar," Gottfried
Kübli said. "You understand?"

"We feel awkward," Frau Kübli said. "But what are old
friends for?"

"*Ach, so,*" Gottfried sighed.

And Frau Kübli said: "We are worried about her."

"The doctor said it was just a question of . . ."

"Not her injuries, her friends," Frau Kübli said flatly, nodding, making up her mind. "A man named Curtis Severing."

Frazer set down his mug. A little of the hot coffee sloshed over the rim.

"The name means something to you?" Frau Kübli asked.

"A boy named Grayling, an American, mentioned it. I met him at the hospital."

"A good boy," Frau Kübli said. "Good for Cindy."

"Severing is also an American," Gottfried said. "A man of your own age, Herr Bradley."

"He came here before Christmas," Frau Kübli went on. "He rented a room from the chalet builder Siebenthal, Gottfried's cousin, in Saanen. Cindy met him the first weekend after New Year's."

"They became friends," Gottfried said.

Frau Kübli glowered at her husband. "Say what you mean, Gottfried."

"Well . . . more than friends." Gottfried looked away from Frazer and blushed.

"How old is Cindy?" Frau Kübli asked.

"Nineteen. You know that."

"Severing is more than twice her age. When he came to Saanen, a woman was with him. They were drinkers. They had violent arguments. Siebenthal is a patient man, but finally he demanded that they either behave themselves or leave."

"The woman left," Gottfried said.

"Siebenthal's wife drove her to the *bahnhof* in Saanen," Frau Kübli said. "She looked a sight. She had been beaten. Siebenthal says the man, Severing, spent three days in his room, drinking, and then he went out. The next weekend he met Cindy at a tea dance at the Olden. Our Frieda saw them there. Cindy met him often after that. Two weekends she spent here with us. The rest . . ."

"At my cousin's chalet in Saanen," Gottfried said.

"With Herr Severing," Frau Kübli said, and they both looked at Frazer.

He knew they expected some reaction from him. They were not telling tales out of school, they were deeply concerned. But what do you say to old family friends when they have just told you that your daughter, whom they've known off and on all her life, is having an affair with a man twice her age?

Frazer said something he immediately regretted. "If you knew what was going on, why didn't you write me?"

Frau Kübli looked at her husband. "*Ach,* the letters we started to write," she said. She sighed and went on with stolid Oberland practicality: "But what we could not do, we could not do, Herr Bradley. What will *you* do?"

"I don't know yet," he said, feeling helpless and frustrated, as he had often felt where Cindy was concerned.

"She is at a difficult time in her life," Frau Kübli said. "More than a child, yet less than a woman. She needs you."

"I'm not going anywhere," Frazer said defensively. "I'll stay as long as I'm needed." The words, his own words, somehow seemed wrong to him. He sounded more like a sympathetic social worker prepared to tackle a difficult case than a father concerned about the welfare of his own daughter.

Perhaps Frau Kübli decided all that could be said had been said. No dramatic change in Cindy's life would occur while she was lying in her bed in the Bezirksspital Saanen. Frau Kübli got up purposefully and said: "You have luggage in the car? Stay with us as long as you wish."

Frazer didn't argue with her. He went outside, got the canvas suitcase, and carried it into the chalet.

"Cindy tells us you are a very important man in Spain," Gottfried said. "For the American government. A very committed man."

"I have my job to do," Frazer said, as defensively as he had stated his intention to stay in Gstaad. He knew what Cindy thought of his particular brand of commitment.

"A man forced to make such world-shaking decisions . . ." Frau Kübli began with earnestness and a little awe, and Frazer cut in deprecatingly:

"I'm not a policy maker. I'm a glorified public relations man."

"Such a man," Frau Kübli went on, as if he hadn't spoken,

"needs a woman at his side." She nodded solemnly, but the earnestness and awe in her voice gave way to guileless teasing. "If you knew how often I have asked myself, when is Herr Bradley going to arrive in Gstaaad with a wife? You have lived alone too long."

"Trudi," Gottfried said reproachfully.

Frau Kübli ignored her husband. "And also for the little Cindy. It would be good for her."

"I'd better unpack," Frazer said.

He took his suitcase into the guest room, set it down on the bed, and lit a cigarette. He still had close to two hours before his appointment with Tommy Grayling, but decided to change his clothes and ride up on the Wasserngrat chairlift early. There were times when Frau Kübli's well-meaning and unspecific matchmaking amused him. Invariably she always got around to the subject on his visits to Gstaad. There were times when it irritated him. There were times, the bad times, and this was one of them, when Frau Kübli's concern over his marital status brought the terrible past hurtling back. He looked out the window at the barely visible towers of the chairlift climbing the flank of the mountain.

You had a wife, he told himself. You loved her, and you killed her, and that's enough.

THREE

He joined the line of skiers and sightseers waiting to ride the Wasserngrat *télésiège*. He watched the two-man chairs rising out of the station, crossing the road, and sliding upward on their cable over the lower slope of the mountain, climbing between the pylons toward the sky. Soon his turn came.

The attendant offered a coarse woolen blanket. Frazer declined, lowering the safety bar across his thighs and settling back as the chair slid forward, rocking slightly, and then cleared the building and climbed across the road. Deep in thought, he watched skiers negotiating the final steep moguls at the bottom of the long run.

There was Wasserngrat here in Gstaad, and the mountain called the Little Egg, and a few kilometers past Saanen along the road to Bern you could ski Horneggli and Rinderberg, and, toward Lausanne in the opposite direction, Videmanette. There was the great Parsenn rising between Klosters and Davos, and the fantastic above-timberline run down from Piz Nair to St. Moritz in the Engadine Valley. There were the fine *pistes* in the Tyrol, and the dangerous Brevent run above Chamonix in High Savoy. With Cindy's mother he had skied them all.

You climbed in an open chair like this, swaying in the wind, or in a four-place cabin or a big cable car, and then you plummeted down on skis, the wide above-timberline slopes at first, then the trails plunging through thick stands of pine. There was fresh powder snow sometimes and the need to lean back a little on your heels and the way the tips of your skis plowed through like the prow of a fast sailboat. There were the hard-packed trails, and you leaned well forward then, speeding down to-

ward the toy village far below, and you felt confident and absolutely free, and you knew this was the only life you wanted,
because flatland was a pretty dull place by comparison, and you
would live with your wife and young daughter in the high Alps,
doing the work you thought you could do, hoping you could do
it well enough to make the life you wanted possible.

There was Arosa, in its high, isolated Shangri-La of a valley
in eastern Switzerland; an early spring thaw, the slopes above
Gstaad sloppy and with bare spots; but Arosa, twice as high,
boasting fine spring snow; the road through Luzern and Zürich
to Chur clear and inviting; the Küblis and their children delighted to baby-sit with Cindy, who was two; the mountains that
ringed Arosa too inviting to resist.

They never did ski there, Bradley Pickett Frazer and his wife.
They had been in Gstaad a year then, the first year after Frazer's GI Bill-sponsored education at William and Mary, the
third year of their marriage. They had four thousand dollars
carefully salted away, most of it a wedding gift from Diana's
parents. The four thousand dollars, in those days, in Switzerland, could and did last them a long time. They skied. They
took brief driving trips through northern Italy and Provence,
when the little sign glued to the rear bumper of their ancient,
prewar Citroën (Help Stamp Out Summer) failed to convince
the weatherman. Frazer and Diana had figured that the four
thousand dollars would last them long enough to see if he had
what it took to become a novelist or a semirespectable ski bum,
depending on which of his passions you took more seriously. For
at least a year, as Diana had eagerly put it, they would be out of
the rat race. Some day they might have to take their places in
the well-ordered, paler world they called flatland. But the time
was not yet.

They stayed the first night in Zürich, window-shopping hand
in hand along Bahnhofstrasse, buying a dozen extravagances in
their imagination. Diana got him a Jaguar. He got her a sable
coat and a Patek Philippe watch. The second afternoon they
were in Chur, wandering through the crooked streets of the old

town. There had been no snow on the highways. It was warm enough to eat lunch out of doors.

"I forgot to mention it," he said. "We have reservations at the Arosa Kulm."

"That's a pretty ritzy joint. Can we afford it?"

"Of course not," Frazer said. "That's why we're going."

Diana's eyes crinkled, and she laughed that wonderful laugh of hers, and she leaned across the tiny outdoor table in the cobbled square near the ancient church and kissed him for the last time. "Nut," she said, and he felt very confident and very much in love. Sometimes—especially when he was on holiday with this beautiful girl at his side, his wife, with her warmth and her openness, with the way any man under eighty would stare at her admiringly and then sometimes at him with grudging envious approval—he would think: How did this happen to me? She's wonderful. We've been married three years, and we have a daughter, and the honeymoon shows no signs of ending.

The narrow mountain road from Chur to Arosa went nowhere else. Built to augment the rack-and-pinion railroad that connected the high Alpine resort with the rest of the world, it climbed more than three thousand feet in twenty-seven kilometers. Theoretically it was open all year, but sometimes it would take the great snow plows, working their way up from Chur, days to clear after a heavy snowfall. It was an impressive engineering feat, that road, clinging to the faces of cliffs, spanning gorges, switching back on itself as it climbed through forests of pine and larch, a narrow, twisting ribbon of asphalt, sometimes wide enough for two cars to pass, sometimes so narrow that the descending driver had to pull over and wait in a bypass.

They started from Chur in mid-afternoon. The pavement was clear and dry, except for an occasional wet patch where a runoff crossed the road. Soon it grew noticeably colder, but the sky was still that incredible high Alpine blue, and the clear air was heady with the scent of pine. Two-thirds of the way up they encountered old snow on the road. A plowing truck, its blade gleaming, was parked in a bypass. The driver waved to them. Diana waved back. The old Citroën forged reliably ahead. They carried a pair of rusty tire chains in the trunk of the car, and Frazer debated putting them on and decided against it. It hardly seemed worth the bother of finding a bypass and jacking up the car. Twenty more minutes of climbing switchback curves would find them in Arosa, where the village streets would certainly be cleared.

"Don't look now," Diana said, "but there's a bee on your leg."

He did look now. It was a small bee with a yellow and black striped body, crawling slowly above the knee of his ski pants. It must have been in the car for some time, he remembered thinking. They had climbed to winter, but down below in flatland it was spring.

With a quick movement he cupped the bee in his right hand and rolled down the window with his left hand. He threw the bee out, turning his head for an instant, feeling pleased with himself, to watch the bee fly away. The car lurched, and the road seemed to swing sharply away to the left as the front right fender of the Citroën caught the guardrail, splintering the heavy wood like a matchstick. The rail was there for a good reason: at that point the narrow road skirted the edge of a cliff, with a sheer drop of several hundred feet. They swung toward it. For an instant Frazer thought they were going over. Then the left front fender, coming around, cashed against the stanchion supporting the guard rail. They stopped suddenly, hanging there, with both front wheels spinning over empty space.

Frazer's chest slammed against the steering wheel, hard. He heard a shattering sound and a scream, choked off abruptly.

Diana had gone head-first through the windshield. She hung there, leaning forward and up, her head beyond the broken glass. Quickly, horribly, the glass was turning red. He tried to pull her back. She was stuck there.

He remembered scrambling frantically from the car. There was barely room to stand on the edge of the cliff. They had come that close to going over. He had to run around behind the car to the other side.

Diana's eyes were open. She was looking at him. Do something, her eyes said. You've got to do something. But she was stuck there, her head through the windshield, the jagged glass at her throat. He tried but couldn't free her. The broken glass was all over red. He tried to pound it loose with his fists. It held.

He ran back to the trunk. The key. Back to the door on the driver's side. Key in the ignition. Trunk again. His hands trembled. A big wrench. Around the car again. He swung the wrench. Red glass shattered. She wasn't looking at him any more. She fell back into the car. He opened the door on her side. She wasn't moving. She was too pale.

Another car stopped. Skiers in bright parkas. A man's face. A woman's. He was sitting. Someone had given him a cigarette—sharp, dark French tobacco, Gaulois or Gitane.

"——" the man's voice said. It was an impossible word.

"Diana," Frazer said in a calm and reasonable voice. "You've got to help me. She . . ."

"——" the man's voice said.

The woman moved quietly off to one side and was sick.

"Diana," Frazer said.

And the man said: "Dead."

The chair made a clattering sound on the overhead cable as it passed into the building of the upper station. An attendant grabbed hold and stopped it from swinging. Frazer sat there a moment.

"Monsieur," the attendant said.

Frazer lifted the safety bar clear of his thighs and got off the chair. He walked out of the building and into the dazzling snow-reflected sunshine and down the path of hard-packed snow to the terrace of the restaurant.

Skiers—their parkas removed, their faces oiled, their boots unlaced—were reclining in the sun. A group of tourists, cameras in hand, were clustered about the schematic drawing of the mountains that could be seen from the edge of the terrace.

Frazer sat down at a plank table. A waitress in a black dress and a frilly white apron came over to him. "Beer," he said, then shook his head. "No, make it whisky."

When it came, he drank the whisky in one gulp.

If they had stayed right here in Gstaad.

If they had gone south over the mountains to the Italian Lakes instead.

If he had driven five miles an hour faster, or five miles an hour slower.

If he had stopped the car before trying to get rid of the bee.

If he had bothered to find out that the windshield of the vintage Citroën wasn't safety glass.

He had broken a knuckle on his right hand trying to smash the glass. They kept him in the hospital in Chur overnight. He rode the train back to Gstaad. Someone had phoned. When he returned they already knew. Frau Kübli took one look at his face and cried. He stayed with them a few weeks. Cindy was told that her mother had gone away. A long, long trip, Frau Kübli said. Diana was buried in the Alps she loved, in the ancient graveyard in Saanen.

He never finished the novel. He read through what he had written, not once, but many times. They were just words. Childishly, melodramatically, he burned the manuscript in the fireplace. You could try to escape from the world, but you couldn't, not really. They never let you.

"You should go back and be among your people, Herr Bradley," Frau Kübli said.

He wrote letters, and letters came back. They offered him the public relations job at William and Mary. He could coach the football team if he wanted. In the late spring he crossed down into Italy and sailed from Genoa with Cindy.

"It looks like we both had the same idea," Tommy Grayling said. He stood over Frazer, his boyish mouth smiling, his eyes hidden behind the dark glasses.

"What?"

"Getting here early. I already took a run and came back up. The skiing's terrific."

Grayling sat down across the table. "Did you ride the chairlift alone?" he asked in a low voice.

"Yes," Frazer said.

Grayling nodded, satisfied. "Look around slowly," he said. "Don't make it obvious. A big man with a bull neck. Heavy and strong as an ox but not fat. Head shaven. He comes on like a loud and extroverted German. See him anywhere?"

Frazer shook his head. "Severing?" he guessed, and then remembered that the Küblis had said Severing was an American.

"What do you know about Severing?"

"Just from the Küblis. They said he was—seeing a lot of Cindy."

Grayling's adam's apple worked. "Yeah," he said. He ordered gin and vermouth from the waitress. "It's the closest you can come to a martini up here," he explained. "Two parts gin to one vermouth—if you're lucky."

Waiting for his drink, Grayling lit a cigarette. The drink came. Grayling tasted it and made a face. "Just what I thought." He watched a shapely girl skier unzip her parka and stretch out lazily in the sun, propping her back against the wall of the restaurant building.

Grayling finished his drink and his cigarette before he asked: "Did you ever hear of Camp King?"

Frazer shook his head

"It's a super-secret U.S. Army installation in the Taunus Mountains in Germany. Curtis Severing used to work there as a debriefing expert."

"A what? I'm not up on the latest jargon, Tommy."

"His job was to interrogate captured East German agents and Communist defectors. He's probably the best man on the Continent with a lie detector. Not only that, but he's been a professional spy most of his life, and he could smell a double agent a mile away. He was born in Germany and lived there until after the war. Spent a hitch with the Wehrmacht when he was just a kid, and saw combat in Yugoslavia. He didn't come home with the defeated German army. Got wounded and involved with the partisans instead—a nationalist group down in Montenegro. Disappeared down there a couple of years, and then showed up in Germany again early in the occupation. He got American citizenship by spending five years in Uncle's Army, most of it in a CIC unit, where he learned his expertise with the lie detector. A devious guy, Curtis Severing, but a valuable one to have on your side."

"What does all this have to do with Cindy?"

"Let me tell it my way, okay? A while back they went sour on Severing at Camp King. Nothing they could prove, but they began to suspect he was working both ends against the middle."

"How do you mean?" Frazer asked. He was impatient, but interested, too.

"Well, suppose a Red defector came over. He gets debriefed by Severing, five or six hours of interrogation a day over a period of a couple of weeks. If Severing's any good at it, and he is, he finds out things even the defector doesn't realize he knows. Like in a football game, Mr. Frazer—you'd be sitting pretty if you knew what signals the other guys were calling in their huddle, wouldn't you?"

"Thanks for putting it on a level I can understand," Frazer said sarcastically.

Grayling grinned. "Hey, lay off. I played quarterback at Dartmouth, Mr. Frazer. I know I'm kind of small, but we didn't recruit our teams in the Pennsylvania coal mines the way you Southern Conference guys did. Anyway, what if the weekend of the big game came along, and you thought you knew the other guy's signals and then found they'd switched them on you? You'd be in the dark and probably worse off than if you hadn't done any snooping at all. Apparently that's the little game Severing was playing. He'd debrief a defector in duplicate—one copy for CIC and one for the Reds. At least that's the way it looked to the brass at Camp King, only they could never prove it. All they knew was that the Reds kept switching the signals on them."

"I don't follow that," Frazer said. "Say a cryptographer came over to us. Wouldn't the other side naturally change their codes? It wouldn't have to mean the debriefing expert was a double agent."

"That's a good example, Mr. Frazer, but you've got to understand one thing about debriefing. When your cryptographer comes over, of course the Reds will figure he'll blow their code. That's why debriefing is so important. You spend two weeks with a defector, or a month or more, you really get to know what makes him tick. He wants to run off at the mouth, and you let him. He wasn't living in a vacuum on the other side. Maybe he can tell you something about the latest in East German missile sites, because he had a friend working on them. Or maybe a defector who used to design missile sites met a guy at a cocktail party, say a cryptographer with a little too much to drink, and he can tell you something about the latest one-time code pads. You get a little here, and a little there, and in the end the Reds don't know what's been leaked—unless they have a Curtis Severing on their payroll."

Sitting there on a mountaintop in the sunlight, watching skiers swoop down and away, staring past Grayling at the wide shining panorama of the Bernese Oberland, waiting impatiently to hear where Cindy entered the picture, Bradley Pickett Frazer was still fascinated. "Why didn't the Army just fire Severing?" he asked. "Or did they?"

"I said we had no proof. We couldn't blow the whistle on him. But he did get a leave of absence, with pay, a pretty common thing at Camp King because you work under so much pressure there. That was CIC's idea, but Dad didn't approve."

"Dad?"

"Department of the Army Detachment," Grayling said. "A pleasant little euphemism for the Central Intelligence Agency." He shrugged philosophically. "We're always butting heads with them, but don't quote me. The difference between tactics and strategy. We're the line companies, they're the general staff. At least that's the way they like to look at things. Their worry was that Severing would get scared and bolt to the other side if we gave him a leave. They wanted him at Camp King, where they could watch him. Our worry was that he was fouling up our operation at the camp."

"He didn't defect," Frazer said. "He's right here in Gstaad, isn't he?"

"In Saanen. Since the beginning of the season. Skiing. Working on a sun tan. Collecting his pay. Apparently not a worry in the world," Grayling said.

"What's he waiting for?" Frazer asked.

"Who the hell knows? Making up his mind about which way he wants to go. Living the good life on three hundred bucks a week. Waiting for the other side to jack up their offer. Search me. Dad's had a roper on him lately though."

"I speak some German, French, and Spanish," Frazer said, vaguely annoyed that this pleasant-looking young man in ski togs should display such cavalier expertise on a restaurant terrace a mile above Gstaad, "but roper's a word I don't know in any language."

"Sorry. A roper's an undercover agent who assumes an elaborate identity to gain the confidence of a suspect. In this case the disillusioned ex-wife of a hard-drinking and tom-catting field grade officer in the U.S. Army. A lady spy, in short, and a good-looking dame if you like your women mature, but she didn't stand a chance with Severing once Cindy came along."

They stared at each other, the disappointed suitor and the worried father, and for an instant Frazer felt sorry for Tommy Grayling, for on mentioning Cindy and Severing in the same breath, he had taken off his glasses and looked desperately young and vulnerable.

"Just like I didn't have a chance with Cindy," he said, "thanks to Severing. She won't see me any more. She's in love with him." Grayling took a deep breath. "Ah, don't mind me. I really went and gummed up the works, didn't I?"

"How did Cindy get hurt, Tommy?"

"That bastard Severing. It's only a guess. He's got a violent temper. If I ever get my hands on him . . . but how the hell can I?"

Frazer saw Cindy's bruised face and the way she had broken into tears in the hospital in Saanen. He clenched his big fists. I, he thought, would love to have a few minutes alone in a locked room with Mr. Curtis Severing myself.

But his voice was calm when he spoke. "Why should Severing do a thing like that?"

"It's still only a guess. Figure Severing's planning to defect. Figure he hopes he can take Cindy with him. Figure . . ."

The theory shocked Frazer. "Take her with him? What for?"

"Are you kidding? A debriefing hotshot at Camp King *and* the daughter of the USIA chief in Madrid? Cindy's politics aren't exactly dead center, Mr. Frazer. Severing must have thought he could talk her into it. He must have tried, and she must have turned him down. Or more: maybe she was afraid for him. Maybe she threatened to get in touch with our people if he tried, and he lost his temper."

Somehow that didn't ring true to Frazer. There had to be more to it than that. "Does she know why you're here, Tommy?"

"A ski bum. She thinks I'm a ski bum, that's all. She thinks Mrs. Hayward—that's the CIA roper—is the ex-wife of a no-goodnik American Army colonel. She thinks . . ."

"Does Cindy know her?"

"Mrs. Hayward doesn't miss a trick, believe me," Grayling said with a trace of envy. "The funny part of it is her assign-ment comes easy to her. She actually was married to a colonel whose idea of how to run a happy marriage was to tom-cat after all the bored wives of all the junior officers."

Grayling, with his concern that was at once professional and personal, was getting too far afield. "I appreciate your taking me into your confidence, Tommy," Frazer told him. "Now let's hear what you think I can do."

For a moment Grayling said nothing. He put the dark glasses back on and scowled. "Here goes," he said. "I have this crazy idea. I told Mrs. Hayward. She thinks I'm nuts, which means no help from her. But if anything else happens to Cindy . . ."

"What else is going to happen to her?"

"Severing. He's been here too long. He's not just mulling things over. He's sweating something out. There's this East German, the big bull-necked guy I mentioned? He goes under the cover name of Leser, Fritz Leser, owner of a camera shop in Dresden. We have a dossier on him in Camp King. Real name: Heinz Glaeske. He's a colonel in the MfS, the East German Ministry for State Security. He's been Severing's contact with the other side ever since he came to Gstaad. I think he's less than delighted with Severing. I think they've been bargaining."

"Bargaining?"

"Severing wants to go over, but he doesn't have enough to offer. Glaeske won't say yes or no, not yet. He wants more than a double agent finally opting for the East. He wants a propaganda coup, and with Severing's help maybe he can get it. He wants the daughter of a high official in USIA, defecting for ideological reasons. He wants Cindy, and if Severing hasn't been able to talk her into going over with him, there's another way. They could kidnap her."

FOUR

A few cars were parked in the lot behind the big chalet in Saanen, Sunday cars with snow piled on their roofs, delivering Sunday visitors to the hospital. Frazer pulled up next to the Küblis' squat little Daf and was taking long strides across the hard-packed snow of the parking lot before Grayling had emerged from the Volkswagen.

Grayling caught up with him. "Hey, take it easy. The place is mobbed with visitors. Be a hell of a stupid time to pull a kidnapping."

The door opened just before Frazer reached it. The Küblis in their Sunday clothes came out, a bouquet of red roses clutched in Frau Kübli's big hand. She smiled at him uncertainly.

"You returned for something, Herr Bradley? The little Cindy's clothing?"

"What? I don't get you," he said in English.

Frau Kübli looked at him earnestly. "Didn't Cindy leave the hospital with you a few minutes ago? With her father, they said. You took her back to the chalet?"

He brushed past her and into the hospital lobby. A few visitors were sitting on hard chairs with fixed waiting-room faces. A new girl was on the reception desk, young and officious-looking. Her close-set eyes glanced up at Frazer. The smallest of reluctant professional smiles touched her prim mouth.

"Where's Miss Frazer?" he said. "She's a patient."

"Not any longer. She left with her father ten minutes ago. He paid cash," she said, pleased with the American father who had settled his account so promptly with the hospital.

"I'm her father."

"You are mistaken," the girl said, dismissing Frazer's claim of parenthood so routinely that, despite everything, he wanted to laugh.

The Küblis came up behind him, and Tommy Grayling behind them. "You see, it is right here," the girl said. She had produced a mimeographed form, typewritten in German, which waived the hospital's responsibility for the early release of the minor patient Cindy Frazer. At the bottom was a line with *parent or guardian* typed in caps under it, and above the line, in a bold and unfamiliar scrawl, someone had signed the name *Bradley Pickett Frazer.*

"She was released in the custody of her father," the girl said, somewhat smugly. "Dr. Herrmann signed the approval, since Dr. Matti is not on duty. Everything is in order, as you can see."

"Is something wrong?" Gottfried Kübli asked Frazer.

"Where do I find your cousin the chalet builder?"

"Why, he will be at our house later this afternoon."

"No, Gottfried," Frau Kübli said impatiently. "Herr Bradley wishes to know where he lives. At the bottom of the Eggli skilift here in Saanen," she told Frazer. "You will see the lumberyard. It is the only chalet there."

Frau Kübli looked at him uncertainly. She held the bouquet of roses out and then withdrew it. She was talking to her husband in a soft voice when Frazer left with Grayling. The name Severing floated out of the hospital after them.

Skiers stood in a long double file on the dazzling snow waiting to mount the Eggli T-bar. The mechanism droned in its shack, and a squat man in a bright orange parka settled each pair of skiers in their places and shoved them on their way uphill.

Maybe, Frazer thought, Severing had to come back for something. Maybe we'll find them here, it's only been a few minutes. It seemed a forlorn hope, though, as bleak as the tall stacks of lumber under their shrouds of snow. Whether Cindy had left the hospital willingly or otherwise, it hardly seemed likely that Severing would hang around Saanen until Frazer found them.

A black Mercedes-Benz with German plates was parked outside the chalet.

"That's Glaeske's car," Grayling said. "Drive past. We'll come back on foot."

Frazer drove fifty yards further and parked the Volkswagen between two huge stacks of lumber. The silence, when he cut the engine, was absolute. A clump of snow fell from the stacked lumber with a faint thud.

"Listen," Grayling said as they got out, "it was the only thing we could do, but I never thought we'd find them here. We ought to call the cops. You ought to. There'll be a phone at the T-bar station. I'll keep an eye on the chalet."

"Cindy's in there. I'm going in."

"Don't be a fool. Glaeske's armed."

"Are you?"

"No," Grayling said, shaking his head.

"Then you call the cops. I'll keep watch."

Grayling shrugged. "I can just see myself trying to explain this one to the gendarmes."

"She's being held against her will, that's all you have to say."

"Sure," Grayling said bitterly. "If she is."

They walked back past the chalet, keeping the stacked lumber between it and them. The snow was deep.

"Just keep watch," Grayling said. "No heroics, huh? I'll have the gendarmes here inside of ten minutes, and I'll be back inside of five. You stay out of sight."

He watched Grayling walk down to the line of waiting skiers and past it into the T-bar shack. He stood in shadow behind the pile of stacked lumber closest to the chalet. It was very cold. He moved cautiously into the sunlight. They still wouldn't be able to see him from the chalet. A minute passed. Two. He wanted to go to Cindy. He waited. A door slammed, jarring the silence like a pistol shot. He peered out from behind the lumber, his face close to it, smelling the resiny smell of the freshly cut boards. Twenty yards away, in the brilliant sunlight, a big, powerfully built man in a gray parka was approaching the Mercedes. He was carrying a pair of tan cowhide valises. He set the valises down in the snow and opened the trunk of the car. Over his shoulder Frazer could see into it: the spare tire, a jack, and a small blue overnight case, which he recognized as Cindy's. He had bought it for her before they left the States last summer.

The bald man put the two tan cowhide valises in the trunk and brought the lid down hard so that the lock would catch. He tested it. His large hands, gloveless, were red with the cold. He rubbed them together briskly. Straightening, he lit a cigarette and looked at his watch. Frazer looked at his own watch. Four minutes had passed. There was still no sign of Tommy Grayling. What was worse, if the big man remained where he was, he might spot Grayling returning from the T-bar station.

Then, suddenly, it no longer mattered. The front door of the chalet opened again and Cindy came out. A tall man was one step behind her. Cindy headed straight for the car, and Frazer had time to think that nobody was twisting her arm. She walked straight and proud in light blue parka and black stretch pants, and Frazer also had time to think, irrelevantly, that his daughter was a grown woman, poised and lovely, even in her latest wild adventure. The tall man locked the chalet door and stood for an instant with his back to it, watching with faintly lecherous approval the way Cindy walked. He was a man of about Frazer's age, with wavy black hair, graying at the temples, and the sort of stylized Continental good looks that young American women on their junior year abroad would find attractive. He had to be Curtis Severing, of course.

He opened the rear door of the Mercedes for Cindy. Frazer, waiting, not knowing what to do, wishing that Tommy Grayling and a carload of Saanen-based gendarmes would make their timely appearance like a troop of Royal Mounted Police, watched for some sign of resistance or at least reluctance on Cindy's part. She did a small and graceful half-turn toward Severing, said a few words so softly that Frazer couldn't hear them, smiled, and kissed Severing's cheek. The bald man, who still stood behind the car, looked up at the sky in exaggerated exasperation. Then Cindy was in the car and Severing got in after her.

The bald man came around the side of the car. Frazer looked across the snow toward the T-bar a hundred yards away: no sign of Tommy Grayling.

He walked out from behind the stacked lumber. He said: "Just a minute here."

The bald man swung toward him. "What do you want?"

It was an oddly rectangular face that Frazer saw, the small eyes staring at him across the bright snow, the brow broad and jutting, the heavy jowls just as wide and solidly meaty.

"That's my daughter in the car." There seemed nothing else to say.

The rear window of the car rolled down, and Cindy thrust her head out. A lock of long hair came down over her injured eye. "Daddy," she said, and her voice was very young and vulnerable.

"Come on out of there," Frazer said, his own voice unexpectedly harsh.

Then he sensed, rather than explicitly saw, movement, and then he did see it, a shadow moving quickly over the snow, and he turned away from Cindy to see the bald man, very close and large, almost upon him, coming fast, one big arm raised, and something dark and solid, a gun, in the hand, swinging down, and he raised his own hand in a tardy defensive gesture, feeling it brushed aside at once by the down-swinging arm as Cindy screamed, her scream exploding visually in a bright burst of light that took the strength from his legs and left him lying in the snow, conscious but unable to move, and somehow outside of time, so that in the same instant the gun struck his head, the car started and drove off leaving its exhaust fumes hanging in the clear, windless air, and Tommy Grayling was there, crouching near him.

". . . took her."

"I know. They drove straight past me. You're bleeding all over the place. Scalp'll do that."

Frazer raised a hand to his head. It came away bloody.

"Severing and the man you described. The German. Leser?"

"Or Glaeske. It figures."

Tommy Grayling did not ask him, then, if Cindy had gone willingly. Frazer did not offer the information. A few minutes later the black and white police Volkswagen came.

FIVE

The first time Bradley Pickett Frazer ever saw the police in connection with Cindy, she had just turned fourteen.

They were living in Georgetown then, together for once, because Frazer was working out of the USIA office in Washington. His job involved frequent flying trips abroad, though, and the father-daughter togetherness bit, as Cindy called it, did not work out too well in practice. They had an apartment on Canal Road and a sleep-in housekeeper named Mrs. Brewer. Cindy, as she saw herself then, was fourteen going on twenty-one. She affected modish clothing and an elaborate ritual of sighs and long, pained looks when Frazer did not understand her, which, he would have been the first to admit, was often.

"These days," Mrs. Brewer said, "they grow up so fast. They grow up too fast, but how's a person going to stop them?" Mrs. Brewer was a plump and placid widow in her middle fifties, very efficient around the house, a good cook, and a harmless secret drinker.

She woke him that night to say he was wanted on the telephone.

It was past midnight. "Cindy home yet?"

"No."

He put on his robe, opened the bedroom door, and joined Mrs. Brewer in the hall.

"It's the police."

He picked up the phone. "Hello?"

"Is this Mr. Frazer? You'd better get on down here to the police station, Mr. Frazer."

"Is it my daughter?"

"Cindy Frazer, yes, sir. She hasn't been hurt. You don't have to worry on that score."

Frazer let his breath out. He hadn't realized he'd been holding it. "What is it then?"

"Just get on down here, please. Ask for Lieutenant Levy."

"Fifteen minutes," Frazer said, and fifteen minutes later he was at the desk of the police station, asking the duty sergeant for Lieutenant Levy. He was directed up a flight of stairs and along a hallway to a pebble-glass door that said, *Detective Squad*. Behind the door was a large room where a small, bird-like man in a rumpled seersucker suit was perched on a corner of one of the desks facing an electric fan that swung back and forth, slowly stirring the stale cigarette smoke in the bullpen. It was a hot night in June.

"Lieutenant Levy? I'm Bradley Frazer. Where's my daughter?"

"Mr. Frazer." Levy got off the desk, and they shook hands. "It figures, you being the first one. Fifteen minutes on the button. The others aren't first-time losers, and they're older. Parents'll straggle in before the night's over. It's going to be a long one. Where was your daughter tonight, Mr. Frazer?"

"Studying. With a girl named Davis. They have finals next week."

"Over at the high school, yeah. No she wasn't, Mr. Frazer— studying, I mean, or with a kid named, what did you say, Davis?"

"Then you tell me where she was."

"Don't snap at me, Mr. Frazer, all right? I'm a cop, and I'm Jewish, and either one of them is enough to make me a patient man or else get an ulcer. Ulcers I can do without. They had a party, a bunch of kids from the high school, all of them sixteen and seventeen except your daughter. They all got a load on, and then six of them piled into a car, and how the boy driving could take them any place at all, when he was too drunk to stand when we found him, beats me. What they were doing, or thought they were doing, was taking your daughter home because she'd passed out at the party. They made it as far as a lamppost on Canal Road, and they wrapped the car around it, which is where we enter the picture. What do you do for a living, Mr. Frazer?"

"Is she all right?"

"Sleeping it off downstairs. They're all fine. Not a scratch on any of them. What's your line of work?"

"I work for the government. USIA."

"Travel a lot?"

"Most of the time."

"What about Mrs. Frazer? She work too?"

"She died when my daughter was a baby."

Lieutenant Levy lit a cigarette and offered the pack to Frazer. "You get kids from a bad neighborhood," he said slowly, "and they get into trouble because their parents are fighting, or boozing it up all the time and don't seem to understand—if you'll excuse my college education showing, Mr. Frazer—what a sensitive mechanism a teenager is. You get kids from a high-rent neighborhood like this one, they ought to know better. But I'll be damned if they do. They're all the time gallivanting off somewhere, and instead of the old man coming home looped from the corner saloon and clobbering the old lady, you have the cocktail party circuit and a kind of in-fighting that's a little more subtle, but it gets to the kids finally. The result is the same, and whatever values the kids are born with, if they're born with any at all, they get too cynical too young and they lose them. The only difference with a high-rent neighborhood, you want to know the truth, is that the mess is handed upstairs to the detective squad instead of being handled downstairs by the guys who run the drunk tank, and we're supposed to take care of everything with kid gloves. Do I look like I'm wearing kid gloves, Mr. Frazer?"

"I don't know yet," Frazer said truthfully.

"You ought to keep a tighter check-rein on those kids. It was just drunken driving this time, and not a scratch on any of them. It could have been different. It could have been a few

sticks of pot or mainlining in somebody's fancy finished base-
ment in front of the color TV set. Or it could have ended up in
the meat wagon."

Lieutenant Levy stubbed his cigarette out with a quick, angry
gesture. "End of lecture. Go downstairs and collect your kid.
She doesn't earn herself a record this time, but if anything like
it happens again, there'll be a file on her. Fair enough? You got
any complaints, see the commissioner."

"No complaints," Frazer said. "What about the car?"

"A kid named Townsend was driving. He's president of the
high school General Organization. It was his old man's car. Ha-
rold Townsend, the congressman. The car's insured, and Congressman Townsend'll show up in a few minutes to give me a
lecture on how we ought to patrol the streets better at night. It's
happened before. Now go on downstairs and get your kid the
hell out of here."

Frazer went downstairs and got Cindy the hell out of there.
He had meant to be parentally stern. No reading the riot act to
her, because being a heavy-handed father had never made sense
to him. Just let her know he was displeased and then work out
some rational punishment, possibly a curtailment of her nights
out of the house for a month or so.

But Cindy could not walk a straight line, or any kind of line
at all without help, when he saw her. Her face was green, and
she was trying very hard to compose herself and act grown-up.
Even the matron who led her to the high desk downstairs was
doing her best not to smile.

"I," Cindy said slurringly in a doom-laden voice, "will never
touch a drop again as long as I live." She hiccuped, the matron
winked elaborately at Frazer, and that was the end of that.

The next time Frazer saw the police in connection with Cindy
there was no Lieutenant Levy patiently staving off ulcers, and no
winking matron.

There was a lawyer named Breeze, a small, intense man too
dapperly dressed, in a black raw silk suit, for the September cli-

mate in Caine, Alabama. It was two years after the Lieutenant Levy episode. Cindy was a student at a girls' school in Massachusetts, because Frazer, though still based in Washington, was overseas more often than not. The toughest job in USIA had been dumped in his lap—that of polling, in twenty-odd countries, the image America was creating abroad. It was a thankless job because, as the director told Frazer, you're damned if you do and damned if you don't. "Conclude that our foreign policy presents a good image," he said, "and you'll be accused of paving the way for higher appropriations next year. Conclude that our activities in such cheerful spots as Viet Nam meet with less than delighted approval in Paris and Mexico City and New Delhi, and you'll be accused of pandering to foreign opinion."

Frazer was back in Washington making a report when he got the call from Caine, Alabama. He drove straight through the hot night to get there, and he saw the dapper lawyer named Breeze early in the morning in the sheriff's substation. Breeze was chief counsel for an organization called AFID—American Fighters for Internal Democracy.

"Sit right down, Mr. Frazer, and I'm sorry the accommodations aren't any better, but Caine, Alabama, isn't my idea of the best America has to offer," Breeze said. Frazer sat right down in a hard chair that faced a fly-specked window and the main street of Caine, a parched street on which an angry crowd was stirring the dust, most but not all of them men, most but not all of them in overalls.

"The question is," Breeze said, "what are you going to do?"

"I'm going to get my daughter out of here and take her home with me as soon as possible."

Breeze's tight mouth made a small moue of disappointment. "Yes, you could do that, Mr. Frazer, and AFID wouldn't try to stop you. But there's a lot more at stake here than whether your daughter spends another night or two in the Caine lock-up. For one thing, there are twenty people involved, none of them quite adult, but all of them quite dedicated. You wouldn't want Cindy to desert her friends, would you? For another there's what

AFID's trying to do. I don't have to tell you, a man of your acumen, what AFID is fighting for."

AFID was fighting to desegregate the Caine, Alabama, high school. Cindy and her twenty friends had car-pooled and/or hitch-hiked their way down to Alabama just before the opening of the school year in Caine and, according to Chief Counsel Breeze's long-distance phone call, had camped on the high school lawn in protest against the school's segregated, all-white student body. When the police came to remove them, some AFID members, Cindy included, had handcuffed themselves to the cyclone fence around the schoolyard. Hacksaws had been used to release them. They had been jailed for trespassing and disturbing the peace.

"I know what AFID's fighting for," Frazer said, and his tone of voice must have disturbed Chief Counsel Breeze.

"Don't tell me you're in favor of segregation?" Breeze asked, shocked.

"What were you doing, Mr. Breeze?"

"What was I doing? I don't follow you."

"What were you doing when Cindy and her friends were handcuffing themselves to the fence?"

"I flew down here as soon as I heard there was trouble."

"That's not what I asked you."

"This is no full-time job for me. AFID's a small organization —so far. I left my practice to be here."

"That's still not what I asked you."

Breeze offered a smile that was part ingratiating and part man-of-the-world. "Don't you think I'm a little old to manacle myself to a cyclone fence?"

"Don't you think Cindy and her friends are a little young?"

"Nobody's too young to fight intolerance any way it has to be fought. Frankly, Mr. Frazer, I had hoped for a more . . . satisfactory reaction from you. A man in your position, if you took your stand shoulder-to-shoulder with the courageous youth that is AFID's strong right arm . . ."

"I want to get my daughter out of here and take her home. How do I go about it?"

"That is your final decision?"

"Just tell me how to go about it."

Breeze said nothing for a while. He looked at Frazer, ready to smile again, and then his face changed, and he seemed, oddly, a dapperly dressed version of the rednecks milling about outside on the main street of Caine, Alabama.

"Do I," he asked, "detect a faint suggestion of the South in your speech, Frazer? Magnolias and hominy and kick the nigger in the ass every chance you get, if you forgive my rudeness?"

Frazer wanted to end the interview. "I was born in Virginia, Mr. Breeze," he said, intentionally drawling.

"I have allowed you to waste my time," Breeze said stiffly. "I should have known better."

He went away. His place in the small, hot, sparely furnished room was taken by a deputy sheriff named Moon, a big sweaty man with a red porcine face and the tiniest eyes Frazer had ever seen.

"Let's see some identification," Moon said, and Frazer showed him some.

"What are you people after?" Moon demanded. He sat down on the windowsill and swung the cartridge belt around on his hip, so that the cracked leather holster and the revolver in it rested on his heavy thigh.

"I'm after my daughter," Frazer told him.

"That's a jailable offense, what she did."

"She's in jail now."

"Ain't seen anybody doing any arraigning yet," Moon said. "What's the matter with you people? You want that daughter of yours to marry some buck nigger and raise a passel of colored brats, that's no skin off my rump, but why the hell you have to bring your sick ideas down here and give us a hard time, that I can't figure."

"If there's a fine, I'll pay it," Frazer said. "If you try to press charges, I'll fight it. I got a lecture from Mr. Breeze, and now I'm getting one from you. I can do without both."

"That son of a bitch," Sheriff Moon said, "is liable to find himself with a bullet through his pea-sized brain one of these days."

"If it happens," Frazer said, wishing he didn't have to defend the objectionable Mr. Breeze before the even more objectionable Sheriff Moon, "and if you keep running off at the mouth like that, they'll know where to look."

"Don't get insolent, mister. Your kid's in a heap of trouble. Why, we could . . ."

"You could do a lot of things, all of them foolish. I said I'd pay the fine if there was one. I want my daughter released in my custody, and I want that now. If your answer's no I'll get a lawyer—and it won't be Mr. Breeze. I know what small southern towns are like because I was born in one, and if you want me to pull a smart lawyer on you to do some digging, don't say you weren't warned."

"You mean to say you ain't no yankee?" Sheriff Moon asked, amazed. "I figured you for a D.C. politician or maybe one of them New York Jew white niggers."

"No," Frazer drawled. "I'm a southern gentleman just like you." He knew he shouldn't be baiting Sheriff Moon, not with Cindy waiting behind bars, but he also knew there'd be a confrontation with Cindy afterward, and being tough with Moon now would make that easier.

Moon took his sweating bulk out of the room without another word. Frazer waited twenty minutes, chain-smoking and wondering what would happen next.

What happened next was a small gray man with rimless glasses and a face as expressive as the back of a filing cabinet. "You sign this, and this, and this," he said. Frazer signed. "You pay a fine. Three hundred dollars in cash."

"And no receipt," Frazer couldn't help saying.

"And no receipt."

Frazer paid. He knew that the papers he had signed were

meaningless. He had not bothered reading them. They might be filed somewhere and forgotten. They might even be destroyed. The three hundred dollars was for Moon and the small gray man. It was cash-register justice, southern style, like the speed traps that line the big Miami- or New Orleans-bound highways in the wide spaces in the road that are the red clay and redneck villages of the South.

A few minutes later he was alone with Cindy. "I'm not going," she said. "You can't make me. It's unfair to my friends. It's disloyal to the cause."

"We'll talk about it later."

"If you make me go, I'll never forgive you."

He took her arm and led her gently but firmly toward the door. "There's a mob outside. They'll be ugly. Walk with your head high. Don't look anywhere but straight ahead. You'll hear some nasty words."

Outside in the harsh sunlight, they moved into the ugly shouting of the words Frazer had predicted. He was proud of Cindy then. She walked like a lady, her steps never faltering. Sheriff Moon and another man in khaki escorted them through the crowd. Moon was wearing a white Stetson hat, which had the right theatrical effect. It made him look capable, and capable of heroics. They weren't needed. The crowd was all red faces and mouths. "This way, miss," a photographer called, and started shooting pictures with a 35 millimeter camera. Cindy just looked straight ahead.

A reporter whose business it was to recognize people like Frazer said: "How you gonna explain this to the folks overseas, Mr. Frazer?" Frazer said nothing.

They went across the dusty street and through the heat, past the used car lot and the five-and-dime and the mail order display window and the trading stamp redemption center, the same storefronts that you saw in Washington or Boise, Idaho, but this could have been another country. It was more foreign than the capitals and the hamlets of Europe that Frazer knew so well. What are we doing here? he thought, how did it get this way?

Will it ever change in my lifetime or Cindy's? He wished the reporter hadn't asked the predictable question.

Then they had reached the car, where Moon and the other man in khaki parted the crowd so they could get in. Frazer opened the door for Cindy. She got in, and he shut the door and went around the back of the car to his side, the slow, stylized gesture to ignore the crowd, and it worked. The words were there, and the threatening gestures, but nobody laid a hand on him.

He started the engine and rolled down the window and placed his elbow comfortably on the sill. Moon leaned close with a broad red-faced smile that was all teeth and face muscles, and he said: "You all come back to Caine, hear? Bring that little whore of yours. I know some buck niggers who'd go a whole Saturday night without moonshine to . . ."

Frazer slipped the clutch and stepped down hard on the gas, and Moon jerked clear as they sped off. It was over.

But it wasn't over. Thirty miles of highway and two towns that could have been Caine flashed by before Cindy spoke. Then she said: "I wanted to stay. My friends are staying. It means as much to me as it means to them. How will I ever be able to face them?"

"Maybe you shouldn't," Frazer said.

"That's a new one," Cindy said. "Are you going to pick my friends for me from now on?"

"You know that isn't true. You're upset."

No more talk for a while.

"May I have a cigarette, please?" Cindy asked.

"Didn't know you smoked." He passed her the pack.

"There's a lot you don't know about me." She inhaled deeply and blew smoke at the windshield. "Daddy, how do you feel, really *feel*, about segregation?"

"Same as you, I guess."

"Let me be the judge of that, okay?"

"Well, okay. This sounds banal, but there just isn't any other way to say it. I think every American ought to have the same rights as every other American."

"Those are just words if you don't do anything about it."

"And, incidentally, I was proud of the way you acted when we walked out of there."

"You're changing the subject. I guess I can't communicate with you at all."

He tried to hide his sudden, irrational, not-quite-called-for anger. "I said I was against segregation. I meant it."

"Are you against polio?"

"Polio?"

"You do something about polio. That's the point. You take the Salk vaccine. What do you do about segregation?"

"Cindy, listen to me. One of the great things about America, it's a country of laws."

"Law? You call what happened in Caine law?"

"I didn't say law. I said laws. We've never had a man on horseback, we've never had the rabble in the streets taking the streets apart to use paving stones as weapons, we've never had . . ."

"Maybe it's time we did."

"This is the middle of the twentieth century, Cindy. We're supposed to be civilized."

"It isn't the middle. Maybe that's your trouble. You're living in the past. It's already the last third of the century. If the ruling classes don't . . ."

"Ruling classes? I wasn't aware we had any in the States."

"What the English call it then. The Establishment. You're very much a part of it. Why rock the boat?"

"Do you really believe that?"

"I don't know what to believe about you any more. I guess I don't see you much."

"I believe," he said slowly, "that there's a climate of violence in the country. I don't like it. I believe we've allowed it to go too far. You're underprivileged and downtrodden, we tell people. It's time you got in your licks. Run wild. We understand. Let off steam. Throw bricks through plate glass windows. We forgive you. Intimidate shopkeepers because their color's different. Overturn cars, with or without occupants. Loot and steal, listen to the demagogues who tell you to obey just the laws you want to obey. Go ahead and demonstrate as a means of bringing your grievances to the light of day. Who cares if the demonstrations infringe on the rights, the constitutional rights, of other people? Or if they break existing laws? You don't like those laws anyway. The rest of the country will condone your breaking the law, we tell them, because you've been discriminated against all your life, and you've had more than your own share of injustice. You've had a bellyful. Now get it out, spit it back at us. That's what I don't like, Cindy. You could call it prejudice in reverse. In the long run it doesn't help the people we're trying to help. It doesn't help them as individuals, and it doesn't help their cause. I can name civil rights organizations that are doing a fine job. But AFID apparently isn't one of them, not with your Mr. Breeze calling the shots."

He glanced at Cindy. She had a faint, wearily superior smile on her face. "End of speech," he said, a little lamely.

"Well, I guess I did ask you."

They didn't speak of it again on the long drive north, and they never spoke of it again afterward. It was as if they had reached an unspoken decision to agree that they could not agree.

Maybe that was part of raising a daughter, Frazer thought. Maybe you couldn't really expect any more agreement than that. But he would have liked to believe something had gone out of their relationship, because at least that would have meant it had once been there.

PART TWO

The Seventh Category

SIX

On Monday morning he drove to Bern with Tommy Grayling. It was just a fifty-mile drive down out of the Oberland, and at Thun they left the mountains behind and most of the snow.

They had very little to say. What could be said had been said last night, after their meeting with the police, after a mild concussion had been diagnosed at the hospital, after Frazer had been put to bed by Frau Kübli. Dr. Matti recommended three days of absolute rest. The police recommended patience. Switzerland, they told Frazer, was a small country. If his daughter and Severing remained within its boundaries, the police would know when they registered at a hotel. If Severing had friends he could stay with, it might take a little more time. If they tried to leave the country, the border police had been alerted. All Frazer had to do was wait. His wayward daughter and the older man she had gone off with would be found, and then Frazer could prefer charges or not, as he wished, for the assault and battery committed on his person by Cindy's lover. That was the story they had given the police. No mention was made of the camera shop proprietor named Leser, real name Heinz Glaeske, real occupation colonel in the East German Ministry for State Security.

Then Grayling thought of the airport in Saanen. He drove there in Frazer's rented Volkswagen and was back at the Kübli chalet within an hour. "They flew out," he said. "Cindy and Severing, piloted by a German named Fuchs. They logged Schaffhausen on their flight plan but never landed there. Schaffhausen's on the German frontier, so you can figure they're out of the country by now. I guess we better go see Dad in the morning. It looks like I blew it again."

The CIA cover in Bern was a travel agency on Marktgasse a block from the clock tower. They parked and joined the morning crowds under the Marktgasse arcade. The dull ache in Frazer's head throbbed with every step he took. Behind the ache, feeding it, was despair. Severing could have taken Cindy anywhere by now. He might hole up in West Germany somewhere, worried that both sides were down on him, if Grayling's guess was right, ready to use Cindy as a pawn in his game with the Reds. He might have to hurt her, as he had hurt her before, if she balked. He might cross into the East Zone, if asylum there was to be his reward for bringing Cindy over. Whatever move he made, it hardly seemed that a visit to a phony travel agency on Marktgasse in Bern could flush him out.

There were the usual posters in the window and a cutaway scale model of a Boeing 707 supplied by Pan Am. The sign on the door said American International Tours, Inc., and there were more travel posters inside the long, narrow shop and a staggered counter with cubbyholes for a receptionist, a cashier, and five clerks. Somehow Frazer had expected the agency to be no more than a front, but it was busy, the receptionist, cashier, and five clerks attending to the needs of the travel-minded public. With Grayling he stood in line at the receptionist's desk. The man in front of them, an American, wanted a round-trip flight to Amsterdam. He was sent down the line to one of the clerks.

"Yes, sir?" the girl at the reception counter said to Grayling.

"*Guten Tag*, miss," he said. "You wouldn't happen to have half a dozen seats to Helsinki, would you?"

The girl shook her head. "Unfortunately, five to Finland is all I can foresee, unless someone forgoes his place, *mein Herr*."

"All right," Grayling said.

"May I have your name, sir?"

"Graph," Grayling said.

"Just a moment, then." The girl left the counter and went through a door behind it.

"What was all that about?" Frazer asked.

"Identification. Dad has a small setup here, just half a dozen people. When someone's in, one of them's on reception. Otherwise I just go away and come back later."

"No, I mean Finland."

"That's what I'm talking about. You open with two languages in one sentence and then give them a bunch of alliterative sounds. I used H. She answers with a bunch of alliterative sounds earlier in the alphabet—she used F—and clinches it with a switch to a second language. That means Dad is home."

"Who's Graph?"

"My cover. Somebody was getting fancy, I guess. Because Severing's a lie detector expert. You know, polygraph? Dad's name for Severing, by the way, is Red Rover. Cute, eh?"

At the mention of Severing's name, Frazer's interest in the mechanics of contact vanished. He lit a cigarette and waited for the girl to return.

"Please use the stairs at the rear of the office, gentlemen," she said.

There were two of them in the small conference room, a man and a woman. The man had a cold pipe in his mouth and wore a Harris tweed suit. He was middle-aged and had a rumpled, befuddled look, like a professor of some esoteric language at a small college in New England. His name, probably his cover, was Gutenberg. "You know," he said half apologetically, "like the printing press?"

The woman was something else again. Her age could have been anything from twenty-five to thirty-five. She might be a talented CIA agent, but the one job she could never pull off successfully, Frazer realized, was shadowing. Seeing her once, you'd remember her. She was too strikingly good-looking. Her dark blond hair fell to her shoulders and framed a high-cheekboned face. She was tall and wore a nubby turquoise suit that emphasized her blue-green eyes. The bones of her face were delicate and there was an almost fashion-model gauntness to it, but her figure was full and very female. She had a low voice, slightly and unaffectedly throaty. "I'm Mrs. Hayward," she told Frazer. "Hayward's not the real name, but it will do. You must be the father." She said that a little antagonistically, as if objecting to the presence of the concerned father among professionals.

Frazer and Grayling sat down. A Neapolitan coffee maker was heating on a hot plate. Mrs. Hayward reversed it and waited for the water to filter through. She didn't offer any small talk, and neither did the man called Gutenberg. They were waiting for Grayling to make his report.

He made it, initially, with just two words: "Severing's gone."

"Oh, my," Gutenberg said, sucking on his cold pipe.

Mrs. Hayward poured four cups of coffee. Grayling was looking at her anxiously. He almost seemed afraid of her.

"Could you give us a few details?" she said, too sweetly.

Quickly Grayling brought them up to date. His face was shining when he finished. He was working on his second cup of coffee. Gutenberg had listened to him with a series of sympathetic grunts and oh my's. He had fidgeted in his chair and unbuttoned the Harris tweed jacket and buttoned it. Mrs. Hayward's blue-green eyes had never wavered from Grayling's face. She left her coffee untouched.

"He waits a month," Gutenberg said in the silence that followed Grayling's report, "frittering away his time skiing in a neutral country, and then suddenly makes his move. Bargaining with Glaeske, wouldn't you say? Apparently they finally came to terms."

"That's the way I figured it all along," Grayling said.

"Well, good for you," Mrs. Hayward said, still too sweetly. "That's really an enormous help. I'm so glad you came to that conclusion early in the game. It will look fine in our final report to Dad."

"Final?" Frazer said.

"We have no more case. The case was Severing, and Severing went over with Glaeske."

"No he didn't," Grayling said brightly. "Glaeske wasn't on the plane."

"Was sent over by Glaeske then. What difference does it make? We've lost him. And we've lost Cindy Frazer too. Glaeske's poeple will have a field day when they surface her, all polished and brain-washed and ready to tell the world—how does this sound?—that it was the nature of her father's work that made her defect. Better prepare yourself, Mr. Frazer: they'll call you an ogre all the way from Berlin to Vladivostok, and the voice they use will be your daughter's."

Gutenberg stood up suddenly and took the pipe from his mouth. It was with a feeling of shock that Frazer realized he was putting an end to the brief interview. "Then that would seem to be it," Gutenberg said, and asked Grayling: "Could you have a written report for us by, say, Wednesday? We'll want to incorporate it in our own wrap-up."

"Now just a minute," Frazer said, aware that his head was throbbing more painfully now, annoyed that his voice wasn't steady, coldly furious at Gutenberg's you-can't-win-them-all attitude. "What do you mean, your wrap-up? My daughter's been kidnapped."

Gutenberg finally lit his pipe, reluctantly, like a man letting himself in for something that he knew would be unpleasant. "I'm afraid that's no job for Dad," he said. "You might try the embassy. I'm sure they'll be sympathetic."

"I don't want sympathy. I want help."

"Just what kind of help did you have in mind?" Mrs. Hayward asked.

The question stopped Frazer short. He couldn't answer it. "I don't know," he admitted. "I thought . . ."

"That we'd send an agent East after them? Where would you suggest he start looking?"

"I don't know," Frazer said again.

"Our job was to keep Severing from defecting. We've failed. Severing's gone. We could have handled it differently, but chose not to. Probably that was a mistake."

"Differently?"

"We could have . . . eliminated Severing," Gutenberg said. "I wasn't in favor of it. Severing just wasn't that important, and every time you use an expert in liquidation, you expose him. It just wasn't worth it."

"I'm sure Mr. Frazer has very little interest in technical problems of that nature," Mrs. Hayward said.

"What do I say now?" Frazer asked sarcastically. "That I'm sorry to have taken ten minutes of your time, and I guess I'll run along because I know you couldn't possibly be interested in my daughter's kidnapping?"

"What do you want to say?" Mrs. Hayward asked him.

"That if Severing isn't important, Cindy is. I don't mean just to me. Grayling knew it. He told you they might try to kidnap her."

"Oh my, no names please," Gutenberg said, scolding Frazer pedantically. "You mean Mr. Graph, I'm sure."

"Mr. Graph is very young," Mrs. Hayward said. "Mr. Graph did the one thing no agent should ever do—he involved himself emotionally. We had to weigh everything he said on that basis."

"Just like you're weighing what I have to say?" Frazer challenged her.

Mrs. Hayward surprised him: "Tell me about your daughter, Mr. Frazer."

"Tell you about her? Tell you what?"

"Then let me tell you. Cindy Frazer belonged for over a year to a group called AFID. That's the American Fighters for Internal Democracy, and it's what they would have called, a decade ago, a Red front organization. Maybe they still do. Unlike genuine liberal groups, AFID has always aimed to sow dissent and disunity, while seeming to pursue liberal goals. On a small scale AFID has been rather successful, wouldn't you say?"

"I'm not going to defend AFID," Frazer said.

"As a freshman at Sarah Lawrence College, Bronxville, New York," Mrs. Hayward went on, "Cindy Frazer took sides in a student controversy by writing a long letter that was published in the college newspaper. In it she took the position that it was ridiculous to paint the adversaries in the Cold War—so-called Cold War, she dubbed it—as black and white. She went on to say that it was equally ridiculous for us to regard a defector from, say, Russia, as a man committing a heroic act on principle while regarding an American defector *to* Russia as a blackguard. She wrote that ideological defection was neither a good nor an evil thing absolutely, and that it depended on the beliefs and the integrity of the defector himself. She wouldn't condemn out of hand an American defector, she said, until she knew his reasons. She quoted Shakespeare prettily: *This above all, to thine own self be true.* She . . ."

"Okay, okay," Grayling said, "so she gets taken in by a phony liberal outfit and she defends an unpopular position regarding defectors. She's only nineteen, for crying out loud."

Mrs. Hayward smiled past him at Frazer, as though equating Tommy Grayling's own youthfulness with Cindy's. Then she stopped smiling. "Are you quite sure your daughter was kidnapped?"

Frazer waited too long without answering, and then Mrs. Hayward was speaking again. "The point is, I've met your daughter, Mr. Frazer. I've talked with her. I was the 'older woman' she thought had a crush on her boy friend. I can tell you this: she was really sold on Severing. Part of the reason, if you don't mind my getting Freudian and casting aspersions on your relationship with your daughter, is that she was looking for a father-image. You weren't around much in her formative years, as I don't have to remind you. The other part is that she felt a strong ideological bond with Severing. Wait, don't interrupt me, please. I got that straight from the horse's mouth, and while I'd sympathize with your attempt to defend her, it wouldn't change anything."

"What are you trying to say?" Frazer asked.

"That even if we were in a position to do something about a kidnapping, very likely this wasn't a kidnapping at all. If she

were taken by force, don't you think Colonel Glaeske would
have gone along to help Severing keep her in line?"

"Maybe Glaeske's got other irons in the fire here," Grayling
suggested.

"In this hotbed of international intrigue? In Switzerland, Mr.
Graph? Don't be silly."

"We're right back where we started," Frazer said. "You're
ready to write her off. I'm not."

"I'm afraid we *have* written her off," Mrs. Hayward said
coolly. "Mr. Gutenberg suggested that you see our embassy here
in Bern. My advice is the same."

Frazer said nothing, and Mrs. Hayward continued: "You do
have something of a problem with the Foreign Service, though,
don't you? Thanks to the work you were doing for USIA before
taking the Madrid assignment. And please don't look at me
quite that way, Mr. Frazer. Of course we put a check through on
you once your daughter was involved in the Severing case. What
did you expect?"

"What did you find out?" Frazer asked right back at her, his
face hot.

"You spent almost three years based in Washington and
touring the world for USIA to poll foreign opinions of American State Department policies. You concluded that, thanks to
such as Viet Nam and the China-UN problem and our general
Asia policy, Uncle Sam was fast becoming a pariah."

"The hell I did," Frazer said.

"The hell you didn't."

"Oh my," Gutenberg said. "we seem to be getting miles off
the track."

"You certainly concluded . . ."

"I merely reported . . ."

"Mr. Frazer. Mrs. Hayward. Please, both of you."

"And, as I recall, you had a few choice words for poor old
Dad, too. You're lucky you won't find us as thin-skinned as the
Foreign Service."

"Sure, I see. Of course not," Frazer said, his voice flat. "You've displayed nothing but admirable objectivity, Mrs. Hayward."

"You mean you wish I were a man so you could take me outside and knock some sense into me?" Mrs. Hayward began to laugh, and at first Frazer thought she was laughing at him, and his anger increased, but then she said, trying not to laugh:

"Forgive me. I'm not laughing at you. I can just see two grown men walking downstairs and trying to beat the stuffings out of each other by the Geiler fountain in front of the stolid burghers of Bern. Can you picture their faces? It's too much."

Her laughter, frank and open, and the gift of imagination that triggered it, broke the tension in the small conference room. Mr. Gutenberg suppressed a giggle, and even Tommy Grayling smiled reluctantly.

Mr. Gutenberg said: "Off the record—oh my, yes, off the record—we wish there were something we could do to help, Mr. Frazer, but there isn't. I'm sure you can appreciate that?"

"See Ellis St. John at the embassy," Mrs. Hayward suggested.

"He's our inside man," Mr. Gutenberg said. "We shouldn't be telling you this, but it will save you some time unless you know your way through the embassy labyrinth better than we do. No hard feelings, Mr. Frazer? I'm sure you can appreciate our position."

In a way, Frazer knew, it was like being kicked upstairs. Ellis St. John would have all the glib, time-tested State Department terminology at his disposal, the big seal of the Department on the wall over his desk, a prefabricated directive outlining every alternative choice of action. Still, Frazer had no choice.

"I'll be staying at the Hotel Arca," he said. "I don't know how long. If you find out anything . . ."

"Naturally we'll inform you," Mr. Gutenberg said placatingly. "We have our own magicians on the other side. They should be able to tell us when and where your daughter is going to be surfaced."

"Not to mention whether she defected because I'm an ogre or because my work for USIA gave her the right dialectical slant on things," Frazer said dryly.

Mrs. Hayward gave Frazer a long, searching look. It was the sort of look he had received before, at diplomatic cocktail parties, when quite accidentally, something he said had cut through the three-martini banter and impressed an attractive woman, so that she seemed to be looking at him for the first time or with a new appraising interest.

Mr. Gutenberg suppressed another giggle and said: "We did seem to be contradicting ourselves there for a while, didn't we?"

"The very least St. John will do," Mrs. Hayward said, "is make sure your daughter gets her consular rights when she is surfaced."

Frazer did not bother pointing out that the United States had no diplomatic relations with East Germany.

SEVEN

He met Grayling for dinner at the Kornhauskeller.

"It wasn't the least Ellis St. John would do," Frazer said, "it was the most. He also explained, in words of one syllable, that if Cindy were surfaced in East Germany rather than Russia, which seems likely since Glaeske is involved, he couldn't even guarantee that. Might have to work through a neutral, he said, probably the Swiss, and he hoped they would play ball. Tommy, I don't know what to do."

"Well, don't get your hopes up," Grayling said, "but I ran into something this afternoon. It's kind of odd, but for lack of anything better . . ." Grayling shrugged. "Would you have known if you were being followed?"

"I doubt it."

"I kind of wandered around like a tourist all day, which is one good way to learn if you're being tailed. I was being tailed all right. I made at least three of them, and there might have been more. I'm pretty sure I could have flushed them," Grayling said, "but I didn't want to."

"Glaeske?"

"Search me, but I guess it figures. It has to be Glaeske, and it has to be you, not me, they're after, unless they're lining me up for liquidation," Grayling said calmly. "But like Severing I'm not that important. It's Glaeske, and it's you they want to keep an eye on. Glaeske wants something."

"What?"

"I don't have the foggiest," Grayling said. "I guess you'll find out. Scared?"

Frazer waited a moment, then said: "The only thing that scares me is the possibility you're wrong."

But outside on the street, after saying goodnight to Grayling, it was different. A cold wind blew down from the Oberland, bringing snow flurries. Snow mantled the roofs of parked cars and there was slush in the street. Only a few people, all moving fast, were out. Frazer turned up the collar of his parka and walked aimlessly, under the clock tower, along the Spitalgasse arcade and past the fountains on Kramgasse. A car went by, too fast, spraying slush. Frazer stood absolutely still. The car's red tail-lights receded. He turned around quickly. What might have been the shadow of a man stopped suddenly under one of the arcades, merging with the darkness. Frazer started walking again. A woman's voice made him jump.

"Ah, so there you are, darling!" she cried in German in a tired parody of a seductive voice. She came out quickly from under the arcade and linked her arm in his. He looked around and saw no one else.

"A night like this, you should be somewhere warm."

He had a foolish impulse to say, Go away, I'm being followed, I want to be followed, but they'll keep away if you're with me. "No, thank you," he said. "Really, no."

"I do not please you?"

They walked together under a street lamp. She was in her late thirties with a heavy layer of pancake makeup that almost hid the pock marks on her face. Her head was bare and her hair covered with snow. He tried to shake her.

"I will make you happy."

"I'm sorry."

The pathetic lilt went out of her voice, and this time when he tried to disengage his arm she permitted it. "I could get you a boy," she called after him, mockingly. He kept walking.

The unexpected contact had unnerved him. His heart was racing. If being propositioned by a whore did that, he wondered, what would happen when the real thing came along? He walked faster, breathing deeply and trying to calm his jangled nerves. Ahead, the cobbled street and the arcades and stone façades of the ancient buildings disappeared, leaving only a double row of street lamps fading into the snow and the darkness. He was approaching the Nydegg Bridge.

He walked across it slowly, listening to the rushing roar of the Aare, looking down at the steeply slanting roofs and the lighted windows of the Old Town. A tram groaned up behind him, its bell clanging. He looked back. He saw no one else on the bridge.

Grayling could have been wrong. Maybe he had been imagining things and hadn't been followed at all. If there was a profession more conducive to paranoid fancies than spying, Frazer had no idea what it was.

He called a halt to his aimless wandering at the bear pit. He leaned on the rampart and looked down into the bear-runs: a drooping tree, its winter-bare branches snow-covered, a large trough like black oil, and the famous bears of Bern, symbol of the city, sensibly out of sight, asleep in their dens. It was cold, not the clear exhilarating cold of the Oberland, but a wet and knifing city cold. I'll give them five minutes, Frazer thought, and after that it's back home to bed.

But home meant his room at the Hotel Arca, and more waiting, and not knowing where Cindy was or what was happening to her, and the five minutes became ten and then almost fifteen. He smoked two cigarettes. It was so still he could almost hear the snow falling.

He ground the second cigarette underfoot in the slush. A car rumbled across the cobbled roadway of the bridge. He waited for it to pass. It didn't pass. The motor idled. Footsteps came toward him. He did not turn around. The tritest of all lines in cloak-and-dagger stories came to mind: This is it. The triteness was chillingly appropriate. There were no other words.

"Herr Frazer?"

He turned then. Two men stood behind him, both in trench-coats as trite as his thought had been.

"You do not have to come with us. Only of your own free will. You understand?"

"Come where?"

"Herr Leser wishes to see you."

He nodded. His voiced choked up in his throat. "Yes," he finally said. "All right."

They fell in on either side of him and returned with him to the car. It was a black Mercedes, possibly the same one that had taken Cindy to the airport in Saanen. A man sat hunched over the wheel. One of the trench-coated figures got in back, and then Frazer, and then the other one. The door shut.

"We regret the necessity of this," the first one said. "Please hold still. Turn your head that way. So." A gloved hand nudged Frazer's jaw. A soft flannel cloth was tied around his eyes. It smelled faintly of oil.

"Comfortable?" a voice asked solicitously. "Not too tight?"

The big car made a U-turn and went back over the Nydegg Bridge. Blindfolded, Frazer could follow it that far. But then it began to turn, and through the flannel cloth light and darkness alternated, and soon there were so many turns that he lost track of them. Within the loop of the river, Bern was a warren of crooked, narrow streets. The driver took a long time getting them wherever they were going. He seemed to know his way well. Twenty minutes, Frazer judged, just before the car pulled to a stop. But Bern was a small city. Without traffic and despite the snow, you could drive clear across it in less than fifteen. They could have been anywhere.

"Out, please. Take my arm."

The slush underfoot again, which meant no arcade. Just three steps to a doorway, which meant a narrow side street. Distantly the sound of a tram, which meant not too far from one of the main streets.

"Careful. The stairs are steep."

Warmth and the faintly stale smell of a poorly ventilated house. He counted the stairs. There were sixteen of them. The fifth from the bottom gave a little and creaked. A door, and someone knocking.

"We have Frazer."

They nudged him. He took two steps forward. "Now stand still."

They removed the blindfold.

EIGHT

The windows were draped with coarse gold burlap. There was a fireplace on the far wall, two red hot logs glowing, but not in flames. A hodge-podge of modern furniture: a pair of armchairs on swivel tripods, covered in green like the sofa, a standing lamp with a garish parchment shade, a round glass-topped coffee table, a high cabinet and a low one, in wood darker than the paneled walls, a large color print on one of the walls, showing what was probably the Jungfrau massif, and on a low bench near the fireplace, his broad back to the room, his eyes brooding on the fire, his bald head glowing with its light, Glaeske.

"Half an hour," he said. "Then come back."

The two men who had brought Frazer upstairs said, in unison, *"Jawohl."* They did not quite click their heels. The door shut, and Frazer heard their footsteps receding down the stairs.

Glaeske turned to face him. He was wearing a heavy wool sweater and a white shirt open at the throat. Frazer again had the impression of a rectangular, waxen face, jowls as wide across as the forehead, the mouth an ascetic slit, the eyes like two dark holes punched in the wax before it had quite hardened.

"Sit down, Mr. Frazer."

He sat on one of the swivel chairs. It moved with the pressure of his body.

"Drink?"

"No, thanks."

"I will have one." Glaeske went to a closet and poured whisky from a decanter into a snifter glass. "Everything, even whisky, should be drunk from one of these. The bouquet adds to the flavor, don't you think?" he said pointlessly, aggravatingly, his words belying the ascetic slit of his mouth. He held the snifter in both large hands, like a votive offering. He sipped. "There is something you want from us?" he asked abruptly.

"You know what I want. I want my daughter."

"Mr. Frazer, have you ever made a study of defectors?"

It was obviously a rhetorical question. Frazer said nothing.

"I have, of course. They are my business. For a bona-fide defector, I have always thought the cloak-and-dagger methods of the Spetsburo absolutely unnecessary. You know the Spetsburo, the special terrorist section of the Soviet Secret Police? We do not intend to use those methods in this case."

"With Cindy you mean?"

"No, Mr. Frazer. With you. The knock at the door at night, the administration of a drug, perhaps pentathol, the quick flight from a small airport—those are too often the methods of the Spetsburo. Sometimes I despair of them. They have so much to learn from us Germans."

Glaeske sipped from the snifter again, still holding it in both hands, warming it. "I have made a very thorough study of defectors. They fall so neatly into categories.

"First and simplest, there is the trouble-prone defector. He may be an American soldier stationed in Germany, in debt perhaps, or serving a term in the stockade for going absent without leave. He is bitter, and he may have access to a small secret or two, but he will get into much the same sort of trouble when he comes over, and he is almost useless to us.

"Then there is the shallow romantic. Perhaps he is an engineer of a very special sort. We want him. He has been sent by his American company to a trade fair in Poland, or in Russia perhaps. We plant a woman. She is very good at *her* work, and if he is the right sort of shallow romantic, pretty soon he does not want to leave. In a way, in a very special way, we have recruited him. He works for us, and in the end he is probably disillusioned because the woman, of course, moves on to other game.

"Then there is the mystic. An aging American who never got

over the ideological conflicts of the thirties, when he was very young and emotionally vulnerable. A Noel Field, to give an example. Imprison him in Budapest, rub his nose in the filth of his so-called capitalist deviations, and he comes out still ranting about the glories of communism. He has brain-washed himself, don't you see?

"The refugee is a similar case, but there the mystic element is missing. More often than you would think, he becomes cynical about his adopted country. He thinks back on the old days, remembering only the good. When he returns to the fold, a somewhat chastened sheep, his propaganda value is of course inestimable.

"The scientist, Mr. Frazer, is a very special sort of defector. In this doomsday world, he is the most pampered of citizens. Whatever you give him, he expects more. And an American physicist, for example, certainly has more in common with a fellow physicist in Russia than he does with the man who sells him groceries at home. Perhaps they meet at a convention in Geneva. They talk, discussing what they have in common. A bond grows. The American received an offer. He knows what it will entail: for defecting, a house in the country, servants, a chauffered car, the very top level of society, reserved in your country for the captains of industry. He defects—wisely, don't you think?

"And then there is the plant. He is an ersatz defector sent on a specific mission. He will stay to perform whatever task he was sent to perform, and then he will redefect." Glaeske finished his whisky.

"That makes six categories, I believe, and there is a seventh. Can you guess what it is?"

"You said half an hour. We've wasted ten minutes already."

"The seventh category, Mr. Frazer," said Glaeske, enjoying his impatience, "is the most interesting. Especially to you, since you belong to it. But first, what about Curtis Severing? As a double agent, he is a classic example of the trouble-prone defector. Taking money from both the East and the West in exchange for information, he inevitably finds himself in an untenable position.

Once the Americans no longer trust him, he is ready to defect. But by then we have no more reason to trust him than you do. Such a man, Mr. Frazer, is a candidate for liquidation by either side, and in the end that is what Severing feared. Until he met your daughter.

"Suddenly he had bargaining power. The daughter of a high official in the United States Information Agency, she with a background of sympathy toward causes we hold dear, her father a controversial figure who had concluded, publicly and in print, that United States foreign policy left a good deal to be desired —you can see the possibilities, as Severing must have seen them. The way to safety and a good life might be open to him if he could persuade her to come over."

Glaeske got up and poured another snifter of Scotch, swirling it as he returned to the fire.

"Our primary interest, of course, shifted from Severing to Cindy Frazer. The shallow romantic, you see, is far more valuable than the trouble-prone defector." Glaeske sipped the whisky. "I hope you don't object to this designation of your daughter. We can blame the shallowness on her youth. The girl is in love with Severing."

"Where is she?"

"She is quite safe, Mr. Frazer, and even, for the moment, happy. The initial period of orientation for defectors is pleasant, almost like a honeymoon. They are where they want to be. The commitment has been made. The uncertainty is over. Unfortunately, the honeymoon does not last forever. How important is your daughter's happiness to you, Mr. Frazer?"

"I'll do anything I have to to get her back," Frazer said, "short of betraying my country."

Glaeske smiled, as though the words had been predictable, as though he had only to press the proper button to elicit them. "Betray your country?" he said mockingly. "Possibly there are a few paltry little secrets you could divulge about the inner workings of your propaganda bureau, but our interest does not lie in that direction. Now that we know the importance you place on your daughter's happiness and the limits of the sacrifice you would be willing to make for it, I would like to know the importance you place on your daughter's life."

"Stop playing games," Frazer said, his voice cold. "You want to strike some kind of bargain. You want me to do something for you. Let's hear it."

"She is at Bautzen. You have heard of Bautzen?"

Bautzen, Frazer knew, was the East German equivalent of Camp King, where Severing had worked. It was where most American defectors were debriefed. "I've heard of it, yes."

"How long she stays there depends on you. Whether or not she leaves there alive depends on you."

"What do you want me to do?"

"The seventh category of defectors, Mr. Frazer, is the smallest, but it is also the most valuable. The self-sacrificing defector, ready to give up his own life for a loved one, the *rara avis* who places human relationships, one particular human relationship, before ideology. This man belongs to the seventh category. You, Mr. Frazer, belong to the seventh category."

Glaeske drained the snifter. "There are no trials and no executions at Bautzen. There are only administrative decisions and sudden liquidation, usually in the form of a bullet in the nape of the neck. Quite painless, and administered without warning. The victims . . ."

Frazer stood up, his head throbbing, his fists clenched. "That's enough," he said. "What do you want me to do?"

"Isn't it obvious? We want you to change places with your daughter."

NINE

There was something oddly static about the rumpled, professorial man who called himself Gutenberg and the tall blond woman who went under the name of Mrs. Hayward. They sat in the same room above the travel agency, drinking what could have been the same coffee, Gutenberg sucking on his dry pipe, Mrs. Hayward looking cool and efficient and more like a former fashion model than a CIA agent.

"And then," Frazer said, "his two henchmen came back right on schedule. They blindfolded me again and took me down to the car. It was a black Mercedes, or did I already say that? I never got a look at the plates."

"What specific arrangements were made?" Mrs. Hayward asked.

"I already told you," Frazer said, vaguely irritated, uncertain whether Mrs. Hayward thought he had left something out or didn't trust him to tell the whole story. "I have three days. They'll expect me Wednesday, Thursday, or Friday on the Hannover-Berlin Autobahn. How I get there is my own problem, Glaeske said. I'm to leave the autobahn, on foot, at the Olvenstedt exit and give myself up at the police station in Olvenstedt. If I don't show up by Friday night, they surface Cindy."

"Olvenstedt is thirty kilometers inside the East German border," Gutenberg said. "How are you going to get there?"

"Thirty kilometers beyond the Helmstedt checkpoint," Tommy Grayling said. "Our guys wouldn't pass you as far as the frontier, and the Vopos wouldn't let you cross it. Not without a cover," he added.

"Assuming you're foolish enough to try it," Mrs. Hayward said.

"That's why I came here. I want your help." \

Mrs. Hayward didn't quite smile. "I've done a lot of things for Dad, but I've never helped a defector go over yet."

"I'm afraid it's quite out of our line, Mr. Frazer," Gutenberg said.

"It doesn't have to be. American Army convoys cross at Helmstedt on the way to Berlin, don't they? Grayling said he could probably arrange it."

"You mean Mr. Graph," Gutenberg scolded.

"If Mr. Graph said he could arrange it," Mrs. Hayward said, "why come to us?"

Tommy Grayling and Frazer exchanged glances.

"A court martial would look great on Grayling's record," Frazer said dryly.

"I was willing to do it on my own hook," Grayling admitted. "I still am."

Frazer shook his head. "I want a green light from this office. It's where Grayling gets his orders, and I want him covered."

"Let me get this straight," Mrs. Hayward said. "What you're asking is our approval for your defection. You intend to walk into East Germany, surrender yourself to Glaeske and the Ministry for State Security, and let them surface you as a top USIA man who is so fed up with our way of doing things that he wants to try theirs. That's an interesting way of winning the Cold War—which, stated simply, is Dad's mission. You don't seriously expect our blessings, do you?"

"Cindy's nineteen," Frazer said. "I'm her father. That's all that interests me."

"It's not all that interests us. An impressionable child or a grown man in a responsible position—suppose you tell me which has better propaganda value for the Reds?"

Mr. Gutenberg lit his pipe carefully with two kitchen matches and squinted at Frazer through the smoke. "Believe me, I can sympathize with you, Mr. Frazer. I have two daughters myself, both in college. Oh my, yes, I can sympathize with you."

Frazer wasn't sure whether Gutenberg's sympathy was directed toward Cindy's abduction or simply toward the fact that Frazer had a college-age daughter. "I can sympathize, but I cannot approve," Gutenberg said. "Have you given a thought to what happens after you surrender to the MfS?"

"We make a trade. They keep me. My daughter goes free."

"What guarantee have you? I hope it's more than Colonel Glaeske's word."

"No guarantee. But Glaeske was more interested in Cindy than he was in Severing, and now he's more interested in me. If Cindy goes free, he gets my cooperation. That's my guarantee."

Gutenberg would not meet Frazer's eyes. "How can we let you, as you say, cooperate with Colonel Glaeske?"

"It's my decision to make, not yours. I've already made it."

"Then why come to us?" Mrs. Hayward asked.

"I told you. To get Tommy Grayling off the hook."

"Mr. Graph," Gutenberg said.

"His name," Frazer said with sudden cold anger, "is Grayling. G-r-a-y-l-i-n-g. He's human, and apparently you're not. He knows what's at stake here. A nineteen-year-old girl, and you sit there and try to tell me her father can't decide what I've decided. You're a pretty poor excuse for a human being in my book, Mr. Gutenberg. Or whatever the hell your name is."

Gutenberg sighed. "I'm sorry you feel that way. We understand your concern, but Dad cannot possibly approve . . ."

"Let's get out of here, Mr. Frazer," Tommy Grayling said. "You're wasting your time."

"And then what?" Mrs. Hayward asked. "Because if you came here for orders, Mr. Graph, here's one: You are not, in any way, shape, or form, to help Frazer defect. Would you like that in writing?"

"Don't bother," Grayling said with a cocky grin. "I have a lousy memory. Which is what I'll tell my court martial."

They were in Frazer's room at the Hotel Arca, Grayling sitting on the bed smoking, Frazer at the window looking down at the red tile rooftops of Bern.

"Just give me the word," Grayling said. "All I have to do is pick up the phone."

"And then what?"

"I have a friend with the five-hundred and thirty-second Recon who owes me a man-sized favor. He could get you on the next convoy through Helmstedt to Berlin and let you off on the autobahn, no questions asked."

"Sure, but what happens to you?"

"Maybe I'm beginning to think the Army's a pretty punk career anyway, if you have to take orders from a dame like Mrs. Hayward. Do I make that call? It's got to be soon, because you can bet your bottom franc Mrs. Hayward is going to call Big Daddy in Frankfurt, and once the word goes out, I won't be able to get you on a bus from here to Zürich. Well?"

Before Frazer could answer, the phone rang. He picked it up, said yes three times with a surprised look on his face and hung up. "That was Mrs. Hayward. She's downstairs, and on her way up. Situation's changed, she said."

Wearing a belted blue trench coat with large white polkadots, Mrs. Hayward stood in the doorway. She smiled at Frazer uncertainly, strangely shy, he thought. Then she saw Grayling in the room and stopped smiling.

"Is it all right if I speak to you alone?"

Grayling took his coat off the bed. "I was just leaving. Call you later, Mr. Frazer?" He looked at Mrs. Hayward. "You never can predict what Big Daddy has up his sleeve, can you?"

"Good-bye, Mr. Graph."

Grayling shut the door softly as he left. Frazer positioned himself behind Mrs. Hayward to take her coat, but she spun quickly, removed it, and handed it to him.

"I thought Grayling was part of the team."

"Of course he is. I really shouldn't feel the way I do about him, but he's so damn young. He'd have been unbearably smug if he heard what I'm going to propose."

"He's going to hear it, later."

"That's your business."

Frazer's offer of a cigarette was declined. He said he could send down for drinks. That offer also was declined. He looked around the small, functional single room: a modular steel chair, the combination desk-dressing table, and the bed. He gestured toward the bed. Mrs. Hayward sat on its edge, crossing her legs. They were very good legs.

She laughed, a little nervously, to break the silence. He was uncertain whether the nervousness was genuine or put on, but her apparent lack of poise pleased him. Get her out of that room above the travel agency, he found himself thinking, and she's human after all.

"What's so funny?" he asked.

"A man, a woman, and a bed," she said promptly. "Put them all together, and there's only one thing that comes to mind in this sex-conscious age. I almost wasn't going to sit here, but I would have felt even more ridiculous if I hadn't. I'll have that cigarette now, please."

He lit it for her and sat on the one chair in the room.

"What's up?" he asked. "You called Frankfurt, didn't you?"

Afterward, looking back on the interview, he was left with the odd impression that there had been three Mrs. Haywards, not one. The first was very professional and just a shade too cynical. The second, unexpectedly, seemed to be a compulsive drinker. The third, even more unexpectedly, was remorseful and unsure of herself.

"Yes, I called Frankfurt," said the professional, too-cynical Mrs. Hayward. "To put a stop to any ideas Mr. Graph might have had of sending you over himself."

"What did they say?"

"Plenty. Our desk men tend to be garrulous. But to sum it up in a word, the answer is yes. They want you to go."

"I'll be damned," Frazer said, and Mrs. Hayward grinned.

"Do you always sound so southern when you're surprised?" She stopped grinning. "What do you know about the camp at Bautzen, where they've taken your daughter?"

"It's their answer to Camp King, isn't it? Defectors, mostly military defectors, are sent there for debriefing."

"Bautzen is a town about ninety miles south of Berlin and not far from Dresden, near both the Polish and Czech borders. You've named one of its functions: the less important one."

"What's the other?"

"Bautzen is a school for spies, literally. It's run by both the KGB and the MfS, the Russian and East German ministries of state security. A fully trained Russian or East German spy, before assuming his phony identity in the West, takes—well, call them post-graduate courses, at Bautzen."

"You mean unarmed combat and how to reduce messages to microdots and so forth?"

"No, those are the undergraduate courses. Germans take them at Main Department II of the MfS in Lichtenberg, Main Department II being the espionage section. Russian spies matriculate in the Karlshorst enclave of Berlin before going on to Bautzen for their post-graduate work. That means learning who won the National League pennant last year and how to hold a cigarette between the second and third finger instead of cupped in the palm of the hand and if a man wears high socks with garters in Peoria, Illinois, he'll look peculiar, and the word gross is in among American teen-agers for anything that is vulgar or gauche, and in Brooklyn—if you are going to be a resident spy in Brooklyn, as Rudolph Abel was—you don't have or get a haircut, you take one. Know what they call the University of Illinois football team?"

"The Illini?"

"Right. What's a user of LSD doing?"

"Uh, taking a trip?"

"Right again. And what would you call him?"

"An acid head?"

"Head of the class, if you'll forgive the pun. How do you say TV in England?"

"The telly."

"But you never say telly in the States. I guess you get the

idea. At Bautzen spies learn how to go native. The course of
study is six months, and no Russian or East German agent becomes a resident abroad, complete with counterfeit papers, until
he passes it. If he does, that means he can talk native, act native,
breathe native, etc. He spends twenty-four hours a day, seven
days a week, and six months in all, preparing. And he has the
best teachers in the world—Western defectors. That's why the
Reds run their post-graduate school for spies at Bautzen. A neat
combination, isn't it?"

Frazer agreed that it was neat. He stood more than a little in
awe of the first, professional Mrs. Hayward.

"Dad has a magician at Bautzen," she said suddenly. Magician, Frazer knew, was a CIA euphemism for an undercover
agent. "A military defector. I wish I could say he was a plant,
but he wasn't. He defected, plain and simple. Then, like so
many defectors, he apparently had a change of heart. Does the
name Major William Halladay mean anything to you?"

"No, I don't think so."

"A career officer, divorced, who got himself involved in Germany with a Fräulein Gerda Grass. Maybe you read about it in
the papers?"

"The Grass case, sure. Now I've got it."

"His commanding officer didn't mind when Major Halladay
spent his entire salary on Fräulein Grass. He began to mind
when Halladay went into debt. He minded still more when
Halladay went around with her openly, while his divorce still
wasn't final, to the Officers' Club, to the general's farewell dinner and so on. Then Halladay took her to live with him and
redecorated their love-nest rather sumptuously with the cooperation of a friend in Supply and at the taxpayers' expense. That
was the sort of thing that could have earned Halladay a court
martial, a reduction to his permanent grade, which was first
lieutenant, and a polite suggestion to get out of Uncle Sam's
Army. It would have, too, only he didn't stop there, not Bill
Halladay. Do you remember seeing a picture of Fräulein Grass?
She was gorgeous, and it's easy to imagine a lady's man like

Halladay wanting her. She was also, unluckily for the major, an East German plant, an agent of the MfS. And Major Halladay, as I think I neglected to mention, was in Military Intelligence. He began to feed her classified information in return for her favors. The result was inevitable. Halladay left Frankfurt, where he was stationed, one step ahead of the CIC. He crossed over with a convoy at Helmstedt, left the convoy and wound up at Bautzen, coincidentally the same route you may be taking.

"Nothing more for almost two years. Which brings us almost up to date, because they finally did surface him last year in Berlin, for the usual TV interview and ghost-written articles denouncing the Western imperialist warmongers. Then he disappeared again. And then, during the last six months, Dad began getting messages."

"You mean from Major Halladay? How?"

"Particularly among the military, the percentage of redefectors is large. About one in three. Bautzen is a camp more than a prison. You can go AWOL from Bautzen as easily as you can from, say, Camp King, and if you're ingenious enough to cross over one way, what's to stop you from crossing back? Sometimes the MfS even helps: a useless defector is just one more mouth to feed, unless you're prepared to shoot him. Anyway, redefectors began to show up with information supplied by Major Halladay. It was their way of trying to get back into the good graces of our side, of course."

"What kind of information?"

"Halladay is a proctor at Bautzen. As a career man in the Army he's been around, and he can supply the background that helps spies-in-training go native. But he also sends Dad the kind of information that will make it easier for our side to uncover Bautzen's graduates once they're occupied with what the MfS calls Westwork. Things like age, physical description, where a spy is going to be posted, whether he'll be an Eastern European immigrant or is good enough to go completely native, likely profession he'll assume—all in all a pretty thorough dossier.

"And that *does* bring us up to date, because last week a redefector named Banks was being debriefed at Camp King prior to being turned over to his own unit for a general court martial. Major Halladay, in the vernacular, has been blown. Banks either doesn't know how or isn't saying. Dad's guess is that Banks did it himself, playing Halladay and the MfS off against each other to get out of Bautzen. Now he's trying to save his own skin by passing the word that Halladay's in trouble. In any event, Frankfurt wants to save him if they can. The best guess is that there's still a little time, because before arresting him, the MfS will want to make sure Halladay's working alone. He is working alone, by the way, and we need him.

"He's been a proctor at Bautzen almost a year. He'd know the camp inside out by now, and his knowledge of it is something Dad would love to get its hands on. So we were going to send a plant over, as a military defector, to warn him. The plant would have been a CIC agent, the idea being for him to warn Halladay and then make a break with him. But a CIC agent's a valuable piece of equipment as far as Dad is concerned. Anyway, as I told you on the phone, the situation's changed."

"I came along."

"You came along. You're a natural. You're expected at Bautzen. You've been invited by Colonel Glaeske. You can warn Halladay for us."

It was the means to the end that Frazer wanted, but the calculated cynicism of it appalled him. Why blow one of your own highly trained agents when you could send a reasonable facsimile instead?

"Could I have that drink now?" Mrs. Hayward said. "I think I'm going to need it."

That was when the second Mrs. Hayward, the one who acted like a compulsive drinker, entered the room.

Frazer called down for a bottle of whisky, soda, ice, and glasses. They smoked cigarettes and sat like two strangers making desultory conversation in a deserted waiting room. The weather, they said. Skiing conditions in Gstaad, they said. I like small hotels, don't you? Bern is probably the most medieval of

Europe's capitals, they said. What's she waiting for? Frazer wondered. Nothing remained but his answer, and there was only one answer he could give.

A dark Italian girl came with the whisky, giving them a knowing look, a man and woman in a room that had been registered as a single, in the middle of a winter afternoon. Frazer made the drinks. He wanted to prolong the feeling the maid's unspoken insinuation had left. The girl was wrong, but in a normal and expected way, and where he was going, where he had to go, the normal and the expected would not exist.

"Bet I know what she was thinking," he said lightly.

"Did you see her eyes? Telling tales downstairs right now, I'll bet." Mrs. Hayward took a long swallow of her drink. "Thanks. You don't know how much I needed that." Two more swallows and the glass was empty except for the ice cubes. She held it out. Frazer refilled it.

"In Bautzen," he said, "if they were being sent to Brooklyn, would they be taught to say 'what's bugging you, kiddo?' "

"Something like that, but kiddo is out. Kiddo is prehistoric."

"Well, what's bugging you?"

"The Bautzen magician. Story within a story." Mrs. Hayward finished her second drink. "I'm ready. At times like this I'm always ready."

Frazer gave her a third whisky, and the second Mrs. Hayward, the possibly compulsive-drinker Mrs. Hayward, went to work on it.

"There was this Bryn Mawr graduate—oh, about a hundred years ago?"

Frazer realized, with surprise, that she meant herself. "Ten maybe?" he said.

"Let me see, thirteen actually. She was recruited, as a lot of bright young college graduates are recruited, by Dad. Flattered and excited by the prospect, she started with a three-year tour in Washington, or rather Langley, Virginia, to learn the ropes, and then off to Germany she went. Department of the Army Detachment, Frankfurt am Main, and liaison work with Army Intelligence. Where, still reasonably wet behind the ears, she met a bright young Army captain." What had been a note of cynicism turning to bitterness, now became a brittle quality in Mrs. Hayward's voice.

"Romance," she said. "The quick, four-week, we're-living-in-an-uncertain-world brand of courtship. Bright young Bryn Mawr graduate gets swept off her feet. Result: marriage. But the captain was what—if you are a student at Bautzen and going to be posted as a resident agent in New England—you'd learn to call a womanizer. The bride, no longer quite so wet behind the ears, got dizzy just trying to catalogue his escapades. Divorce in process," Mrs. Hayward said lightly, too lightly, not meeting Frazer's eyes, "when along came promotion for the captain and the last and most flamboyant of his escapades. Her name you already know—Gerda Grass. We live on a rather small planet, don't we?"

Frazer finished the drink he had been nursing. "Okay, you married a wrong guy," he said impatiently. "Let's get on with it, shall we?"

The harshness of his words brought the third Mrs. Hayward, the remorseful Mrs. Hayward, into the room. "I'm sorry. I had no business telling you my troubles. That's not why I'm here." Then for a moment the first Mrs. Hayward was back. "But thank you ever so much for being so understanding."

"All right. I'm sorry. I didn't mean to snap at you."

"No. It's my fault. How can I blame you for being impatient?"

Mrs. Hayward—Mrs. Halladay—got off the bed. She went to the window and stared out. Frazer watched her, and he thought: It isn't really cynicism, it's professionalism. He had accepted Colonel Glaeske's trade, hadn't he? They would simply implement it for him. It was the only way he could get Cindy out of there.

A weak winter sun had broken through the overcast. Frazer came up behind Mrs. Hayward and stared over her shoulder at the lambent yellow light and the tile rooftops of Bern.

"It's so beautiful," she said. Her voice was oddly subdued. She was, Frazer realized, close to tears. If what they had in mind was to be relentlessly professional, he wondered, why did they have to send her?

"Hey," he said gently, "take it easy. You know what my answer's going to be. Of course I'll do it. Does Halladay still mean that much to you?"

She turned on him almost savagely, and there were tears on her cheeks. "Halladay? *Halladay?*"

"Then what is it?"

"I don't know. Leave me alone. You're exactly the right man for the job. I ought to be pleased with myself. I talked you into it, didn't I?"

"No you didn't. No sales talk necessary."

"You're capable, and if you don't mind a word that always manages to seem corny these days, you're heroic, and you're going to give yourself up for a daughter who may not be worth it, and . . . I'm sorry, I shouldn't have said that."

She was crying openly then, and her head came against Frazer's shoulder. He patted her hair with a large, awkward hand.

She looked up into his eyes. Her own eyes were angry and hurt and, somehow, accusing. "It was so easy," she said. "It was so damn easy. Why couldn't you have said no?"

TEN

When they crossed the German border north of Schaffhausen the snow turned to a pelting rain.

Mrs. Hayward sat very competently behind the wheel of her Opel Kadett, watching the drab winter landscape roll by: a curving stretch of road with old snow on the shoulders, a stand of beech trees, some pines, here and there on the dead brown fields a farmhouse.

"I guess it takes a long time forgetting," she said. "I was only a little girl during the war, but I still get the feeling there ought to be Panzer battalions clanking along the road and at every crossroad a sentry, with a swastika armband, directing traffic. The Germans! I don't think they even understand themselves."

"There's one thing they'd better understand," Frazer said, oddly relaxed for the first time since he'd flown up from Spain. He was glad to be driving north through the rain with this attractive woman, knowing what lay ahead, but able to put it out of his mind because the arrangements were being made for him, now, in Hannover, while they drove. It was still thirty-six hours until he crossed over, thirty-six hours which belonged to him. "I think they're learning it," he said. "They've learned it better than the French have anyway."

"Learned what?"

"Europe's not the center of the world anymore. The time when they could call a tune the whole world had to dance to is gone. There's a giant to the east of them and another to the west, and you can stick all of Europe into Russia west of the Ural Mountains or the States east of the Mississippi. For better or worse, we're the pipers now, and the Russians."

"That sounds almost condescending."

"Not meant to be. Western Europe is playing the role Greece played around the time of the Roman Empire. They're where it all began, and even if we're bigger, we're less cynical and still willing to learn from them."

"Then what you're saying makes Russia and China the barbarians, hungry and ready to pounce. But what does it make us?"

"That's easy," Frazer said. "We're the Romans. Jet planes for imperial roads, and a lot of waste and maybe decadence, but a cockeyed dream of a world of law, the same law for every man."

"I see what you mean. But to borrow a phrase from Mr. Gutenberg—oh my. Because when Greece went under, Rome had its couple of centuries in the sun, and after that the barbarians were pitching their tents all over the place."

"Sure, but they became Hellenized and Romanized."

"Do you think we're going under too—the way Greece and Rome did?"

"I don't think it matters a whole hell of a lot. I like to think it's more important what we do while we're around. No civilization lasts forever, except in what it . . . well, contributes."

"The tragic view of history. And *not* the depths of tragedy but the heights. I like that. It ought to make the Europeans feel smug. They've contributed so much. That is, if you can forget Germany's particular contributions of the first half of this century. Do you like it here?" Mrs. Hayward asked abruptly.

"Where? Germany?"

"No, I mean all of it. Europe. I love it. I mean, I go on feeling very American, very patriotic and proud of my heritage, but put me down in a small town in Provence or a village on the Italian Riviera, and I really come alive. It's like your ancient Romans all over again—going to Greece to find out what it was all about. What's your favorite place in all of Europe, if you had to name just one?"

"Tall order," Frazer said. "The Oberland feels as much like

home to me as Tidewater, Virginia, where I was born. But when I'm feeling jaded, the only sure cure is Spain."

"You're stationed there now, aren't you? I've never even been there."

So Frazer talked for half an hour and forty kilometers about Spain. It was, in a way, oddly like answering Cindy's question in the hospital in Saanen: "Tell me about Spain." Even while he talked, even as he framed himself in the picture of Spain that his words produced, the events of the past three days flashed through his mind—Cindy in the hospital, Grayling, the way Cindy looked at Severing and kissed him before they drove to the airport, Glaeske hitting him with the gun, the frustrating meeting with Gutenberg, the melodramatic meeting with Glaeske, the unexpected cooperation of Dad, the final meeting with Gutenberg, Grayling flying directly to Hannover to make arrangements for the convoy that would take Frazer through the checkpoint Thursday night, Mrs. Hayward's odd insistence that she drive north through Germany with Frazer, and Frazer's quick agreement, because waiting a day and a half in Hannover would have been sheer torture.

". . . Santillana del Mar," he was saying. "Every old Europe hand has his own candidate for the most perfectly preserved medieval town in Europe. That's the Spanish Director General de Turismo's, and it's mine."

"Small argument," said Mrs. Hayward. "Have you ever been to Rothenburg ob der Tauber?" Frazer shook his head. "It's *my* candidate and . . . I have a great idea! Get down the map, will you?"

He took the map off the sun visor.

"Where are we among all these ghosts of Panzer battalions?"

"Place called Mengen coming up. South of Ulm."

"It's a long way to Hannover, and we've got to spend the night somewhere. Why not Rothenburg? It's hardly out of the way at all, and you'll love it. There won't be a tourist in sight in March."

When Frazer said nothing right away, Mrs. Hayward shook

her head and told him: "Please forgive me. I'm sure you have too much on your mind to leave room for sightseeing."

"No, Rothenburg sounds fine." He meant it. Another stolen moment, he thought, probably the last, before he crossed over. It made Thursday night seem a long way off.

"Hey, pull over," he said, smiling, feeling very young, letting the deal with Glaeske go out of focus again. "Let me do some driving."

When Mrs. Hayward had parked on the muddy shoulder of the road, he got out and ran around the car through the rain while she slid across the seat. Then he was driving north toward Ulm and beyond.

They took two single rooms at the Hotel Eisenhut inside the Rothenburg city walls. Night had come by the time Frazer had shaved, bathed, and gone down to the lobby to wait for Mrs. Hayward. It was all dark wood paneling and a fireplace big enough to roast a wild boar and the firelight shining on casques and long lances and suits of armor on the walls. The concierge, his thumbs under the crossed keys of his calling on his lapels, smiled at Frazer.

"The lady is in the bar," he said.

Frazer found her. "Sorry I kept you waiting. I thought I'd be first."

"The usual woman syndrome?" she said with a smile. "I usually take longer. I was in a hurry to get down. The rain's just right, makes everything seem even more medieval, don't you think? They make a very good martini here, by the way. Don't you, Hans?"

Hans, from his station behind the bar, beamed at them. They were the only customers.

"Two of them, then," Frazer said. "Very dry and straight up."

By the time the drinks were ready, they had moved from the bar to a small table across the room.

"Just one drink," Mrs. Hayward said. "Or maybe two. I warn you, I want to go walking in the rain. Unless you want to rest? Tomorrow night's going to be rough."

"I want a drink and your walk in the rain and a good dinner. If you want to know the truth, I feel something like a condemned man waiting in his cell."

"Does that make me the warden?"

"No, I'm glad you wanted to drive up with me. I mean that."

"All right, but just for the record I had a selfish reason, and I'm not quite sure I understand it myself." Mrs. Hayward's head turned toward the arched doorway, and her voice changed. "That would be one of Colonel Glaeske's minions," she said.

A pale, scrawny man entered the bar. He looked at them once, very briefly, the way you look at the occupants of a bar as you come in, and sat down at a table near the archway. He ordered a beer and a newspaper and opened the newspaper on its stick and began to read.

"How do you know?"

"I've been outside already. A gray Ford Taunus with German plates. I saw it in Ulm and again right after lunch. Glaeske would want to keep an eye on you, of course."

"It never occurred to me." Frazer looked at the pale, scrawny minion of Colonel Glaeske, who put the stein of beer down, smacked his lips, glanced quickly at Frazer and away, and returned to his newspaper. "He doesn't look very ominous," Frazer said.

"He's not meant to be."

"On the other hand," Frazer said with a quick grin, "I was never tailed by a real live spy before. No, that's not quite true. I was in Bern."

"You probably were when you did those public opinion surveys for USIA. That may give you some trouble, by the way, when you go over."

"What kind of trouble?"

"You're tailor-made for Glaeske. He'll say you began to see the light when you learned exactly the same thing in country after country—namely, that Uncle Sam was regarded as the biggest heavy since Adolf Hitler was incinerated in the Führer-bunker. Finally you couldn't take it any more, so you defected. That will be Glaeske's story, and it's why Dad couldn't consider helping you—until my ex-husband was denounced. Which gives you an idea of just how important his information is."

"And how unimportant I am."

"Not at all. Dad had some trouble deciding, believe me." Mrs. Hayward lit a cigarette. She still hadn't touched her drink. She looked at Frazer gravely. "They would have written off any CIC agent who went over after Halladay. They're writing you off the same way. They hope Halladay can get out, and they hope you can get out with him, but they're not counting on it."

"Then why try at all?"

Mrs. Hayward averted her eyes. "They have nothing to lose —except you. Also, I thought you'd like to know I'm disobeying orders.

"By telling me this?"

"I was supposed to give you something. Marching powder, we call it."

"Marching powder?"

"A cyanide capsule. Almost painless, I'm told, and absolutely permanent. You bite down on it and you're dead inside of two seconds."

"They wanted me to take it?"

"They wanted you to have it handy if the situation got bad enough."

"Ouch," said Frazer, and forced another grin.

"You're going to fool them," she said. "You're going to come back."

"All right, Mrs. Hayward. You talked me into it."

"You sound bitter."

"I thought they were cynical before."

Nothing else was said for a while. Colonel Glaeske's minion ordered another beer.

"Martinis are getting warm," Mrs. Hayward said. "And look: forget about Mrs. Hayward or even the former Mrs. Halladay. My first name is Jane. Okay?"

"Okay, Jane."

"And I have another confession to make. Rothenburg was no brainstorm. I wanted to come here all along."

"Why here?"

"Let's have our drinks first, if you don't mind."

They had them, and ordered another round. Just as Hans brought the fresh drinks, a woman walked in. She was tall and statuesque and looked enough like Ursula Andress to be her twin. She was gorgeous.

"I'll be darned," Jane said. "Even her."

The woman who wasn't Ursula Andress sat down and was brought a carafe of white wine without asking for it.

"She lives here," Jane said. "Her father owns the hotel. The amazing thing is she's hardly changed at all."

"You know her?"

"I've seen her before. Beautiful, isn't she?"

Frazer nodded. "She's the second best looking dame in the place."

"Oh now, come on. I'm reasonably attractive, but really. Maybe I just ought to say thank you, sir, and let it go at that. I like your southern upbringing."

"Where are you from?" Frazer asked.

"Bryn Mawr, Pennsylvania—the town and the college. My father taught philosophy there. You know something? You remind me of him a little. I have a hunch you can be pretty hard when you have to be, but there's an old-fashioned gentleness that keeps coming through. I like it. And I guess I'm ready to tell you now. Bill Halladay went over on a convoy through Helmstedt and wound up in Bautzen. You'll be taking the same route. *And* I was in Rothenburg just once before, with Bill, on our honeymoon. It's silly, I know, but I just had the feeling I wanted to extend the parallel as far as possible. Second time lucky, as far as you're concerned. I *want* you to come back."

"I'll come back," Frazer said lightly. "I'm beginning to like it here."

"Talk about parallels. That girl. We'd driven here from Frankfurt after our wedding, and we'd just settled down with champagne, and she came in. I was young, remember, and excited but a little frightened, as a bride ought to be. The groom gave her one of those long, lecherous looks that I'd get to know much, much better, because he used them regularly on everything in skirts not old enough to be his grandmother, even if they didn't look like that. I tapped his shoulder and said something like, 'Hello, I'm still here,' and he said in a bored voice— it must have been pretty funny, but I didn't see the humor at the time—'Oh, it's you,' and we both managed to laugh, but he couldn't get his eyes off her all through the champagne and later in the dining room. Well, anyway, this is getting pretty involved, but that's the way it started, on our wedding night, and the only way it changed was to get more so."

"I kind of stared at her somewhat too," Frazer said, surprised that he should be defending Major Halladay.

"So did I. There are stares and stares. Yours didn't make me feel that I was sitting at your table by accident."

"I told you. She's the second best looking dame in the place."

It was, Frazer realized, no line. The words came naturally, and they were words he wanted to say. His southern upbringing, as Jane had suggested? Or because it was one more moment he could snatch before he crossed over and all such moments ran out? Jane Hayward, or Halladay, he thought, was one hell of an attractive woman, and he wanted to be here with her, in the bar with its darkly paneled walls, with the rain drumming outside, having a second martini, knowing he would be walking out there with her soon, in the rain, through the ancient cobbled streets of the town, in another century, when there had been no Colonel Glaeske and no camp for defectors or school for spies at Bautzen. But that wasn't all. There was something strangely,

touchingly vulnerable about this woman, despite the professionalism, despite the sometime cynicism. There was a very human
uncertainty in her, like her whim of returning to Rothenburg,
as though that could help, as though that could be the touch-
stone for a magic bigger than any CIA magic and could somehow guarantee his return. It was something you could pity. It
was something you could love.

He had a moment of acute awareness. It was the wrong time
and the wrong place, and the one thing he had to do, the one
thing that was everything, was cross over and get Cindy out, and
anything that made that harder to do was something he had to
avoid. But he knew, he absolutely knew, that here, sitting at this
table with him on his last night of freedom, was a woman with
whom he could fall in love. That had not happened since Diana
had died. It was a commitment he had been unable to face
again. He had loved once, with all of himself in the loving. And
he had killed her.

"Hey, you're staring at me. You look like a little boy who just
woke up."

"Let's take that walk."

They ran the last few hundred yards, through the rain, across
the worn cobblestones, past the dark buttressed façade of the
Franziskaner Kirche and the broad empty market square, still
floodlit, though there were no tourists, and not a single car was
parked in it to spoil the illusion of having gone back five hundred years. Jane lost her footing on the slick cobblestones. Frazer grabbed her hand and she came against him jarringly, so
that they both almost fell. She was breathless, but laughing. He
could feel the softly firm womanness of her through the polka-
dot trench coat and smell the perfume of her wet hair.

"High heels are just the thing for a jaunt like this," she said.

"Hold onto me."

She held his hand, and they slowed to a trot as they neared
the Eisenhut with its limp sodden flag hanging outside. Still out
of breath they entered the lobby. The door banged shut behind

them. The concierge, his head nodding over the high desk, looked up suddenly, blinking.

"A warm drink, perhaps?" he suggested. "Hot milk or mulled wine? We could serve it in the bar."

"I'm starving," Jane said. Her hair was plastered to her head, rain water was running down her cheeks, and her blue-green eyes were sparkling.

"I regret, *gnädige Frau,* but the dining room is closed. It is almost midnight."

"Midnight?" Jane repeated.

The door opened and banged shut again. Colonel Glaeske's scrawny, sallow-faced minion came in dripping wet. He looked very unhappy.

It was Jane who started laughing first, but soon Frazer joined in, and the concierge watched them with patient uncomprehending politeness, two Americans, drenched, in the middle of the night, laughing so hard that they couldn't talk.

"Dinner," said Colonel Glaeske's minion peremptorily. "Schnitzel and fried potatoes. And a bottle of Dortmunder."

"I am sorry, *mein Herr,* but the dining room is shut," the concierge said.

"I am a paying guest here." Raising his voice: "I want my dinner."

"I am sorry, sir."

"I demand my dinner."

"The dining room . . ."

"The director. I demand to see the director."

"That is impossible. In the morning, sir."

"Then you will not serve me?"

"I cannot serve you. I regret it."

"The director will hear of this in the morning," shouted Colonel Glaeske's minion.

"As the gentleman wishes."

The gentleman wished for his key. He snatched it from the concierge's hand, muttered under his breath, and stalked off upstairs, casting a final baleful look back at the concierge, Frazer, and Jane.

"Friendly fellow," said Frazer.

"All good cheer and an even disposition," said Jane. "But darn it all, he has a point. I'm starving."

The concierge smiled at them. "Under the circumstances, I can no longer serve you in the bar. The gentleman might return. But hot mulled wine in your room first and perhaps I can find a steak somewhere? Bread and a green salad? A bottle of Beaune, 1957 perhaps, and afterwards some Viennese pastry and Italian coffee? I regret that the dining room is closed and hope that will be satisfactory."

"You're wonderful," Jane said. "My mouth's watering already."

"I am a frustrated chef, *gnädige Frau.* Half an hour then? He took down both room keys. "Which room shall it be?"

Frazer looked at Jane. "Whichever one has a light under the door," he said.

Jane pushed back from the table with an exaggerated gesture of satiety. Her eyes glowed in the candlelight. "I don't know when I enjoyed a meal this much."

The concierge had brought two candles in antique silver candlesticks to make their dinner more festive. He had served everything with a proud flourish and had made a point of saying he would return for the dishes in the morning. He had seemed just as determined to make everything right for them as he had been determined to give Colonel Glaeske's minion a case of apoplexy, as Jane had put it, to go with his hunger.

"There's more coffee," Jane said.

"There's more wine."

"I guess I'll have the wine."

The concierge had even brought two crystal snifters to develop the fragrance of the wine. "You don't even have to drink it," Jane said. "All you have to do is take a deep breath."

The snifter glasses made Frazer think of Colonel Glaeske. Jane looked at him. "What's the matter?"

He told her about Glaeske and the snifter of Scotch.

"I'm sorry. I was trying to keep your mind off it. Mine too. Tomorrow at this time . . ."

"I want it to come. I want to get it over with."

"Over with," she said.

There was a long and awkward silence. The meal had mostly been silence, but none of it awkward. Without the need to talk they had shared their delight over how good it was to be hungry and have a fine dinner set before them. But this was different.

"You must love her very much," Jane said finally.

"Cindy? Sure I love her."

"Would you mind me saying you sound a little bit . . . defensive?"

"I've let her down. I've always let her down, damn it. Just a shade too late, or a shade too little, or a shade too much. It's always been like that. I haven't been much of a father to her."

"Stop talking that way. Probably every good father who ever lived felt like that."

"It's not going to be like that this time."

Another silence, even more awkward. Then:

"Brad? What if she doesn't want to come back?"

"Doesn't want to?"

"What if she prefers staying behind the Iron Curtain with Severing?"

"That's impossible."

"All right. I suppose you know your own daughter."

He finished the last of the wine in a quick gulp and lit a cigarette. "No," he said slowly. "I wish I did. I hardly know a damn thing about her."

"I said stop that. You still sound like every concerned father." She looked at him. "I never should have brought it up. I know you have to do it. I know you have to go. And I know you're going to come back . . . somehow. But listen—you want to know just how selfish I can be? I'm glad your daughter went over."

He had not known what was coming. He just stared at her.

"Because we wouldn't have met otherwise. Because I never would have known you, or even known you existed." She was talking quickly, her eyes downcast, the candle flames making golden highlights in her still-damp hair. "I'm being selfish, because I have no right to say this at a time like this, but can you understand that if it was any other time I never could have said it at all? I want to see you when you come back. I want to get to know you better. There. Now I said it. Now I'm really embarrassed. Now you can go to sleep chuckling over your little conquest. Now *please go,* and we'll drive to Hannover in the morning as if I'd kept my big mouth shut."

He stood up. He felt nothing, and then all of a sudden he felt everything. Her eyes were still downcast. "Jane," he said.

Her head lifted slowly, golden highlights moving from her hair to her eyes. Her eyes smiled first, and then her lips. He leaned down and kissed the smile.

For a moment she froze. "Divorcées," she said. "They're so easy."

"You cut that out," he said.

Then she really smiled. "You always sound so southern when you're all serious like that."

She rose slowly, the blue silk dressing gown rustling with her movements, and came into his arms eagerly, as eager as he was. At first he thought, immediately hating the thought, that it was the ultimate gift a woman could give to a condemned man, the gift of her body and her passion. Then he thought it was exactly the right gift, whatever her reason, and then he thought that she was taking too, not just giving, and that made it, finally, neither a giving nor a taking, and he could stop thinking and begin to feel.

PART THREE

The Magicians

ELEVEN

The cell is perhaps ten feet square. There is no window and no furniture.

The opaque wire mesh of walls and ceiling, the bare wood planks of the floor, the door reinforced with metal strips, all flicker on and off capriciously. Sometimes darkness and light come and go so quickly that the effect is that of an old silent movie. Sometimes the darkness remains longer. It is an absolute darkness bringing vast and frightening distances into the cell. Sometimes the light remains longer and glares rheostatically brighter until it is painful, until it is the light of a thousand suns, until it stabs and scorches even through shut eyelids, until it brings odd animal sounds from the parched lips.

Bang! bang! he shot me down bang! bang! I hit the ground bang! bang! that awful sound bang! bang! my baby shot me down!

The sounds come in darkness or in light, sometimes so softly that he strains to catch the words that, a moment before, have blared loudly enough to threaten his eardrums with damage, even though he sits on the bare floor with knees up, elbows on knees, and palms pressed hard against his ears. And there are the terrible pregnant silences, either in light or in darkness. The silences are very bad because he knows sound will come screeching from them unexpectedly, the banal insistent unsubtle rhythm of electric guitar and bass, the railroad train thundering through a tunnel, the high treble laughter of little children, the caterwauling rock-and-roll again *here it comes! here comes your nineteenth nervous breakdown!*

In the early minutes, even in what he assumes are the first few

hours, he is amused. But his watch has been taken, and he cannot judge the passage of time. In the alternating darkness and
light, in the noise and the silences, there is no reference point.
Though the floor is solid under him, though he can get up,
giddy and disoriented, to touch the wire-mesh walls (light and
sound pour from walls and ceiling, again there is no reference
point), he begins to feel that he is floating in space. Nor can he
sleep. Sometimes periods of darkness and silence come together,
and they are tantalizing. They bring him to the edge of sleep,
but he comes hurtling out of it *roar of jet plane taking off* and
realizes that his amusement is itself amusing. If this goes on long
enough, he knows that they can break him. He is not sure why
they wish to do so. It is a strange Pavlovian game, but how can
he play it if he does not know the rules?

Think, he thinks, in the darkness and the light, in the silences
and buffeted by the sound effects, they have placed you here,
outside of time and space, and unless you find and hold on to
those reference points, they will certainly break you. A man will
come through that door, Colonel Glaeske perhaps, and darkness,
light, sound, and no sound will all go away, and you will be so
grateful you will be absolutely at his disposal for anything. That,
he tells himself, is what it is all about. That is what they wish in
this game which you either don't understand or understand all
too well.

So he plants the feet of his mind in memory, but it is hard to
concentrate *little girls gigglingly laughing louder than thunder
inside his head,* but he knows he must try.

On the train to Bautzen the defectors said: "You think I was
about to spend a couple of years in Leavenworth for breaking
that bastard's jaw, you're nuts."

And they said: "A little poker game. Just a cruddy little
penny-ante game, but they put something in the goddamn
drinks and all of a sudden I was playing way the hell over my
head. Then they tried to collect, and they weren't kidding.
They like to bust my arms for me, one at a time, and then start
on my legs."

They also said: "MP's swarming all over the place, I swear. So maybe I talked a little too much. How should I know she was working for the Reds?"

And some of them said: "Shut the damn window, will you please? What do they run this train on anyhow, dried cow dung?"

And at some time or other most of them said: "So this is the People's Paradise. It looks pretty crummy to me."

Those were the talkative ones, the Army defectors, half a dozen of them, all young, all nervous, but with built-in sneers, all, Frazer realized, talking to keep up their courage, a collection of punks who would have found more trouble than they could cope with on the streets of New York or in the red clay country of Alabama.

There were also the silent ones, brooding as they sat on the hard wooden benches in the train, staring out morosely at the snow and the bare, unplowed fields and the tidy East German villages and the copses of spruce and pine along the right of way. Among the silent ones were a man and a woman, both reasonably good-looking, traveling together. They looked at their fellow defectors and at the landscape rolling by with the stunned bemused indifference of punch-drunk fighters, but at one another with searing, implacable hatred. Frazer wondered what quirk of fate had brought them, together, hating each other, to the collection point for defectors at Olvenstedt.

Frazer himself was one of the silent ones. He had been surprised by the number of defectors waiting under guard in Olvenstedt. His arrival had made it an even dozen. Two hours later they all had been piled into an old bus and driven to the railroad station. It was a long train. The last car was just being shunted into place by a coal-powered engine, and several hundred East German troops were lined up on the siding, waiting to board. The defectors themselves, along with two guards bundled in greatcoats and carrying machine pistols, boarded the first car behind the coal-cab. It was a creaking, rickety old coach with crude wooden benches and tables, a relic of fourth-class passage, at least thirty years old, and looking it and feeling it. The train began to move . . .

She loves you yea! yea! yea! she loves you yea! yea! yea! she loves you yea! yea! yea! yea! in the light this time, repeated, louder and louder, and then, just when he can bear it no longer there is the sudden darkness, and silence. He wonders if they are watching him. A judas window somewhere that he cannot see, or a television camera behind the wire mesh on the ceiling, and Colonel Glaeske (is there a Colonel Glaeske?) or someone working for Colonel Glaeske, seated in a comfortable chair before the screen, smoking perhaps, and smiling at the way he covers his ears. Would they know the moment he breaks? Would they come then?

He finds a cigarette butt on the floor, in the darkness, and carefully straightens it. He searches his pockets but cannot find his lighter. The two drags he can get from the butt are suddenly very important. He crawls about on all fours looking for the lighter. He is trembling. He does not find it in the now flickering dark-light-dark-light-dark-light, and he freezes, on hands and knees, as the banal lyrics blast all other awareness away *gonna make you, gonna make you, gonna make you all mine, gonna love you, gonna love you, gonna love you all the time,* until the light comes rheostatically, bright, and then brighter, and then impossibly brightest, descriptive, comparative, superlative, think, remember the morning in Rothenburg with Jane, waking warm and snug and as close as two human beings could ever get, but also somehow like strangers in the big bed together. There was the strained confusion of dressing in the same room, and once or twice the attempts at embraces that were as awkward as the silences. Breakfast downstairs, alone in the dining room of the Eisenhut except for Colonel Glaeske's sallow minion. Climbing into the car, Frazer driving, and Jane subdued at his side, and the words he wanted to say, only he wasn't sure he wanted to say them, remaining an unspoken burden that added to the strain of the mostly silent drive.

There was Grayling in Hannover, and a final good dinner at the Hotel Intercontinental, Grayling apologizing because there were things he had to tell Frazer regarding the arrangements, even while he sensed, but did not say he sensed, that Frazer and Jane would have preferred a final dinner for two. Sensing that, Grayling had been both right and wrong. A final dinner for two might or might not have recaptured the shared feeling of the night before. But all Frazer wanted was to reach Bautzen and Cindy.

Jane had said good-bye at the hotel, not going with them to where the convoy was assembling outside Hannover *look at that stupid girl! I'm not talking about the way she combs her hair look at that stupid girl* in the white-hot brightness and he retreats into memory again with a white-helmeted MP poking his head into the back of the two-and-a-half-ton truck.

"Travel orders," the MP said, and the man sitting nearest the tailgate on the left side produced a sheaf or papers.

The MP held his flashlight on the papers and thumbed through them without reading anything. "Okay," he said, *"gute Fahrt* and say hello to the bright lights of the K-damm for me." He handed the papers back and the sergeant thrust them into his trench coat pocket as the canvas flap dropped over the tailgate and the two dozen soldiers sat in darkness, cigarettes glowing. The rain, which had kept falling all the way from Rothenburg to Hannover, was still coming down. The convoy had assembled in the rain and cold, a dozen two-and-a-halfs and three jeeps, and had driven from Hannover to Helmstedt on the rain-drenched autobahn, and was now entering East Germany in the rain. It was two o'clock in the morning, and if it got any colder, Frazer thought, the rain might turn to snow.

He was seated halfway along the bench on the right side of the truck wearing an Army trench coat and a pair of OD slacks over his own parka and the ski-pants Grayling had supplied. The 532nd Recon sergeant, Frazer knew, was carrying two sets of mimeographed orders, one for the Helmstedt checkpoints and another for Berlin. The number of soldiers in the truck would tally with the first set at Helmstedt and with the second at Berlin.

The truck began to move, rain drumming on its canvas roof. "Jesus H. Christ on a totem pole," the soldier next to Frazer swore. "You might have known she'd spring a leak on a night like this. Shove over, will you, buddy? I don't want to drown." Frazer shoved over.

"You're new with Recon, ain't you?"

"Temporary duty," Frazer said, wondering what the GI would think when he learned, further along the autobahn, just how temporary the duty was.

"Thought I never seen you before. This outfit ain't just snafu it's fubar. You'll see," the GI said ominously. "Smoke?"

Frazer thought he was being offered a cigarette, then realized he was being asked for one. He supplied it and settled back while the truck covered the few hundred yards between the MP checkpoint and the East German border control. They stopped again, and when the tail-flap was raised, Frazer could see floodlights outside and the skeletal structure of a watchtower. Far off in the cold rain a dog barked.

The sergeant showed his papers again—the doctored set that included Frazer in the number of enlisted men aboard the truck—this time to a Vopo in a gray-green uniform. The Vopo seemed as bored with the necessary formalities as the MP had been, but a second Vopo with a rifle weather-slung over his shoulder was waiting behind him. The first Vopo poked here and there in the truck with a flashlight.

"Cut it out, Charlie," the sergeant said. "You're not authorized to do that."

The Vopo grinned and killed the beam of his flashlight. He returned the papers to the sergeant. Frazer heard the truck ahead of them begin to grind forward in first gear. The Vopo stepped back and the tail-flap dropped. They rolled forward slowly into the German Democratic Republic.

Less than an hour later the truck had stopped again. "Ullman and McCarthy," said the sergeant. "Outside and check that left rear tire."

"You've got to be kidding, Sarge," said the GI next to Frazer, who was either Ullman or McCarthy.

"On your feet. Get going."

The autobahn was deserted at this hour, but in the unlikely event of a Vopo patrol car passing, two men checking a tire on the now snow-slick road would provide the cover Frazer needed.

Ullman or McCarthy said to Frazer: "See what I mean? Fubar." He got up, reached the tailgate, and dropped out.

"Okay, mister," the sergeant said. "Snap it up. We want to get rolling."

Frazer quickly took off the Army trench coat and the OD slacks. There was a sudden silence in the truck.

"Okay, okay, stop gawking," the sergeant said. "One of you guys put that gear in your duffel."

As Frazer approached in the narrow aisle between the knees of sitting GIs the sergeant stood. He removed a glove and stuck out his hand. "I don't know what it's all about, mister, and I guess it's none of my business. But good luck to you. I figure you'll need it."

A few moments later Frazer was standing in the snow and watching the taillights of the convoy recede around a gentle curve in the autobahn. Then there was nothing but the broad divided highway and the cold and the brightly lit blue sign over the exit ramp that said OLVENSTEDT—*nach* MAGDEBURG.

Frazer started walking *turn off your mind relax and float downstream this is not dying this is not dying!* loud like a jet taking off and the citizens of the housing development organize a committee to ground jet planes at certain specified suburban hours call that progress try to explain it to rich progress-oriented Caracas once it had come up at a press conference *this is not dying!* it was dark again and still snowing when their car was uncoupled at the big railway station in Dresden. They were fed sausage, dark bread, and bad coffee in a room off the station buffet, and the expected cynical comments were made concerning the high cuisine of the People's Paradise. But the banter as they approached their destination, Frazer observed, was subdued and less spontaneous. Nobody had much to say when they were led outside the station and boarded a small bus for the short drive to Bautzen, the two greatcoated guards still riding fore and aft with their machine-pistols.

The bus climbed into mountain country. Diesel-powered, it groaned resolutely up the steep, twisting road. The driver was a fat woman with a face like raw dough. She chain-smoked all the way to Bautzen, and was still smoking when they filed from the bus not quite two hours after they left Dresden.

Then Frazer found himself standing in the snow again, this time with eleven other defectors to keep him company.

Ten minutes passed. Fifteen. A cold wind blew down from unseen mountain peaks. Faintly through the snow came the sound of music and a voice wailed in nasal English a lament about a lonely woman who kept her face in a jar by the door. There was little to see except the falling snow, and the dim, dark silhouettes of a few shedlike buildings nearby and, further off, long low barracks with their windows lighted.

It was a good trick, Frazer had to admit, stamping his feet to keep them from going numb. If the defectors were kept waiting out there long enough, they'd be grateful for whatever happened next.

What happened next, after almost an hour, was the sudden appearance of a man with a flashlight, flanked by two more guards. He walked down the line of defectors, saying nothing, and then about-faced and walked halfway back, stabbing at an occasional face with the beam of the flashlight.

"Hey, how's about letting us in out of the hot sun?" a voice called plaintively.

"Welcome to Bautzen!" shouted the man with the flashlight. "That you have come this far . . . is a tribute . . . to your good sense . . . and the strength of your convictions."

Died in the church, wailed the voice.

"Bedding will be issued at the supply shed . . . and toilet articles . . . for those who need them," declaimed the man with the flashlight. "You will be expected . . . to keep your quarters . . . spotless and ready for inspection . . . at all times. Personal interviews and testing . . . begin tomorrow. I want again . . . to stress . . . the importance of these sessions . . . in regard to your own future. After three or four days . . . we shall know each of you . . . as an individual. After a week . . . we shall know . . . where best you can serve the German Democratic Republic . . . and its allies. Obey instructions . . . cooperate . . . at all times take your processing seriously. I am Sergeant Schmidt . . . your cadre. Have you any . . . questions?"

Three or four days, a week, the dry bored voice of Sergeant Schmidt shouting at them as if they were new recruits at an induction center—the prospect was so far from what Frazer had expected that he could not allow himself to be marched off with the others. He had to see Colonel Glaeske. He had to see Cindy. He had to know what arrangements were being made for her release.

He stepped forward. Sergeant Schmidt immediately shot the flashlight beam on his face. He blinked. His teeth were chattering with the cold. Step back, he thought. Go with them for now. You're tired and overwrought. You're in no condition to argue.

"You have a question?"

He did not step back.

"Hey, knock it off, pal, let's get inside first."

"It is his right to ask a question," Sergeant Schmidt allowed in a faintly irritated voice, using the old army trick of making a maverick toe the line by sympathizing with the group whose comfort was adversely affected by the maverick's behavior.

"I want to see Colonel Glaeske," Frazer said.

He turned his head away from the flashlight beam. The light followed him.

"You want what?"

"Colonel Glaeske is expecting me."

Silence. The light. A long wait. Grumbling from the other defectors.

"What name did you say?" asked Sergeant Schmidt.

"Glaeske. Colonel Glaeske. My name is Frazer."

The light left his face suddenly. He could see absolutely nothing.

"You will fall back into line with the others and march to the supply shed. There is no Colonel Glaeske here at Bautzen."

But he had refused to fall back into line. Sergeant Schmidt had conferred with one of the guards, and he had been marched off, alone and at gun-point, to the nearest shedlike building.

Where the cell was waiting for him THEY'RE COMING TO TAKE ME AWAY HA-HA THEY'RE COMING TO TAKE ME AWAY HO-HO THEY'RE COMING TO TAKE ME AWAY

TWELVE

"Boy, I've really got to hand it to you," an ingenuous American voice said. "They'll be talking about this for a long time."

There was light, just plain, ordinary light from a single source in the middle of the wire-mesh ceiling. Bradley Pickett Frazer looked up warily. The light remained unchanged. A figure stood over him, a man in gray-green pants and a gray-green wool shirt open at the collar. The pants were tucked neatly into short, highly polished boots. The shirt was covered by an unzipped fleece-lined windbreaker. The man had a cheerful, freckled face and a thatch of unruly sandy hair. He was smiling down at Frazer.

"It's one for the books, all right. How'd you do it? Thirty hours, minus a few minutes. You took the treatment thirty hours without breaking. Nobody else ever came close." He laughed. It was an ingenuous laugh, to go with the ingenuous voice. "Do you *like* yé-yé music or something?"

Frazer's lips were parched. He was terribly, consumingly thirsty. "Drink of water," he said.

"Presto," said the sandy-haired, freckle-faced, ingenuous-looking man. He produced a canteen. Frazer took it from him and drank deeply. The water was cool. "They always ask for water," the man said. "Never something to eat, just water."

"You've been through this before?"

"Both ends," said the man. "Your way only once. I lasted, I think, six hours. Then I started climbing the walls. Boy, I've really got to hand it to you," he said again. "Want a smoke?"

Frazer nodded.

"They're Kazbeks, Russian cigarettes. Kind of strong like

Gaulois, but you get used to them." The man smiled and winked. "I've got an in with the camp commander." He crouched and lit Frazer's cigarette. "What did you go and do? To deserve the yé-yé treatment."

"I was hoping you could tell me," Frazer said.

"Me? I only work here." The sandy-haired man was still crouching near Frazer. His left eyelid twitched, and the eye shut and then opened quickly. He did not seem aware of the nervous tic. His eyes were a friendly, innocent, baby blue. The tic came again. "But I'll tell you this—they don't waste the treatment. Whatever you did or didn't do, they figured you deserved it."

"I wanted to see Colonel Glaeske," Frazer said. "A German named Schmidt said there was no such animal, and I insisted."

The sandy-haired man laughed. It was open, friendly, infectious laughter that almost brought a smile to Frazer's own face. "I've been here, let me see, over a year this time, and I've seen Colonel Glaeske exactly twice. You see Colonel Glaeske when Colonel Glaeske wants to see you, not the other way around. No wonder they leaned on you."

"There was some kind of a mixup. I came here to see Glaeske. He's expecting me."

"Everybody has his own reason for coming over, but once you're here all that matters is what Glaeske says matters. It's funny, because he isn't even the camp commander. Commander's a guy named Vladimir Denikin, a colonel in the Russian KGB. He's a friendly little man, sort of an intellectual, and scared blue of Glaeske, who's second in command. Another cigarette?"

"Thanks. Can we talk?"

"What do you think we've been doing?"

"I mean, I get the idea the place isn't bugged, the way you're talking."

"Oh, it's bugged all right," the sandy-haired man said. "Would you rather it wasn't?"

Surprised, Frazer nodded.

The sandy-haired man got up, stared at the ceiling a moment, and then suddenly raised both hands over his head, pressed something, and removed a foot-square section of the wire mesh. He poked around behind it for a while, said, "We're signing off, Ivan, go have a cup of tea," and yanked at something.

"No more bug," he told Frazer. "They trust me. What's on your mind?"

It could have been a trick, Frazer realized. The sandy-haired American, after all, worked for the Bautzen authorities. What better way to gain the confidence of an inmate of the cell than to apparently disconnect the listening apparatus? But what difference did it make? Even without the bug in operation, the sandy-haired man could still give a verbal report of their conversation.

"Do you know who I am?" Frazer asked.

"Bradley Pickett Frazer, former wheel with USIA. You came here to collect your female offspring, who came over with a double-agent named Severing. She's a doll, by the way."

"How is she? When can I see her? When does she go back?"

"Whoa," laughed the sandy-haired man. "Slow down. I said I had an in with the camp commander, but I don't exactly run the joint. The last I saw of her she was fine."

"Is she . . . living with Severing?"

"That's the American father talking, all right. I don't know what their sleeping arrangements are. And while we're at it, I don't know when you can see her either, and I don't know when she gets to go back. I can take a pretty good guess, though. Denikin will want something from you first, as proof of your good intentions. My advice is to cooperate, because if you cooperate with Denikin, you don't have to tangle with Glaeske."

"What will he want?"

"Beats me. The usual defector propaganda stuff, I guess. Funny thing, but even though a guy comes over of his own free will, he still balks at making like a turncoat at the beginning. After a while it comes easy. You'll see. They have a way of holding Glaeske over your head like a club."

"What if I say no dice until Cindy's back in the West?"

"You'd be making a mistake, believe me. You'd get Glaeske.
Play ball with Denikin, and you won't regret it. He's a pretty
good joe. Once I realized that, I had it made." The sandy-haired
man offered Frazer a third cigarette, which was declined, and lit
one for himself. "The name's Halladay, by the way," he said.
"But you might as well call me Bill. Everybody does, sooner or
later."

That the ingenuous, baby-blue-eyed American was Jane
Halladay's former husband came as a surprise to Frazer. Somehow he had expected a man at once more sophisticated and less
open.

"If you're Halladay," Frazer said, "you better be sure nobody
can hear us. Because I have a message for you."

"I said so, didn't I?" Halladay seemed insulted. "Nobody else
is listening, believe me. What kind of message?"

"You're sure?"

"Come on, give, will you? This is one of my jobs, first man
into the yé-yé cell after decontamination. I know the joint inside out. We're unbugged."

"A redefector named Banks came back with the news that
you're blown. Dad wants you to get out as soon as possible."

The tic in Bill Halladay's eye became more pronounced.
"Hell, I remember Banks. A mean little pimply faced son of a
bitch. He wanted to redefect almost the minute he got here."

"Did you help him?"

"Me?" Halladay asked innocently. "Why should I have
helped him?"

"You've been doing Dad a few unasked-for favors lately, the
way I hear it."

Halladay waited a long time before replying. He finished his
cigarette, dropped it on the floor, ground it to shreds with the
heel of his boot. "Unasked-for but not unappreciated, I hope,"
he said finally.

"They sent me to warn you you've been blown. Banks probably did it. Glaeske and Denikin won't lower the boom on you
until they're sure you're working alone. Then look out."

Again Halladay was silent. He lit another cigarette. The tic was still more pronounced. He laughed nervously, almost a girlish giggle. "I'm in no sweat," he said at last. "Dad's being overpaternal. The Reds know a good thing when they see it. I wouldn't be the first double-agent they decided to keep around because he did them more good than harm."

"Then why send your messages to Dad at all?"

"Because I won't be here forever. I've got connections. I can walk out of Bautzen any time I want and be back on the other side of the curtain inside of twenty-four hours."

"Could I go with you?" Frazer asked.

"Hey, one thing at a time. I thought you came to change places with the offspring."

"I mean after that."

"Slow down, boy. You're too fast for me."

Maybe, Frazer thought, he was too fast for his own good. He couldn't help it. He hadn't realized how much effect the treatment had had on him until now. But now he knew he was talking too much. A blown double-agent like Halladay was the last man he should trust. But the aftereffects of thirty hours in the cell were like the immediate effects of a shot of pentathol. Colonel Glaeske must have counted on that, and the obvious audience for such compulsive talking would be an apparently sympathetic American. Even the disconnecting of the bugging apparatus had been an effective ploy. Still, he hadn't said anything about himself that would come as a surprise to Glaeske. He was no voluntary defector. It was natural that he had no intention of staying among the magicians in Bautzen, or going docilely wherever they sent him. It was natural that he wanted out.

"What else do you do around here?" he asked Halladay.

"You mean aside from turning off the music and holding your hand when it's all over? I'm a proctor. I teach the local magicians how to go native in the land of the big PX. There's only one guy I know can do the job better, and that's because he sees it from our point of view *and* theirs. Old Vladimir Denikin."

"How can he see it from our point of view?" Frazer asked, determined now to stay on safe ground.

"Ever heard of Rudolph Romanovich Radek?"

"Colonel Radek, sure. He was a Russian spy they caught in New York a few years ago."

"Eight years ago, in Greenwich Village. He wasn't just a spy, he was the Chief Resident Agent for North America. He got blown because they sent him an alcoholic assistant who got to hate Radek's guts because Radek worked him too hard. Radek —real name, Denikin—got forty years in jail in the federal pen in Atlanta. He's a funny number, as you'll see. Loves Mother Russia, but he kind of got to like the States, too. He had his own life there, his own friends, and a career as a portrait photographer. His Village friends had seventeen different kinds of fits when they read in the papers that their pal Rudy Radek was a Russian spy. His accent wasn't perfect, and he was posing as a Latvian immigrant. He got pretty popular and respected there in the Village. Always doing favors for people, lending little sums of money, like that. A ham radio nut, too, the so-called ham radio being one means of communication with the motherland. Wrote poetry, and from what I gather it was pretty good stuff, so he even fit in with the Macdougal Street coffeehouse crowd. And meanwhile he was setting up Russian apparats in half a dozen cities and sending classified information out on microdots in letters to a phony aunt in Berlin. He was probably the best spy Russia ever had."

"So now, logically, he runs a school for spies."

"In a way it's like being kicked upstairs. He got to like the States too well. I'm not sure they trust him. I sure as hell know Colonel Glaeske doesn't. Glaeske's your totalitarian personality with a capital T. There's nothing he'd rather do than ream old Denikin. He thinks Denikin's too soft."

"Is he?"

"He's not relentless enough to suit Glaeske. He thinks he had a pretty fair trial in New York. He was defended by a big-shot lawyer named O'Reilly, a former wheel with the OSS, who served a term as junior senator from New York a while back. As for his five years in the federal pen, Denikin was treated like what he was: a soldier whose luck had gone sour. He's a bridge fanatic, an odd thing for a Russian, and he taught bridge in Atlanta. He also gave language lessons to any cons interested enough to take them. He was a trusty after a while. And, most important, O'Reilly liked the guy, acted as a go-between for messages from his family, and even visited him every now and then. They became friends, which is another gold star Denikin gives the American Way of Life.

"Denikin's my ace in the hole," Halladay admitted. "He says I remind him of O'Reilly. That's all right with me, especially since O'Reilly was the guy who finally got him his freedom. On an odd kind of swap, remember? It made all the papers."

Frazer remembered. There was an American graduate student named Roberts or Rogers, something like that, studying in Germany. He had taken a summer off for a tour of the Soviet Union, and CIA had contacted him. Would he keep his eyes and ears open and report when he got back? Rogers or Roberts agreed, only he did more than keep his eyes and ears open. He kept a diary and took the wrong kind of photographs, or the right kind if he hadn't been caught at it, and got picked up by the Committee of State Security in Leningrad. Though he was an amateur and Radek-Denikin a professional, his trial, unlike Denikin's, was a railroading. He got fifteen years at hard labor. He served two of them in Vorkuta, and then O'Reilly, visiting Russia at his own expense, arranged the trade. There had been some criticism, because we were exchanging a master spy for a kid wet behind the ears, but Radek-Denikin and Rogers, six weeks after O'Reilly's trip to Russia, marched past each other on foot, on a bridge over the Mittelland Canal between the two Germanies, and Rogers went back to obscurity, while Radek-Denikin, Frazier now knew, became commandant of the world's most expert school for spies.

"Denikin owes not only his freedom but his life to O'Reilly," Halladay said. "At his trial they were asking for the death penalty, but in his summing up O'Reilly made the kind of speech old Clarence Darrow would have been proud of. I can see a future time, he told the jury, when some American in circumstances similar to Colonel Radek's may be held behind the Iron Curtain. Our compassion now might give that American his life then. It kind of worked out just the way O'Reilly predicted, didn't it? Up to and including the trade. Colonel Denikin is grateful, believe me. And if you don't think I capitalize on my resemblance to O'Reilly, you're nuts. Like I said, Denikin's my ace in the hole. So thanks for bringing over Dad's mayday. I appreciate it, but I won't lose any sleep over it."

Halladay actually seemed calmer, as though he found his own voice soothing. The facial tic was less pronounced. "Now I've got some advice for you," he said. "They're going to give you a shower, a shave, a good meal, as much sleep as you want, and a change of clothes. Then they're going to spring Denikin on you. If you want to see that kid of yours on her way back home, cooperate. Denikin's a reasonable guy, and he understands patriotism because he's a patriot himself. But don't push it too far. He has a job to do, and getting you to play ball is part of that job. Play ball with Denikin, or you get Glaeske, and believe me Glaeske you can do without. They have a name for him around here. They call him the Gravedigger."

Halladay smiled. His left eyelid jumped. "Well, see you around," he said, and opened the cell door and was gone.

THIRTEEN

Bill Halladay was right about their springing Denikin on him, but wrong about the shower, the shave, the good meal, sleep, and a change of clothes.

Five minutes after Halladay left, Frazer heard footsteps outside. The door was unbolted, and two uniformed guards, polite but toting rifles, came for him. They escorted him outside into the cold, clear night, and he realized that he had lost track of time. He had expected daylight, not darkness. He did not know what night it was. He felt the hard-packed snow underfoot. Every step he took jarred him. His body was aching with fatigue. His eyes stung. Ahead in the starlight loomed a great stone pile of a building on a hill overlooking the far side of camp. They took him there, and inside, and through damp corridors, their hobnailed boots ringing on the stone floors, to a massive wooden door, and an office beyond it, where Colonel Vladimir Denikin was waiting behind a big, untidy desk, in the middle of the night, as though he normally kept such strange hours. If the intention was to disorient him even more, Frazer realized, it had worked.

Colonel Denikin of the KGB was a round, pudgy little man, wearing the same not-quite-uniform that Halladay had worn, gray-green wool shirt open at the collar, gray-green wool trousers and short boots. He wore no insignia or shoulder boards to designate his rank. His watery eyes behind the hexagonally cut lenses of his glasses seemed, oddly, both friendly and cynical. He had a large, untidy mustache and softly curving lips, like a woman's. His hair was gray, and he needed a haircut. Flakes of dandruff were sprinkled on the shoulders of his shirt.

"So you are Bradley Pickett Frazer," he said in excellent Eng-

lish, heaving his rotund body up from behind the large and in-
credibly cluttered desk. There were stacks of papers; three
books, open, lying face down; a small portable typewriter, all
but hidden; an assortment of pencils, most of them with their
points broken; two telephones; a pair of in and out trays, overflowing; an empty ink bottle; half a dozen maps, all partially
unfolded; several newspapers; a photograph of a homely woman
and two gap-toothed children, smiling fixedly at the camera.

Denikin shook Frazer's hand enthusiastically. His hand was
soft and slightly damp. An ink stain colored the fleshy part of
his nose. "It is a pleasure, sir," he said, "truly a pleasure. You
are well rested? If there is anything you require . . ."

"The only thing I require," Frazer said slowly, "is your assur-
ance that my daughter is on her way out of here. Or, if she's still
here, I want to see her."

"In this office," Denikin said in a dry scholarly voice, "I often
feel I've stepped back half a dozen centuries. This building is an
old fortress, of course. Bautzen was once the capital of Saxony. A
strange place for a defectors' camp, is it not? Do you play
bridge, Mr. Frazer?"

"What?" Frazer said.

"Do you play bridge? There aren't many sound bridge players
here. I have been studying the Italian system. Ingenious, but of
course it needs a thorough understanding . . . but forgive me.
You weren't brought here to discuss bridge. Another time perhaps?"

Denikin's soft plump hand rummaged on the cluttered desk.
He found a newspaper and extracted it from a pile of several
others.

"What would you say about this?" he asked, handing the
newspaper over. He chuckled. "Aside from the fact that it is
probably the newspaper with the longest name in the world?"

Frazer looked at the paper. It was a copy of the *New York
Herald-Tribune International The Washington Post*, the biggest selling newspaper published for Americans abroad. The
copy in Frazer's hands was dated the previous January, a little

over a year old. There were the usual headlines, some of them still meaningful and some like news from another planet. BATTLE FOR SOUTHEAST CHINA AREA, ASSAULT ON SHANGHAI MAOISTS SEEN, the screaming headline said. There was a wire-photo of Red Guards in an armored truck, touring the streets of Peking. SEN. FULBRIGHT OFFERS HIS "ALTERNATIVE TO VIETNAM," another headline said, and there was a photo of the senator, looking quizzical but unafraid as he offered his alternative. FREE FLOW OF WORLD CAPITAL ASKED BY WESTERN BANKERS, read another headline, and there was a four-column cut of the finance ministers of five countries out for a stroll at Chequers.

The two-column headline at the upper left said: AMERICAN FOREIGN POLICY DISTURBS USIA PROBER. Under it and to the right of the text Frazer saw a one-column cut of himself, smiling straight at the camera and holding a homburg in his hand.

"What is this?" he said.

"Read it," Denikin suggested with a pleased smile.

Frazer read the article. It was datelined Paris, and he had indeed been in Paris at that time, concluding a tour of a dozen world capitals to assess foreign reaction to State Department policy. Paris, he remembered, had been the most unsatisfactory stop on the tour. The French then, as now, were castigating America for their own inadequacy. But the article, supposedly an AP release, quoted him as saying things he had never said, things he did not believe then and did not believe now. He was quoted as recommending that we pull out of not only Viet Nam, but all Southeast Asia. He called NATO an aggressive military alliance. He spoke of the admission of Red China to the UN as a certainty and suggested that Chiang Kai-shek's government be booted from the Security Council in the process. He said that the massive and almost unanimous resistance of American youth to the draft indicated, better than any words, the attitude of the younger generation back home regarding our foreign policy. He was asked, on the page two continuation, if he contemplated resigning from USIA. He admitted that he wasn't sure.

"What is this?" he said again, his face hot.

Denikin chuckled. "Rather expertly done, don't you agree?"

"It's a fake," Frazer said unnecessarily. "I never held such an interview."

"A fake?" Denikin said. "But then, Mr. Frazer, I must ask you: What is fake and what is real? Here is this newspaper. You are holding it in your hands. You have read it. And, as the interview suggests, the seeds of your own defection were planted over a year ago. You have defected, haven't you? And can you honestly say all those viewpoints are so alien to your way of thinking? My job, you see, is to bring the Bradley Pickett Frazer sitting before me into complete agreement with the Bradley Pickett Frazer quoted in that newspaper. When that happens, of course, we won't have to counterfeit the first and second page of the *Herald-Tribune,* not to mention various other news media I could show you. I hope you won't make my job too difficult for me."

"It isn't just difficult," Frazer said. "It's impossible."

"But then why, Mr. Frazer, do you think we have brought you here? Your physical presence without your intellectual co-operation is rather meaningless, isn't it?"

Frazer made a motion to toss the newspaper on Denikin's desk, but the colonel said: "Wait, please. You will notice the expert quality of the work. I refer of course to the typography. You can't tell it from the real thing, can you?"

Reluctantly Frazer looked at the newspaper again. He could not distinguish it from the copies of the *Herald-Tribune* he had read every afternoon in Madrid. "No, it's a good job," he admitted.

"It is a perfect job," said Denikin with some pride. "That is another function of the camp here at Bautzen. We counterfeit not only western newspapers but various documents said to have fallen into our hands through the successful enterprises of our magicians abroad. I ask you again. What is fake? What is real?

"Here behind the so-called Iron Curtain there is a mounting thirst for news from the so-called Free World. We gave up jam-

ming your Voice of America a long time ago, and indeed I must
congratulate you on the reasonably objective approach of your
news commentators. But unjamming the Voice of America serves
an ingenious purpose, don't you see? It is a known fact that the
Voice is a government-sponsored medium of propaganda, just as
it is a known fact that newspapers such as the *Herald-Tribune*
are not. If enough people see our version of the *Herald-
Tribune,* they will take the Voice broadcasts with rather a large
grain of salt. You would be amazed at the readership of the
newspapers we produce here at Bautzen. You would be further
amazed at the credence given what these newspapers report."

"Okay," Frazer said, rubbing the stubble of beard on his jaw,
trying to concentrate, "you're doing a good job. Why bother
telling me?"

"So that you understand your position, Mr. Frazer. You have
defected. That is fact. We have you here. That is fact. What
happens next depends on you. You can choose to cooperate with
us, in which case the news released from this office and the news
reported in the West would be identical. Such news would be
real, in your somewhat antiquated terminology. Or, you can refuse to cooperate, in which case I turn you over to Colonel
Glaeske and a routine administrative decision would be made.
What is at stake is your life. Do you seriously think you have
any choice?"

Frazer said nothing. He could have fought a veiled threat; a
veiled threat usually leaves bargaining room. He could have accepted a heavy-handed threat and maybe even physical violence;
it was what he expected, and might still get, from Glaeske. But
it was more difficult to cope with a threat presented so blandly
by the plump Colonel Denikin. How could he hope to fight
Denikin's matter-of-fact objectivity?

He remembered his conversation with Colonel Glaeske in
Bern, and his rather pompous statement that he'd do anything
to get Cindy back except betray his country. Now, in Denikin's
office in Bautzen, the statement seemed not only pompous but
meaningless. Anything they wanted him to do would be betray-

ing his country. The degree of betrayal seemed his only bargaining point.

"We will arrange a schedule for you," Colonel Denikin said. "A television interview in Berlin, a tour of provincial cities here and in Poland, eventually an appearance in Moscow. After that we can talk about your daughter's freedom."

"How long does all this take?"

"Two weeks would be enough for our purposes."

"And then what happens?"

"The girl goes free, as promised. As for yourself, that depends on you. I could guarantee you a job in Moscow commensurate with your ability and experience, and all the trappings that go with such a job. A good salary, a fine apartment, a car, perhaps eventually a house in the country. You could be a valuable man, Mr. Frazer. We are prepared to coddle you. The alternative, should you refuse, would be . . ."

"What you so politely call an administrative decision," Frazer finished for him.

"Precisely," Denikin said.

Frazer stood up, towering over the desk and the plump little man seated behind it. "Let's get one thing straight," he said coldly. "You get zero cooperation from me until Cindy's released."

"I already told you . . ."

"I know what you told me. Now I'm telling you. You tried to trick me. Cindy should have been on her way out of here the day I arrived. Now you're holding her over my head. How do I know you won't continue to do that? Two weeks, you said. What about two months, or two years? No, Colonel Denikin. I don't play ball unless you do. First Cindy. Then we'll see."

"That's impossible, Mr. Frazer," Denikin said in a faintly apologetic tone.

"Then at least I want to see her," Frazer heard himself saying, knowing he'd backed down. "I want to see she's all right. Then we can talk again."

"I'm afraid that is impossible too," Denikin said.

"Why? You won't give a goddamn inch, will you?"

Denikin fidgeted behind the desk, shifting his weight from side to side, running a hand through his unkempt gray hair that sent flakes of dandruff drifting down to his shoulders. "Please don't hover over me, Mr. Frazer," he said. "You are making me nervous."

He leaned forward across the desk, looking up at Frazer as though beseeching him. His left elbow knocked a book to the stone floor. Frazer looked down at it: it was John O'Hara's *Butterfield 8*.

"I wish I had known New York then," Colonel Denikin sighed. "The hansom cabs in Central Park, the speakeasies, the double-decker buses on Fifth Avenue—New York before it became self-conscious."

Denikin leaned over, grunting, to retrieve the book, and stared at the tattered dust jacket for a moment. "New York," he said. "A cold city, but strangely a city with heart if you know where to look for it. Moscow is not such a city. Moscow is simply there. You can never love Moscow. Leningrad perhaps, when the Neva is frozen over. . . . You know New York well, Mr. Frazer?"

"Well enough," Frazer said.

"Macdougal Street in the Village? I lived there three years," Denikin said with a strange sad pride. "If you walked south, just a small distance south, all of a sudden you found yourself in Italy. A little further, Chinatown. Sunday mornings I would ride my bicycle to Wall Street and the Battery," he said rapturously, his eyes shut. "The silent waiting canyons of a dead city, longing for Monday. It was poetry in concrete and steel." Denikin chuckled softly. "It was also the only time you could ride a bicycle safely in New York."

Frazer found himself picturing the small, plump, lonely figure wending its way through the deserted streets of the financial district on a bicycle.

"I liked it there," Denikin said plaintively. "But I did my job. Where one is born is an interesting accident, don't you think? Born five thousand miles to the east, you would have been a Russian. Do you know what my job was, in New York?" "Yes," Frazer said. "Halladay told me."

Colonel Denikin pushed his chair back and stood. His legs were extremely short, almost dwarfish. The green wool trousers were rumpled and tucked sloppily into his short boots. He waddled around the desk and approached Frazer uncertainly, almost shyly. "I wish," he said, "that we could start all over again. I wish that we could be friends. I like Americans, they have an open quality that is appealing. I couldn't help thinking, though I knew it was foolish, that we might reminisce about places we have both known in the United States of America." There was something touching and pathetic about his careful pronunciation of the entire name of the country.

Be careful, Frazer thought. Despite his maudlin sentimentality, Colonel Denikin was no fool.

"However," he was saying, walking past Frazer and around the other side of the big desk, "we seem to be at loggerheads. You won't cooperate, will you?"

"I told you how to get me to cooperate."

"Out of the question," Denikin said vaguely, staring off into space. "Absolutely out of the question. I wish I could help you, Mr. Frazer. Because if I could help you, you would help me."

Frazer took a gamble. "Who runs this place," he said slowly, "you or Glaeske?"

Denikin, seated again, drew his small rotund figure up straight and stared coldly at Frazer. "Please remember that you are a long way from home, Mr. Frazer. There is no one here who will help you unless you help yourself."

"I know just how far from home I am," Frazer said. "Apparently you don't. Or do you?"

Denikin slumped in the chair a little. He went vague again. "What do you mean?"

"This is Glaeske's country, not yours. You're afraid of him, aren't you?"

"Glaeske is second in command here," Denikin said stiffly. "I run Bautzen."

"You only think you do—*if* you think you do."

"I think," Denikin said in a very soft voice, "that Bill Halladay talks too much."

"Then show him he's wrong. He said I'd better do business with you because if I didn't I'd get Glaeske."

"My dear Mr. Frazer, that is precisely what I instructed him to say. I have found using Colonel Glaeske as a club a very effective technique when necessary."

"Then use him now," Frazer said.

"If you force me to, I have no choice."

Frazer said nothing.

Denikin reached, reluctantly, for one of the two telephones on the cluttered desk. His hand paused just over it. He looked at Frazer.

"You really would be better off dealing with me, you know," he said in his apologetic voice.

"You haven't showed me that yet."

"Glaeske's methods are brutal. He believes in brutality as an instrument of policy. He . . ."

"And your methods are devious. At least with him maybe I'll know where I stand."

Denikin sighed. His eyes turned away from Frazer. He looked like a man who had just shoved his last chips into a poker pot in which he knew he had the second best hand. He touched the telephone, but did not pick it up. "Why are you doing this to me?" he asked. "Colonel Glaeske has his methods. I have mine. You can work with me, or you can work with him. There is no third course open to you."

"Let me see my daughter, and I'll work with you."

Denikin picked up the telephone. "Get me Colonel Glaeske," he said.

FOURTEEN

Colonel Heinz Glaeske's desk, unlike Denikin's, was not cluttered. It was an anomalous steel and linoleum desk in a large, stone-walled dungeon of a room, and on its surface was a single telephone and a file folder, open, which Glaeske was reading. He did not look up when the guard who had brought Frazer left him standing in front of the desk. His massive shoulders hunched forward, he just went on reading.

The windowless walls of the room were made of unmortared stone blocks, the ceiling low, the single source of illumination an unshielded light bulb hanging from a braided cord over the desk, the only furniture Glaeske's desk and chair. There was the door Frazer had come through and, behind the desk and to the left, another, smaller door, both of heavy wood planking. The room was like something out of an off-Broadway play, Frazer thought, a stage setting for the not-quite-reality of Ionesco or Beckett, with a minimum of props in a setting of eerie gloom counterpointed by the modern, functional desk, a room that Kafka might have put in his castle, a room for a modern Torquemada, a room in which the administrative decision that snuffed out a human life could be made routinely.

All right, Frazer told himself, cut that out. The setting is effective. It was meant to be effective, and Glaeske will probably keep you standing here, not looking up, not acknowledging your presence, in a fifteenth-century dungeon, with Glaeske's bald head, and his modern desk, and his file folder the only realities, until you show your gratitude—when he finally looks up, and

either smiles or doesn't smile in acknowledgment of your ex-
istence—by bowing to his will.

"What is the population of China?" Glaeske said in a dry,
bored voice, without looking up.

He did not wait for an answer. "The population of China is
roughly eight hundred million people. Some Sinologists place it
as high as a billion, which would make one out of every three
people on this planet Chinese. A disquieting thought, isn't it? A
billion people in a country barely the size of your own, gather-
ing strength to burst out and run rampant over the entire
world. The Yellow Peril, Mr. Frazer. Do you lose sleep over the
concept of the Yellow Peril? I don't. I never will. Would you
like to know why?

"Because in imagination and drive the so-called civilization of the East has never equaled the civilization of the West.
The Orient is inward-looking, the West outward. We do not
contemplate our navels, Mr. Frazer. We are not content with a
few hundred pithy aphorisms of a Confucius and the mystical
unworldliness of a Lao-Tze. We strive. They merely exist. China
will never learn to rule the world because China has never
learned to rule herself. Despite the ridiculous saber-rattling in
Peking, their outlook is essentially passive. Our outlook is essentially active. Things happen to them. We make things happen.
Does that make sense to you, Mr. Frazer?"

Frazer felt his mouth stretching in a yawn. His eyelids were
lead. "What are you getting at?" he asked.

"You fail to see the relevance? What a pity. On the one side
the striving, Dionysian West. On the other, the existing, Apol-
lonian East. Yin and Yang. And what lies in the middle?"

Glaeske stood up suddenly, a big, wide-shouldered man, the
bald head and rectangular face catching the light of the single
bare bulb, the eyes set so deeply in dark sockets that Frazer
couldn't see their color, the cheekbones highlighted and the
wide jaw in shadow, the teeth gleaming in the thin slit of a
mouth. He doesn't look human, Frazer thought. He looks like a
robot. It was a frightening thought. You might have expected

compassion from the befuddled intellectual sentimentality of a Colonel Denikin, though none had been forthcoming. You could expect none from a Heinz Glaeske.

"Russia lies in the middle," Glaeske said. The green wool shirt and bloused trousers that had fit Denikin so poorly fit him like a cleverly tailored second layer of skin. Clipped to his belt was a small black holster, the leather soft and shining, and from the bottom of the holster protruded the last inch of a revolver barrel.

"Do you know the derivation of the word 'Slav,' Mr. Frazer?" he asked. "It comes from the classic Greek for slave. That is how the Greeks, our own cultural ancestors, regarded the inhabitants of the Crimea and the Ukraine. They were slaves. They had the mentality of slaves, and a certain brute physical strength that is an admirable quality for a slave to possess. I have seen no indication that they have changed in the two thousand five hundred years since the word was coined. I grant Russia its brief time in the sun, and that time is now, but ultimately the world belongs to the striving West. It belongs to me, Mr. Frazer. And it belongs to you. The active, conquering Teutonic temperament—the German and the Anglo-Saxon and even the American mongrelization of both. But the Anglo-Saxon is too idealistic and the American mongrelization includes some unfortunate additional strains, which dilute the blood.

"We Germans have always been a practical people. We can recognize that the totalitarian framework of communism is just as satisfactory for our purposes, and certainly less odious to certain large segments of world opinion, as the old totalitarian framework of Nazism. In the end we Germans will thank the Russians. We will let them pave the way for our inevitable return to power."

Frazer stood there, in front of the modern desk, in this medieval dungeon of a room in the old Bautzen fortress, with a fixed, attentive look on his face. He was fascinated, the way a doomed animal is fascinated by the spreading hood of a cobra. He was listening to a madman.

"I give you as a case in point," the madman said, "Colonel

Denikin. I give you Bautzen for a microcosm. The Slav, hope-lessly trapped geographically between East and West, and the Teuton. Colonel Denikin wanted to break you himself. It meant a great deal to him. He failed, as I knew he would fail. Now it is my turn. Do you think I will fail, Mr. Frazer?"

"Go ahead and answer your own question," Frazer said. "You're pretty good at it."

"Would you say whether I succeed or fail depends on one thing? On one specific factor?" Glaeske asked with an almost fe-line smile.

"You know it does."

"And what would that factor be?"

"You know the answer to that one too."

"The girl?"

"My daughter, yes."

"But you are wrong, Mr. Frazer, as wrong as Colonel Denikin. Whether I succeed or fail depends on one thing only—the strength of my will as opposed to the strength of your will. The purebred Teuton and the mongrel American—it hardly seems a fair contest. However, we shall see. Right now the telephone is going to ring."

Obediently, the telephone on Glaeske's desk rang.

"Yes? Then send him in," Glaeske said, and the door that Frazer had come through opened, and Bill Halladay came into the room, the friendly, open, boyish smile belied by the nervous tic in his left eye.

"You sent for me, Colonel?"

"How considerate of you to be on time, Bill," Glaeske said warmly, and Frazer was instantly alert. He did not know what was coming, but he knew it would be bad. The spurious warmth in Glaeske's voice contained a warning note.

"But then," Glaeske went on in the same warm vocie, "tardi-ness was never one of your faults. You know Mr. Frazer?"

"Yeah, sure," Bill Halladay said. "I didn't expect to see you again so soon, Frazer."

The fact that he had nowhere to sit bothered Bill Halladay.

He shifted his weight from one foot to the other. He looked anxiously at Glaeske and then away. He looked at Frazer and tried a smile on for size. He cleared his throat. The muscle under his left eye jumped.

"Mr. Frazer and I," Glaeske said, "were in the midst of an interesting discussion—the fact that Colonel Denikin had failed to win his cooperation. I pointed out that Denikin had wanted desperately to do so, as a means of proving something to himself and about himself. Would you consider that a fair statement of the situation?"

"I guess so," Bill Halladay said uncertainly. "I don't know what you're driving at, Colonel."

"At the difference between Colonel Denikin and myself. There is a difference, isn't there, Bill?"

"Putting it mildly," Halladay said with a forced laugh.

"What would you say that difference is?"

"You're stricter," Halladay said, laughing again, nervously.

"Stricter. Yes, I see. Cleverer, would you say? Please be honest with me, Bill."

"Well, he's a pretty intelligent guy," Bill Halladay said after a while. He had glanced at Frazer before answering, as though hoping Frazer could tell him what to say.

"And you like him?"

"Sure, I guess so."

"Then you would say that the difference between Colonel Denikin and myself is such that you could never like me? That it makes a feeling of dislike on your part inevitable?"

"I . . . I don't understand," Bill Halladay said, a little desperately.

"It isn't important, Bill. Don't worry about it. Would you say Colonel Denikin is softer than I am?"

"Softer?"

"More easily swayed. Less relentless. Sentimental even."

"He's a nice guy."

"If, for example, he became aware that one of his trusted lieutenants had been deceiving him, what might you expect him to do?" Glaeske asked calmly, and Frazer knew it was going to be very bad.

The muscle on Bill Halladay's left cheek really jumped. "I don't know," he said in a hoarse voice. "I don't know what you mean."

"We'll get back to it. Would you say Colonel Denikin places more importance on human relationships than I do?"

"Yes, sir," Bill Halladay said, feeling himself on safer ground. "I'd have to admit that."

"Thank you for your candor, Bill. I'm sure all this is very instructive to Mr. Frazer. Would you say another way of comparing us is to say that Colonel Denikin is a talker and I am a doer?"

Bill Halladay cast a cocky grin, his last grin of any kind, in Frazer's direction as he said: "Well, you've been doing a lot of talking yourself, Colonel."

"An excellent bit of repartee, Bill," Glaeske said. "I am delighted that our conversation pleases you. I would hate to think that you found your last little talk with me disappointing. But to return to Colonel Denikin. I believe I can reproduce the interview he had with Mr. Frazer here. Not verbatim, of course, but in substance. Do you think you could?"

"Gee, I don't think so," Bill Halladay said.

"Colonel Denikin would have dwelled on the subject of administrative decisions. Of course you know what an administrative decision is, in our terms here at camp?"

"Yes, sir," Bill Halladay said.

"Tell me."

"It's a round-about way of saying . . . you know . . . execution." The muscle under Bill Halladay's eye jumped and jumped. He was blinking.

"That's right, Bill. The euphemistic term, by its very understatement, was meant to frighten Mr. Frazer, to bend his will. But it failed. Can you tell me why it failed?"

"He, uh, doesn't scare easy? That's it, sure. He's a guy who doesn't scare easy."

"You disappoint me, Bill. Your answer is irrelevant. Obviously what we are interested in is Colonel Denikin's technique, not Mr. Frazer's ability to withstand threats. Would you care to try again?"

"I think you kind of lost me there, Colonel," Bill Halladay said.

"I was trying to suggest that the threat, no matter how deftly made, is insufficient unless reinforced promptly with an example. We learn by example after all, don't we? Is that easy enough for you, Bill?"

"Yes, sir."

"Say it."

"We learn by example," Bill Halladay said.

"And the more obvious the example, the more readily we learn? Would you agree to that?"

"I guess so," Bill Halladay said.

"What would you say is the most obvious example Colonel Denikin could have employed?"

"I don't get you, sir."

"If he wanted to terrorize Mr. Frazer with the words 'administrative decision.' "

Bill Halladay said nothing.

"Come now, Bill," Glaeske chided. "Take a guess. If you're wrong we won't hold it against you. Would we, Mr. Frazer?"

"Well . . . you know . . . deeds not words," Bill Halladay said.

"Be specific."

"You mean, uh, he'd let Mr. Frazer witness one of those . . ."

"Say it," Glaeske urged in a friendly voice.

"Administrative decisions," Bill Halladay said, and his entire face seemed to be jumping.

"Correct," Glaeske said. "But unfortunately, we don't find the need for administrative decisions every day. Do we, Bill?"

"I guess not."

"Colonel Denikin, had he been a stronger individual, could have provided one. There is an overdue administrative decision here at Bautzen. Colonel Denikin knows that as well as I do. I believe we have delayed it long enough, Bill. Don't you? Especially since it would serve a double purpose now. The second purpose being to bend Mr. Frazer's will. Can you tell me what the first purpose might be? Never mind, Bill. You look desperate. A man cannot think clearly under the burden of such strong emotion. Let me tell you: the first purpose would be the removal of what Colonel Denikin would rather picturesquely refer to as a *shavki,* a hungry mongrel. In plain words, a double-agent. I believe it is apt that the *shavki* in question is an American, a representative of that most mongrelized of all races. It is still more apt, because the witness whose will we are trying to bend is also American."

Bill Halladay finally understood what he had not wanted to understand. "Wait," he said. Tic. "Listen. You've got to give me a chance to explain." Tic. "I've been a good worker here. I did a few things." Tic. Tic. "A few things I shouldn't have, but Christ, a guy living this life, he's got to play both ends against the middle. A few little things because I felt sorry for some guys who came over and changed their minds, it wasn't so much, if they wanted to go back they wouldn't have been much good to you anyway. I'm a loyal defector, I swear I . . ."

"A loyal defector," said Glaeske, smiling thinly. "What an interesting, self-contradictory term. Loyal to whom, Bill?"

Tic. "If you just give me a chance, I could explain it all to you, I won't do it again, you've got to listen . . ."

"But you're wrong, Bill. I don't have to listen. This is no trial. There are no trials at Bautzen, only administrative decisions."

"I could tell you things," Halladay said. "I could tell you . . . Frazer, even. Sure. I could tell you. CIA. He works for CIA. They sent him here to warn me. He's an agent. He told me. His daughter was only an excuse." Tic. Tic. "You've got a CIA agent right in your hands, and I gave him to you."

"Bill, Bill," Glaeske said. "If all you did was send a few unsatisfactory defectors on their way home, why would CIA go to so much trouble on your behalf? As for Frazer, of course he came over with the cooperation of CIA, since he did not have my cooperation. And of course they would use him to deliver a message to you. But his first interest is the child. Once he sees the futility of one of his missions, he will realize the futility of the other . . . unless he bows to my will. Do you agree, Mr. Frazer?"

Frazer did not answer immediately. His mouth was dry, his palms moist. Here, in this room, in the next few moments, cold-blooded murder would be committed, an overdue administrative decision, as Glaeske had put it, but whether or not the administrative decision would have been implemented at a later date was something Frazer would never know, unless he could prevent its implementation now. Bill Halladay was a few moments away from death because Frazer had said no to Colonel Denikin.

"You've made your point," he said to Glaeske. "I'm willing to compromise. I start working for you as soon as I know Cindy's . . ."

"Compromise is not a word in my vocabulary," Glaeske said. "Do not mistake me for Colonel Denikin."

"All I want to know is that my daughter . . ."

"We'll get to your daughter later. Bill?"

Tic, tic.

"Please get a grip on yourself, Bill. All you have to do is go to the door behind my desk and open it. Quite simple, really."

Bill Halladay began to cry.

"You will go to the door behind my desk and open it."

Bill Halladay stood there crying.

"There are not two doors. Just one. No decision for you to make at all. *You will go to the door and open it. Now."*

Bill Halladay looked at the door. He stood perhaps twenty feet from it. Six or seven steps. He started walking, slowly, one slow step at a time, looking down at the stone floor in front of his feet. When he had taken three steps, Glaeske came up behind him. Bill Halladay did not react. He took a fourth step and a fifth. He was very near the door. He took a sixth step and a seventh. They placed him directly in front of the door. He waited just two or three seconds, not looking back at Glaeske. He reached out for the door latch. As his fingers touched it Glaeske withdrew the revolver from the soft black leather holster. He raised it behind the nape of Bill Halladay's neck. Bill Halladay tried to pull the door. It did not open that way. He pushed it and it swung away from him on creaking hinges. Beyond it was a staircase going down.

Glaeske placed the muzzle of the revolver in contact with the nape of Bill Halladay's neck, and still Halladay failed to respond in any way.

Glaeske pulled the trigger once. The revolver made a surprisingly small, flat sound.

Bill Halladay tumbled down the stairs.

Frazier watched Glaske pull the door shut, watched him replace the revolver in its holster, watched him return to the desk.

"I would like you to have some time to consider this," he said. "We will talk again. But there is one thing I want you to understand. Cooperate with me and there will be no need for any further administrative decisions. Fail to cooperate and naturally the need may arise again. I am not talking about an administrative decision concerning you, Mr. Frazer. You are too valuable a property. I mean your daughter."

FIFTEEN

Cindy stands at the open door with her back to the big dungeon of a room. Glaeske comes up behind her with the revolver. He makes no sound. Mr. Gutenburg and Jane Halladay come rushing in.

Frazer is standing to one side. He cannot move. "Stop him," he says. "He's going to kill Cindy."

"It is merely an administrative decision," Glaeske says calmly.

"He is going to kill Cindy," Frazer shouts.

Mr. Gutenburg waggles a finger in front of Frazer's face. "Please, Mr. Frazer," he says chidingly. "How many times must I tell you? No names. Do not call her Cindy. She has a code name. Severing is Red Rover. She is Red Rover Two."

While Mr. Gutenburg is talking, Glaeske fires the revolver. He turns calmly as the body tumbles down the stairs. "Next," he says. "Who is next?"

"But I thought he shot Bill," Jane Halladay says.

"Please," Mr. Gutenburg tells her. "How many times must I remind you, no names?"

Frazer came out of the dream sitting up and wide awake. He was sweating. The bright sunlight streaming through the window hurt his eyes. He looked around the small room. A large wardrobe took up one wall. His clothing had been piled in a heap on the single straight-backed chair. Near it was a wire book rack, crammed with paperbacks, and beyond that an alcove hidden by a faded, black and gold striped curtain. On the back of the door hung a calendar with a picture of an enormous-breasted nude throwing a month-old February snowball.

Frazer remembered vaguely being led to one of the barracks by a pair of guards. They had walked through a dormitory with double-decker bunks on either side of the narrow aisle. Up a flight of stairs to a hall, and along the hall to this room. The guards had left him.

He got out of bed and went to the window, naked, squinting against the sunlight. There were three other wooden barracks buildings on a snow-covered quadrangle. A few figures trudged by, wearing the familiar gray-green. A small car drove past with tire chains on the rear wheels. In the distance Frazer saw mountains. He opened the wardrobe. There was a shelf of underwear, socks, and towels, a pair of boots on the floor, and wool shirt and trousers, gray-green, on one wooden hanger and a loden coat on the other. The book rack next: American paperbacks, mysteries and sex novels mostly, all of them old, their garish covers faded and creased. The curtained alcove: a toilet, a shower nozzle in the center of the ceiling, a sink with soap, toothbrush, toothpaste, razor, and shaving cream set out on a shelf under the small mirror. He used the facilities. The shower ran as hot as he wanted to make it. He made it very hot and then very cold. He used a towel to wipe the moisture from the mirror, shaved, brushed his teeth and drank a quart of water straight from the tap. The mirror showed him a Bradley Pickett Frazer who looked like he had just come off a three-day bender.

He dressed in the clothing they had provided. It was a good fit. There were footsteps in the hall occasionally, and distantly the sound of rock-and-roll music, which made him wince. He waited. He expected someone to come for him. No one came for him.

He looked at the door nervously. He was afraid of the door, and the fear annoyed him. I don't want to go out, he thought. It's warm in here, and secure. They'll come for me when they want to come for me.

He went to the door, the boots clomping loudly on the bare floor. He almost hoped the door would be locked.

The door was not locked. It did not open into the room. It opened outward. He remembered Bill Halladay, opening another door that way. His hand began to shake.

"Now cut that out," he said, aloud. It's a door, he thought. You open it and you see what the magicians have provided for your delectation. Get the shakes now and Glaeske will have you exactly where he wants.

What the magicians had provided for his delectation was a narrow hallway with many doors, like his own door, on either side. One of the doors opened and Frazer checked an impulse to flatten himself against the wall and hope he wasn't seen. A man emerged, not young, not old, with a round, deeply-suntanned face. He grinned at Frazer.

"Did you know," he said, "that no one can be considered for the Baseball Hall of Fame in Cooperstown, New York, unless he played ten years in the major leagues? Pretty good, huh?" The round-faced man seemed very pleased with himself. He did a little jig in the hall. "Are you from Dixie?" he said, not quite singing it.

"As a matter of fact I am," Frazer said.

"Then who knows, maybe we'll be meeting somewhere south of the Mason-Dixon line one of these days." The man looked at Frazer, and the self-satisfied smile left his face. "You can't kid me," he said. "You're a proctor, I bet. Where's your southern suntan, boy? New, ain't you?"

"Yes, I'm new," Frazer said.

"But still a proctor," the man insisted suspiciously. "Lordy, the way you guys try to trick us up! How's my accent?"

"Peachy," Frazer said dryly.

"Which kind of means I talk too much, huh? Well, good for me, boy. What I'm supposed to do. I'm gonna be a garrulous old fart in the state of . . . uh-uh, boy, not me. Thought I'd spill it, dincha? That garrulous I ain't. Gonna dabble in politics though. That's the general eye-dea. Well, me for some chow. You coming?"

It could have been a greasy-spoon cafeteria in New York. There was a long counter with hot dishes on steam trays and cold dishes bedded in crushed ice. White celluloid letters on a display board announced the daily specials in English: franks and beans, chipped beef on toast, lemon meringue pie. You took a little ticket when you entered the line and a plump woman in a white uniform punched it at the checkout counter.

"What do I do now?" Frazer asked his companion. "I don't have any money."

"Friend," the man laughed, his southern accent less pronounced, "you really are new. This here's the land of make-believe. Nobody's got a nickel. What happens next is you sit down and eat. Ennis is my name, Harvey Ennis. Harvey Beauregard *Lee* Ennis, suh."

"Bradley Pickett Frazer."

"Are you from Dixie?" Ennis sang, and they moved with their trays to a table where four other men were already eating. The cafeteria was crowded.

". . . Cape Kennedy?" one of the men at the table was saying.

"Cape Canaveral," another man said promptly.

"What about Kennedy International Airport?"

"New York International or Idlewild."

"May I have the mustard, please?"

"May I have is okay. But say pass. It's better."

"Pass the mustard."

"And what happens if I take some first, like so?"

"Uh, boardinghouse reach?"

"Nope. That's making a grab for something across the table. What I'm doing is called shortstopping."

"Who was the shortstop for the Brooklyn Dodgers before they became . . . what *did* they become?"

"Los Angeles Dodgers. And Pee Wee Reese."

"Gimme a piece of bread."

"Gimme, that's okay. What else is bread?"

"Money."

The conversational ball was being tossed back and forth. It was like a game, and the men at the table seemed to be enjoying it. At first Frazer assumed that those asking the questions were the proctors, but soon he realized they all were taking turns asking and answering.

"Welcome to Little America," Harvey Beauregard Lee Ennis said, and everybody looked at Frazer long enough to establish the fact that he did not have two heads before the quizzing was resumed.

"What's the main drag of Philadelphia?"

"Broad Street."

"Hollywood?"

"Sunset Boulevard."

"Williamsburg, Virginia?" Harvey Ennis said triumphantly. Blank looks greeted the question. "Duke of Gloucester Street," Frazer said.

"Are you from Dixie?"

"Who's Edward Albee?"

"Playwright."

"Name a play."

"Uh, *The Dark at the Top of the Stairs?*"

"Nope. That's William Inge."

"*Who's Afraid of Virginia Woolf?* And *she's* a novelist."

"Bart Starr, anybody?"

"Pro football player. Not to be confused with soccer."

"David Brinkley."

"TV commentator."

"From Dixie," said Harvey Ennis. "In a twosome with?"

"Chet Huntley."

"Who's Eugene McCarthy?"

"Senator from . . . the West Coast somewhere."

"Minnesota."

"*Charlie* McCarthy?"

"Ventriloquist's dummy. But that's ancient history, man. Who did the talking?"

"Edgar Bergen."

"Daughter name of?"

"Candy. Candy Bergen. Actress."

"Name some candy bars."

"Milky Way, Babe Ruth, Nestlé's Crunch, Mounds."

It went on like that, one idea triggering another, until the cafeteria began to empty.

"You got your program yet?" Harvey Lee Ennis asked Frazer.

"No."

"Didn't think so. You bug me, man. Usually I can tell."

"Tell what?"

"Proctor or student. Could you tell, at the table there?"

"Not without a scorecard," Frazer said.

"Not without a scorecard, that's pretty good. If you're new you gotta be a proctor. You know too much. But on the other hand," Harvey Ennis said.

"On the other hand what?"

"Come on. Do I hafta tell ya? KGB sticks a guy in to do some listening sometimes. How's the accent now? I'm versatile."

"Brooklyn?" Frazer said.

"Not bad. I was thinking the Bronicks. Why don't you come around with me this afternoon? It's the usual drill, somebody showing you the ropes the first day. Then I'm supposed to make a report."

"A report?"

"Evaluation, pal. If you're a proctor or a student. My guess is supposed to tell something about me, how well *I* know the ropes. They don't miss a trick. Are you dorm or private room?"

"Private room."

"That's right, I saw you coming out. Well, proctor or student, you're a wheel, same as me. I was afraid of that. It's gonna make it tougher for me. Let's go."

Frazer attended two classes with Harvey Beauregard Lee Ennis. There were between fifteen and twenty men in each group auditing a forty-five-minute taped lecture in a room in the big fortresslike building on the hill. The first lecture, complete with motion picture, was in a course called *Suburbia, U.S.A.* The lecture, and the movie, dealt with supermarkets.

"The average suburban American male," the taped voice began, "does twenty-eight percent of the family marketing, usually on weekends. The important thing here is for you to feel at home in the supermarket. Shopping is done in a leisurely fashion and market attendants usually won't assist you unless you ask for their aid. The supermarket carts, stacked in rows as you enter. . . ."

The movie started with the parking lot and façade of an A&P in Rye, New York. The taped commentary was done smoothly and even with some humor, but Harvey Ennis and his fellow students took it seriously, studiously writing notes. After the movie ended, and the lights went on, there were fifteen minutes of supermarket conversation among the students, with questions thrown back and forth as in the cafeteria. Then the taped voice made a brief announcement: "Tomorrow we will study the suburban bowling alley, which is as much a social center and meeting place as it is a sports facility. Good afternoon, and thank you for your attention."

The second class was in a course called *The American Automobile.* Once again taping protected the anonymity of the proctor. There were two films, the first called *At the Service Station.* "It should be stressed at the beginning," the taped voice stressed at the beginning, "that the American driver, unlike his European and particularly his Russian counterpart, doesn't know a thing about automobiles. He can change tires and maybe clean spark plugs, but in general is ignorant of the workings of his vehicle. The issuance of a driver's license does not depend, in any state in the Union, on the ability to strip down and reassemble an automotive engine. You are supposed to be ignorant about such matters. Expertise would be a mistake, except verbal expertise. You can talk like an expert, you can boast about your ability to tune an engine, but when you get down to cases, let the service station attendant do the work. The movie you are watching shows. . . ."

Film number two was *The Used Car Lot*. "Bargaining and incredulity are the key words, should you have either to buy or to sell a used car," the taped voice said. "Any ready acceptance of terms would be suspicious behavior." The movie, in color, showed a geographically unidentified used car lot called Sam's Superbargains. The taped voice provided an imaginary conversation between Sam and his customer. The customer, a balding man in jeans, hands shoved into the pockets of his windbreaker, ambled under the signs that said Miraculous Offer! Sam Is Nuts But He Has a Heart! Come And Get Them Before the Little Men in White Coats Come for Superbargain Sam! The customer looked around suspiciously and finally homed in on a fairly late model Ford with Would You Believe 850 Bucks! soaped on the windshield. He kicked a front tire. He opened a door and shut it. He tried out the front seat for sags. He peered at the brake pedal for wear. He made a slow circle around the car while Superbargain Sam, a dead cigar in his mouth, came beaming in his direction.

"Hiya," said the customer. "What I really wanted was a . . ."

"One owner, a new set of brakes, fifteen thousand miles on the speedometer and it's the true figure we never alter nothing here, you can drive right out with it," said Superbargain Sam.

"One owner," said the customer suspiciously.

"He was a schoolteacher, drove on Sundays only and a mile and a half back and forth to work."

"Looks like a traveling salesman's heap," said the customer.

"I wouldn't steer you wrong. Look. Not a scratch on the finish. You ever see such a shine before in your life? Eight hundred and fifty bucks," said Superbargain Sam, "and you don't have to tell me I'm nuts."

"I'll give you four hundred cash," said the customer.

"*Gonif*, go on, get out of here, you're wasting my time."

"Suit yourself," said the customer, and started walking off.

"Eight hundred, if you pay cash."

"Ha, ha, ha."

"Make me an offer. A sensible offer."

"Four and a quarter," said the customer reluctantly.

"You call that an offer?"

Eventually the car was sold for six hundred dollars. Super-bargain Sam was almost in tears. The customer was furious. They shook hands, went to the office shack, signed papers, and parted friends. The lights went on. The conversation commenced.

"I'm all through for the day," Ennis said. "What's on your docket?"

"Nobody told me," Frazer said.

"No orientation lectures? No personality tests? I don't get it. How long you been here?"

They went outside. The sun had slid down toward the distant snow-capped mountains.

"One thing surprises me," Frazer said.

Ennis laughed. "Only one? Now I know who you are. You must be the guy Old Man Denikin takes his orders from."

"No women," Frazer said off-handedly, as if it wasn't very important.

"Horny already? You must have been here longer than I figured. Don't worry, you'll be able to wet your wick. Old Man Denikin thinks of everything. They got a house in town, and the girls are clean. You get two visits a week if you want."

"No, I meant students and proctors. Where do they hide the women?"

"There's a few old dames do clerical work in the castle and checkout in the cafeteria, and like that. Petrified old virgins," Ennis said. "There ain't no joy juice there."

"But no students?"

"The days of Mata Hari," said Ennis gravely, "have long since passed. No dames matriculating here, friend. What difference does it make?"

"I was just wondering."

"There's a few married couples I seen around," Ennis said. "I figure them for proctors. They got part of the second floor of the barracks right across from ours. Private rooms and a big sign that says 'off limits.' What's on your mind?"

"Nothing in particular," Frazer said. "Just curious."

"You want some advice, go visit the townies a couple of times a week. There was a guy here a couple of months back got a yen for a cute little redheaded Mrs. Proctor. He made a pass at her, and she allowed as how she might be interested. Take three guesses what happened, and the first two don't count."

"I don't know," Frazer said. "What happened?"

"The Gravedigger made one of his administrative decisions. Hell, for once you can't hardly blame him. There's enough tension here as it is. Not that you could notice it. On account of everybody does his bleeding internally. You figure it out. There are maybe four hundred students in camp, and maybe a hundred proctors. I'm just guessing, but those figures are close. The proctors, natch, are defectors, and they didn't give up their lives to come over and spend their time incognito in Bautzen before getting a job in a factory. A defector, he's a little bit like . . . well, an assassin. He wants to be noticed. He wants to feel important. Where your assassin will kill for recognition, your defector will become a traitor to his country to get it. They're all of them hoping to get a real plum: a propaganda job in Moscow, maybe an assignment to go back over as a double agent, like that. But only a few of them'll get the plums. The rest'll be hacks here in Bautzen, and then afterwards desk jockeys doing a dull and stupid job wherever Denikin and his staff send them, or maybe they'll land a factory job and spend their time assembling bicycles in Dnepropetrovsk. Depending on their work here in Bautzen they get the plums or they get Dnepropetrovsk, and there ain't a whole hell of a lot of plums ripe for picking. That's what I mean by tension, friend. They're being evaluated every minute of every day, and it ties the insides up in tight little knots.

"It's worse, if anything, for the students. Four hundred of 'em, and how many resident spies you think are needed in North

America? Half a dozen? Ten? It's a steeplechase, boy. They were hand-picked by the KGB and they come here with high hopes, but maybe one out of forty will get to go all the way. Everybody evaluating everybody else, and the top two percent wins, and the rest of them know they haven't made it, their upper limit has been found, and it ain't good enough. Everybody spying on everybody else is how it works in practice, and the guy who can stick the knife in deepest and break it off is the guy who comes out on top. Very pretty. Your resident agent, when he finally gets over there, is one tough cookie." Ennis grinned suddenly, letting his mask slip back into place. "I told you I was in training to be a garrulous old fart."

Frazer said nothing.

"You don't talk a whole hell of a lot, do you?"

"When I have something to say."

Ennis' eyes narrowed and the round face took on an expression that was both mean and uncertain. "Meaning I talk too much? Meaning that goes on the old punch-card? Harvey Beauregard Lee Ennis talks too much, courtesy of Bradley Pickett Frazer, one courtly old suthren gentleman to another? Well, I got news for you, boy. I'm supposed to say what I said. You get to get it from one of the inmates so it really sinks home. Then I get to evaluate your little old reaction, which as far as I can see wasn't any. Too complicated for you, boy? Is that what goes on your punch-card? He got warned and it confused him?"

Ennis laughed. "Or try this on for size. Maybe I did talk too much, purposely, and told you I didn't, and whichever way you decide to evaluate it is what goes on *your* punch-card. Or maybe I ran off at the mouth and what I'm trying to do is cover up now. There ain't nothing simple at Bautzen. Am I a proctor? If I am, there'll be guys around who came over when I did, and some of them are bound to pass the word to newcomers. Or then again maybe they'll pass the word and it won't be true on account of you're supposed to figure things out for yourself. Am I a student? Then would I waste all this time giving you the poop if I figured you for a proctor? Which are you? Maybe this is my way of finding out. I got to make a report after all. You want to know the truth, I can't figure you out. But don't get to feeling pleased with yourself, like a little old catbird sitting in the cat-bird seat, because my admitting I can't figure you out could be a ruse too. Maybe I got you all figured out and tied in a pack-age with a red silk ribbon on it. Maybe I'm laughing inside fit to bust a gut. So I'll say welcome to Bautzen and I'll see you around, boy. Don't look behind you. Don't you never look be-hind you. Somebody might be gaining on you. Satchel Paige."

SIXTEEN

Nobody was gaining on Frazer when he crossed the snow-covered quadrangle to the barracks where Ennis had told him the few married couples among the proctors lived.

The sun had dropped behind the western mountains, but the sky was still bright. The snow had hardened with the abrupt late afternoon cold; it rang under his boots now instead of creaking. The clear, sharp air was tainted with the smell of the soft coal fire that heated the barracks. Frazer reached the door and opened it quickly, striding through purposefully, like a man who knew where he was going and why. He heard the hum of conversation, muted behind thin walls, and the ubiquitous rock-and-roll music. The hallway was empty. He walked through it to a flight of stairs. Posted on the wall, as Ennis had predicted, was a sign that said: OFF LIMITS TO ALL BUT AUTHORIZED PERSONNEL. Frazer went up the stairs quickly, half-expecting someone to materialize out of thin air and challenge him.

No one did. The stairs led up to a door that was locked. Frazer knocked, not very hard. There was no response. He felt, and fought off, a sense of relief. He could go downstairs, hoping no one spotted him leaving the off-limits area, and return to the frustrating Kafka-esque waiting. Glaeske or Denikin or some other magician would pull a rabbit out of a hat when they were ready to pull a rabbit out of a hat.

He rattled the door latch and banged on the door with the flat of his hand. The door jerked inward suddenly a few inches, and a woman stared at him owlishly.

"I'm coming, I'm coming, baby. *Voilà* I'm here," she said in a hoarse whisky voice. She blinked at Frazer. "Ooo, where did you come from, handsome? This is much more like it, I don't wanna play solitaire any more, I'm going nuts here, come in, come in."

She opened the door wider, latched onto Frazer's sleeve, and tugged him inside, slamming the door shut and smiling up at him moistly. She was a very drunk woman of about thirty, with blue eyes, faded blond hair, uncombed, and a plump figure under the gray-green shirt and trousers. Frazer was sure he had seen her before but didn't know where.

"I know," she said brightly, "you are selling magazines to work your way through spy school. I'll take *Look*, the *SatEve-Post* and *Reader's Barf*. And also we're all alone, I always arrange it so we're all alone when handsome undergraduates come around selling magazines."

She lurched away from Frazer and caught his arm again quickly to keep from falling. Past her he saw a living room that might have been furnished from a mail order catalogue in the States thirty years ago: overstuffed chairs and sofa in green velour festooned with antimacassars, blond wood tables and chests that looked Japanese by way of Cedar Rapids, a hook rug on the floor and Currier & Ives prints on the walls.

"Now I have it," she said, flinging her face and tousled blond hair in his direction, and pressing the soft weight of her breast against his arm. "The train."

"The train?"

"From Olvensburg or Olvenstadt or whatever the hell it's called. I was with Lover Boy, maybe you noticed what a happy couple we are because Lover Boy's got all these big plans that just fill a girl's life with dandy surprises. Lover Boy," she said, wafting a vodka breath at Frazer that belied the breathless claims of the American vodka importers, "is now being interviewed to determine which factory or mine he will spend the rest of his life in."

Frazer remembered the couple on the train from Olvenstedt then, staring at each other with implacable hatred as they rode across East Germany to a new life together. This was the woman.

"Are you and your husband alone here?" he asked.

"Three other couples. Or two now. They're out. Everybody's out. Come on in and sit down in the communal living room. I'd offer you a little drinkie only I drank it all, it's supposed to last all six of us a week. Ain't that a laugh?"

The woman sat on the sofa, patting the cushion next to her. Frazer sat on one of the overstuffed chairs facing her, and she made an exaggerated moue of disappointment.

"What are the other couples like?" Frazer asked.

"Traitors," she said solemnly. "All a bunch of goddamn traitors, it's enough to make you barf. I used to think I was true blue red white and blue, only I'm not. What I am, I'm a lush. Call me Marge," she said. "That's my name. You know, Marjorie? I am also Mrs. Sergeant Marvin Rice." She waggled a finger in front of her face. "Better make that Mrs. ex-Sergeant Marvin Rice. He had great plans, Lover Boy had. We were gonna get rich." She made a raucous squawking sound. "I should live so long. He's a born loser. What a stupid, stupid, stupid idea, and of course he got caught. Or would of got caught if we didn't defect.

"He's in Personnel," she went on. "*Was* in Personnel. Every GI's final papers go over his desk, and he has to fill in how much leave time was taken. You can get a month a year, and if you don't use it all up you get some dough instead. Not enough to retire on, but it can amount to a few hunnerd bucks over a two-year hitch. Marvin started in doctoring the papers. 'You only took ten days leave,' he'd say, and they'd say they took the full sixty. 'No you din't,' he tells them. 'Look, it says so right here. Ten days. Fifty days leave time left, that's three hunnerd and frammis bucks, you sign right here.' They signed, because they wanted the dough, or because they just wanted out without any fuss. That's when Marvin sinks the hook into them. 'The split,' he says. 'Hunnerd fifty for you, hunnerd fifty for me. Meet me in a latrine this afternoon after you see the finance officer, we'll make the split.' They've been conned. They already signed, and what they signed, it wasn't kosher. Most of them meet him for the split, and Marvin salted away twenty thousand bucks in the American Express bank in Hannover that way. Had a great thing going for him, he said, and then he picks a pigeon who is honest. 'I can't do that,' the pigeon says, 'it ain't legal. MP's,' he says. 'Okay, forget it,' Marvin says. 'CID,' the pigeon hollers. He's got Marvin, and Marvin knows it. We pack a bag, one lousy bag for all our stuff, and we run for it. Know where the money is? Our nest egg? It's sitting in the American Express bank in Hannover and we'll never touch a nickel of it. Why doncha come over here and sit down nice and cozy?"

"When are the others coming back?" Frazer asked.

"Don't worry about it, handsome. They're all having interviews after classes, they won't be back till dinnertime. One of them's going to Budapest, I think. He's being interviewed by the Hungarians anyhow. They need a, you know, a journalist, and he worked for PIO in Frankfurt, so that makes him a journalist. Ain't it a laugh?"

Marge Rice was, finally, getting around to talking about the other couples in the barracks. Frazer leaned forward in the overstuffed chair. "You really have your finger on the pulse of what's going on around here," he said admiringly. "What about the rest of them?"

"Well, I keep my eyes open," Marge Rice said. "We got another fellow that was a cook at the R&R center in Garmisch. He married a fraulein, a refugee from East Berlin that got homesick. Cookie follows her around on a nose-ring, but it's ironical because she'll never see Berlin again. They're gonna make him a cook right here in Bautzen."

Marge Rice got up and lurched toward the table where the empty vodka bottle stood. She found a pack of cigarettes, examined it, and crumpled it. "Empty," she said. "You got a cigarette, handsome?"

"I'm all out myself," Frazer said as she lurched back across the room and turned suddenly and dropped, a boneless, leaden weight, onto his lap. "Ooo," she said with a slow, moist smile, "how did I get here?" Then she was all over him, kissing his face and his mouth wetly, stroking his shoulders, running her fingers through his hair. For a confused moment Frazer wondered how he was going to stop her without insulting her and wondered what else, aside from his financial dealings, Sergeant Marvin Rice had had to contend with in Hannover, and then her wandering hands became too insistent and too intimate and he got up quickly, depositing her in a breathless heap on the floor. She looked up at him vaguely, her eyes out of focus, a strand of hair down over one of them. She giggled. "Scared, handsome? You don't hafta be, you're big enough. You could break Marvin in half."

"It isn't that," Frazer said, wondering how he could get the conversation back to the barracks couples. One was still unaccounted for. Hadn't she said something about a couple that had left?

Marge Rice remained where she was on the floor, looking up at him. "I know," she said, "you're scared if the school authorities find out."

"That's it," Frazer said.

"If they find out, they'll send you to Lower Slobovia or somewhere, making widgets in a widget factory." She giggled again. "I must be running out of luck. That makes two of you. *He* was afraid they might pull an administrative decision on him. At least that's what he said, but I know when a guy's just being polite. His wife was a little doll," Marge Rice said reluctantly. "*If* she was his wife. What I'd give to be her age again, knowing what I know now. A big handsome guy like that, he looked a little like you, I always go for a certain type. Lord, what I'd give."

Her meandering, drunken speech had suddenly riveted Frazer's attention. "You mean the fourth couple?" he said. "The ones that aren't here now?"

"Left this morning. He was a winner. I mean it, you could tell."

"Where'd they go?"

"Search me," Marge Rice said.

"Didn't they say anything?"

"Why the frantic interest, handsome? Is little Cinderella your girl friend or something? And you came over and followed them here?"

"You're right about me coming after them, but she's my daughter."

"I'll be damned," Marge Rice said, her eyes big and pitying. His statement of the relationship seemed to sober her. She got up and sat on the arm of his chair. "You poor guy, they're not here any more, they really did leave."

"When?"

"I told you. This morning."

"What makes you so sure they left?"

"Because I was all ears. It ain't every day the camp big-shot pays us a visit."

"Who, Glaeske?"

"No, I mean the Russian, Colonel Denikin."

"He went away with them?"

"Nope. Told them they were going. He just said pack your stuff and get a move on, I've got an assignment for you."

"It could have been here in camp," Frazer persisted.

"No it couldn't. Catching a noon plane out of Dresden? I heard him say that much. He thought the apartment was empty, I guess."

Frazer felt drained of everything. He had come as far as he could. He was here in Bautzen, a defector and a traitor in the eyes of the world whenever Colonel Denikin decided to surface him. The one man who might have been able to help him leave had been killed before his eyes, and now Cindy was gone. A noon flight out of Dresden, he thought. A noon flight to any-where in Eastern Europe, and all the alien, uncooperative, hos-tile Iron Curtain countries to search, assuming he could leave Bautzen, which he couldn't. Before, what he had set out to do, what he had had to do, seemed difficult and dangerous. He had accepted the difficulty and was willing to face the danger. But what had seemed merely difficult and dangerous was now impossible.

He heard himself asking, "Did she seem happy?"

"Who, little Cinderella? She was happy all right. You could tell they were in love a mile off. I must of been nuts to . . . well, never mind. I'm sorry, handsome." She made a face. "After a while it gets to be a habit; you're married to a wrongo, you have too much booze, you make a pass. You poor guy," Marge Rice said. "I wish there was something."

But aside from Marge Rice's belief that Cindy had been happy, there was nothing.

SEVENTEEN

Walking across the now dark quadrangle to his own barracks, he felt tense and tired, but reckless, too, the way a man must feel, he supposed, before he commits an unmotivated crime of violence. He felt quite capable of striking out, pointlessly, at anyone who crossed his path. Once before he had felt that way, after Diana had died. But then he had had the long ski runs to drain off his recklessness, and the warmth and understanding of the Kübli family to curb his unreasoning anger.

Upstairs in the long hallway a door opened as he passed, and Ennis came out. "How's the boy?" he said. "I figured it might be you."

"What do you want?"

"Don't bite my head off," Ennis said in an injured tone. "I was just curious, is all. You got yourself a visitor waiting in your room. Bet you'd never guess who. It's Old Man Denikin. Go tell him how to run Bautzen."

Colonel Vladimir Denikin turned quickly from the window and came waddling across the room, a small unkempt figure of a man. His watery eyes looked sad and ineffectual.

"Where is she?" Frazer said.

Denikin raised a stubby finger to his lips and shook his head frantically from side to side, sprinkling dandruff on the slouched gray-green shoulders. He pointed past Frazer to the door. He put the stubby finger against his lips and shook his head frantically again. Then he found paper and pencil in his pocket, scrawled something and held it up in front of Frazer's face. He had written: "Room bugged. Outside. I'll meet you."

Shrugging, not knowing why the commandant of Bautzen feared one of his own listening devices in the small, functional room with its wire rack of gaudily covered American paperbacks, Frazer turned, retraced his steps down the hallway past Ennis' room, down the stairs and outside. The night had turned very cold. Frazer thrust his gloveless hands into his pockets and paced back and forth. He could feel the constricting thickness in his nostrils as the moist tissues froze with his breathing. He heard the door behind him and turned and saw Denikin's stocky figure walking across the snow.

"Where is she?" Frazer asked again. "You really proved who was in charge here today, didn't you? Why'd Glaeske want you to send her away?"

"Glaeske?" said Denikin. "Please try to calm yourself, Mr. Frazer. It wasn't . . ."

"Just like the treatment you got in the States, wasn't it?" Frazer said angrily. "A fair trial, prison as comfortable as they could make it, and eventually O'Reilly setting up the trade so you could come back here and prove you were a no-good bastard after all."

"Mr. Frazer," Denikin said gently, untouched by Frazer's angry words. "Do us both a favor. Walk over there. Five or six steps will do. Shout. Call me names. Get it all out of your system. And then we will talk."

"I turned my back on my country. I defected. For just one reason: to get my daughter out of here. You never intended living up to your part of the bargain, did you?"

"Mr. Frazer," said Denikin calmly, "you are shouting again. How can I explain, if you don't give me a chance to talk?"

"Tell me where she is. Tell me I can go there. If you have anything else to say, shove it."

"She is in Yugoslavia. You can go to her."

"Because if you think . . . what did you say?"

"Your daughter is in Yugoslavia. You can go to her."

Frazer allowed his arm to be grasped by the short, pudgy man. They walked together across the hard-packed snow.

"Are you serious?"

"Glaeske deceived us both: me about Bill Halladay and you about your daughter. I am a patient man, Mr. Frazer, but even my patience has limits. Now will you listen?"

"I'll listen," Frazer said in a subdued voice.

"You know my friend Senator O'Reilly in the United States? He was the lawyer appointed by the court to defend me. For months he employed all his talents, all his time, all his energy in my defense. There is a considerable element in the United States that believes the defense of a Russian spy is in itself a crime. Senator O'Reilly received threatening letters, threatening phone calls. He sent his wife and children to the country and hired a private detective to protect them. All this for an intruder in his country, a spy, and I think the state of New York was paying him one dollar a day while he defended me. I could not understand why, Mr. Frazer. I asked him. He said his defense of me was really a defense of the American way of life. He said that America was an open society, quite prone to being invaded by spies. He said that if they had the ill fortune to be caught, they still had the right to a fair trial and civilized treatment. That was part of the concept of an open society.

"Later, after we became friends, he said a man could be both a good American and a good human being. He wondered if the same could be true of a Russian—particularly a Russian in my profession. It was a strange question to ask me then, because by then my trial was over and I had been sentenced to forty years in prison. I said that I thought a man could be a good Russian, even a colonel in the KGB, and a good human being. 'I expect you to remember that,' he said. I expect you to remember that, those were his exact words. Five years later I was walking across the bridge over the Mittelland Canal in Germany.

"I told myself I would remember. I owed my freedom to Senator O'Reilly, possibly even my life. I promised myself if the time ever came . . .

"The time came with Bill Halladay. I had known for some weeks that he was a double agent. I knew it before Colonel

Glaeske did, and then Glaeske found out. Try to understand my position, Mr. Frazer. Suddenly I had become Senator O'Reilly, and Bill Halladay was Vladimir Denikin. Somehow, no matter what, I had to save him. I arranged for Halladay's transfer to a less critical job, as subeditor of one of our English language magazines. But he never learned about it.

"When you came here, Glaeske decided to kill two birds with one stone: Halladay, punished sufficiently in your presence, would guarantee your cooperation. Sufficient punishment, to Colonel Glaeske, meant death. You saw Bill Halladay die."

They had been walking for some time along one of the main roads of the camp, toward the darkly looming silhouette of the old medieval fortress. A guard appeared suddenly out of the darkness, barring their way with his rifle.

"Identify yourself," he commanded.

"I am Colonel Denikin," Denikin said gently in German.

"Your identity papers," shouted the guard.

Denikin took out his wallet. The guard, holding the rifle in one hand and a small flashlight in the other, studied the papers.

"And this man?"

"He is with me."

"Colonel Glaeske's orders are that all personnel abroad at night should produce identity papers."

"Colonel Glaeske," said Denikin, "takes his orders from me."

The guard considered that, shrugged, saluted, and marched off across the snow, very stiff-backed, very German, convinced that all foreigners were either fools or enemies.

"I'm glad you witnessed that, Mr. Frazer," Denikin said. "Nominally I am commandant of Bautzen. But the camp is staffed not by my own KGB, but by the German Ministry for State Security. Aside from the students, there are no more than ten Russians in residence. There are several hundred Germans. And whether Glaeske and the MfS or Denikin and the KGB are in actual control of Bautzen, that is a question I have been afraid to answer.

"In your own case, everything had been arranged by Glaeske.

I knew nothing of your arrival until you were already here. When Glaeske finally told me, I asked him what provisions had been made for the girl's release. He laughed in my face. Her release? he said. Then just how do you expect Frazer to cooperate with us?

"I might have done nothing about it. But then Colonel Glaeske made a very grave mistake. He made his administrative decision regarding Bill Halladay. What has since happened, what is going to happen, you owe to that. To that and to Senator O'Reilly's simple statement: 'I expect you to remember.' I remember, Mr. Frazer."

Denikin's voice did not quite break, but he began to walk faster, the small, pudgy sentimentalist waddling quickly across the snow, the incongruous, oddly likable Soviet master spy who could not forget what had been done for him in the country he had been sent to spy on. He stopped walking and turned to Frazer, his voice under control again.

"I have clothing waiting for you. Identity papers. Money. All you will need. My own driver will take you to Dresden. A hotel room has been reserved. You will fly from Dresden to East Berlin in the morning. A lawyer named Vogel will meet you at the airport and arrange your entry into West Berlin."

"What I don't get is why Glaeske sent Cindy and Severing to Yugoslavia."

"Glaeske? Who said anything about Glaeske? I sent them."

"*You* did?"

"Of course. Colonel Glaeske has what almost amounts to an obsession. He wants to break your will. With your daughter in Bautzen, he might have succeeded. I know Glaeske. He would have tried anything, including the infliction of pain on the child in your presence. Could you have withstood that?"

Frazer did not have to think about it. "No," he said.

"Then the first thing I had to do was get your daughter safely out of here. But it was not that simple. There was another consideration. Namely, my own career. Does the name Mitrović mean anything to you?"

"Mitrović? No, I . . . wait a minute. Mitrović, Yugoslavia,

sure. Ernest Mitrović. Tito's Interior Minister, wasn't he? And some kind of a disagreement, with Mitrović winding up in jail?"

"Mitrović was released from prison unexpectedly a few days ago." Denikin smiled. "Apparently he had his Senator O'Reilly, too. His crime against the state was a desire to set up an opposition party—what the British call the loyal opposition. But Tito feared him. Mitrović had been a young *partisan* during the war, and he was too popular. The people idolized him, almost as much as they idolized Tito himself. There is room for only one leader in the cult of personality, Mr. Frazer. Mitrović spent eight years in prison. Now he is out, with Tito's blessings. The Marshal is no longer young, and there is even talk he is grooming Mitrović as his successor. It is possible that Tito is mellowing, but it is also possible he intends using Mitrović as a Judas ram to uncover other dissident elements within the party. Moscow wants to find out. Especially in the event that Mitrović has been forgiven, Moscow wants to learn where he stands on certain issues—China, the Warsaw Pact, the possibility of Yugoslavia returning to the Russian fold."

"You sent Severing to find out?" Frazer asked in amazement.

"I was asked by Moscow to send someone quite unofficially to get a line on Mitrović. Why not Severing? It is quite logical. If Mitrović favors closer ties with the West, he would be more likely to admit it to an American than to a Russian. Severing was never surfaced here in Bautzen. I have supplied him with the necessary papers. Curtis Severing is visiting Yugoslavia as an American journalist."

"And you expect him to come back here of his own free will? Severing's a man on the run, Colonel, in hot water on both sides of the Iron Curtain. Yugoslavia could be just what the doctor ordered for him."

"He may come back. He may not. It would be no great loss, and all I would be guilty of is faulty judgment. Moscow routinely calls on me to supply agents for such jobs. It is one function of Bautzen. If I guessed wrong about Severing, I can weather the storm. His dossier says he speaks Serbo-Croat fluently. That's all the protection I need. Besides, Moscow will be attacking Mitrović from several other angles—the embassy in Belgrade, the Military Intelligence Directorate, our own *Pravda* and *Izvestia* correspondents. With or without Severing we will get what we are after. The important thing is that your daughter is in Yugoslavia, out of Glaeske's reach."

"What about me?" Frazer said. "Won't Glaeske hit the roof when he finds out you let me go?"

Denikin stopped walking then and turned to face him. "I am commandant of Bautzen," he said with dignity. "If I decide a defector is useless to us, I send him back. I am sending you back. I don't want you here, any more than you want to be here. But I am pleased that it matters to you," he said in a softer voice. "Perhaps, then, you will be willing to do something for me? When you return to the United States of America with your daughter, I want you to see Senator O'Reilly. Will you do that?"

Frazer said he would do it.

"I want you to tell him," Colonel Denikin said, "that I remembered."

PART FOUR

The Island

EIGHTEEN

The afternoon flight from Belgrade, a rear-jet Caravelle, trimmed with the white and blue of JAT, the Yugoslav national airline, came in on time.

Seated on the terrace of the Čilipi airport with the warm March sun at his back, Frazer stared past the glass of mastica on the table to the Karst Mountains looming gray and stark like cardboard cutouts beyond the tarmac. He looked impatiently at his watch. It was three o'clock. He hoped the on-time arrival of the Belgrade jet was an omen. Maybe the flight from Zürich would be on time too. It was due in fifteen minutes. Jane Halladay would be aboard.

A sudden gusty wind sprang up and the Caravelle's passengers leaned into it and hurried across the concrete, through the gate in the wire fence, and into the terminal. The flight crew, in dark blue JAT uniforms, came after them, two men and a girl carrying a clipboard and smiling.

After the flurry of activity the airport settled back to its afternoon calm. Frazer moved to an inside table with his glass of mastica when the wind persisted. He glanced at his watch again. Just three minutes had passed. The JAT crew came upstairs, the girl still smiling. They sat at a small round table next to Frazer's and ordered. They spoke animatedly in Serbo-Croat, toasting one another when their drinks came. The girl looked briefly in Frazer's direction, then interested herself in a story one of her companions was telling with broad, elaborate gestures.

A large man approached Frazer's table. He had a shambling, bearish walk, a florid face with wide Slavic cheekbones, and an unruly thatch of thinning white hair. He was wearing a dark suit, a white shirt, and no tie. The necktie, one symbol of the capitalist world, Frazer had observed in his twenty-four hours in Yugoslavia, was out.

"May I sit here?" the large man asked in English. He nodded, as though answering for Frazer, showed several gold teeth in a fleeting professional grin, and sat, tilting his chair back on its hind legs and studying Frazer. The chair came forward with a thump and the large man produced a billfold, open, with a card showing in a plastic window.

"Babunović," he said. "State Security Agency. You are Frazer, Bradley Pickett. American. Guest at Hotel Epidaurus in Cavtat." The chair tilted up and back again, Babunović balancing precariously. The billfold disappeared. "Why are you here, Mr. Frazer?"

"I didn't know I needed a reason," Frazer said.

"No, of course not," Babunović said apologetically. "Usually not necessary, sir. Yugoslavia has eliminated tourist visa. We welcome guests." The chair came forward again. "Why are you here, Mr. Frazer?"

The JAT airline crew had stopped talking to listen to the more interesting conversation at the next table. Frazer took out a pack of cigarettes and offered one.

"American cigarettes," said Babunović. "Good. I like them." He lit both their cigarettes with a little waxed match.

"I'm meeting a friend," Frazer said.

"Of course. American woman, Hayward, Mrs. Jane. You register also for her at Hotel Epidaurus. Adjoining rooms," said Babunović in a gold-toothed smile that accepted and approved of the pleasant inevitability of adjoining rooms. "But still I am asking why you are here."

"I'm employed by the United States Information Agency," Frazer said.

"Ah, you are journalist then?"

"More or less a journalist, yes."

Babunović waggled a large index finger. "You are not registering as foreign journalist, Mr. Frazer. Why is this? We have special problem here. Carefulness is necessary, due to arriving Ernest Mitrović. You understand? Ernest Mitrović, as all great men, has many friends. Also many enemies. Which are you, Mr. Frazer?" The gold teeth gleamed.

"Neither. I'm just a journalist."

"You are not registering as foreign journalist," Babunović repeated in a scolding voice.

"Didn't know I had to. I'll do it when I get back to Cavtat with Mrs. Hayward."

"She is journalist also?"

"No. Just a friend."

"You can show me United States Information Agency identification?" Babunović asked.

Frazer produced his ID card. Babunović studied and returned it.

"You are heading mission in Madrid," he said reproachfully, and turned to stare through the window-wall of the lounge as the whine of a jet engine reached them. Flaps down, another JAT Caravelle was dropping toward the runway at the southern end of the airfield.

Babunović turned back to Frazer. "Zürich flight," he said proudly. "On schedule." He pronounced schedule the British way and added, in the same tone of voice, as though as proud of his knowledge of geography as he was of the efficiency of the Yugoslav airline: "We are long way from Madrid."

Frazer drank what remained of his mastica slowly, wondering what to say. He decided on the ingenuous bureaucratic approach. "USIA's a big organization," he said. "I do what I'm told. And Ernest Mitrović was sprung on the world rather suddenly, Mr. Babunović."

"Suddenly, yes. You speak Serbo-Croat?"

"No," Frazer said.

"Then you know Yugoslavia?"

"I've been here before."

"Many times?"

"I was in Belgrade two years ago."

"Officially or holiday?"

"Officially," Frazer said, glad that he could say that much. Belgrade had been one of many stops on his USIA swing around the world. He had remained in the Yugoslav capital only three days.

"Good, good," Babunović said. "I am relieved." But the smile he showed Frazer was too open. "You are knowing Salt Lake City, Utah?"

"I've been there once or twice."

"I have brother there, American citizen, civil engineer, married to American woman from Phoenix." Babunović pronounced the diphthong as two separate syllables.

A woman's voice blared something over the PA system in Serbo-Croat and repeated it in German: "Yugoslav National Airlines announces the arrival of flight fourteen from Zürich."

The Caravelle had taxied close to the terminal. Two white-uniformed men wheeled the flight stairs across the tarmac toward the plane. The door opened, and a stewardess peered out into the sunlight. Passengers began to emerge.

"Is crowded with foreign journalists like yourself," said Babunović. "All registering properly," he added with just a touch of malice.

Then he watched Frazer's face, until he caught something in its expression and turned to look at the flight stairs again.

"That is Hayward, Mrs. Jane?"

"Yes," Frazer said.

"Beautiful. Like sunny day on Jadran," said Babunović. "Adjoining rooms at Hotel Epidaurus. You are lucky, Mr. Frazer." Babunović got to his feet and leaned down to shake hands. He shambled off as Frazer watched Jane Halladay pass through the gate. Then Frazer paid for his drink and hurried downstairs.

Jane came through customs carrying an overnight bag and the blue trench coat. Standing with the small crowd on the other side of the customs barrier, seeing the long-legged stride and the blond good looks of her, watching the smile light up her blue eyes and spread to the rest of her face, Frazer felt suddenly shy.

"Hello," she said. "Hello."

She had her plane ticket with a yellow baggage check stapled to it in her hand. Frazer took it. "Here, let me get that."

He stood in line at the baggage counter, busying himself lighting a cigarette while the luggage arrived. Jane was at his side.

"Have a good flight?"

She looked up at his face and laughed lightly. "Just the slightest bit bumpy over the Azores, darling," she said in an exaggerated British accent, and then Frazer was laughing too, and although there still was what had to be told about Bill Halladay's final minutes of life, he knew it was going to be all right.

He exchanged the claim check for her suitcase, in dark blue leather that matched her coat. They turned together toward the exit and caught a glimpse of the gray, convoluted mountains.

"It really is rugged country," she said. "And almost spring already, after Switzerland. It's been so quick. Where exactly are we?"

"Southern Dalmatian coast," Frazer said. "Montenegro starts a few miles south of here. That's where you can't read the road signs because they're in Cyrillic. Here's the heap."

They had crossed the parking lot to the car Frazer had rented. He tossed Jane's suitcase in back and opened the front door for her.

"It looks like one of those little Italian cars. A Fiat?"

"It's called a Zlastva here. Assembled in Yugoslavia, but it's the same car. Great for these mountain roads."

They left the anomaly of concrete and steel that was the airport terminal behind them and drove on the new coast road through stands of umbrella pine and cypress. On their right they could see the mountains and on their left occasional glimpses, through the green and silver of olive groves, of the Adriatic. Here and there a sand-colored stone cottage squatted on the landscape. A woman in an elaborately embroidered white peasant blouse was leading a donkey laden with brushwood along the edge of the highway. She waved at them good-naturedly, and Jane waved back.

"It all looks so unspoiled," Jane said. "Except for the airport. As if they jumped into the twentieth century skipping over a few hundred years. The Yugoslav Great Leap Forward."

"Not just Yugoslav," Frazer pointed out. "All over the Balkans, and that includes Greece and Turkey. Not to mention Spain on the other side of the continent. It reminds me of Spain a little. The same stark . . ."

"Have you seen her?"

"No, not yet. I flew in by way of Belgrade and just missed her this morning. Mitrović went on a motorcade to Titograd and the whole press corps, Severing and Cindy included, went along. They're expected back in Cavtat tonight."

"Is that where we're going?"

"It's Mitrović's home town. An old town, and it looks it. Older than Dubrovnik up the coast. Twenty-five hundred years ago the Greeks called it Epidaurus. All of a sudden it's on the map again because Ernest Mitrović has come home. What are you going to do when you see Severing?"

Jane shrugged. "There isn't an awful lot I can do. Point out a few things to him. If he comes back, we forgive and forget, and I've been told to okay a pretty big severance check for him, courtesy of Dad. If he stays here and keeps his mouth shut— provided he also kept it shut in Bautzen—Dad closes the books on him and that's that. If he thinks he can earn himself a place in the sun here by telling what he knows about Camp King, he gets the full defector treatment back home. Not that it would bother him much. He has no known relatives in the West. Did you know he was born in Germany, by the way?"

"Grayling mentioned it," Frazer said, flipping on the turn-indicator. "Cavtat's down there." They turned down a narrow road twisting and descending to the left. The broad, deep blue expanse of the Adriatic came into view far below them, and the weathered stone buildings of the village of Cavtat on a head-land jutting out into the sea.

"It's lovely," Jane said.

"It's also in a holiday mood," Frazer said. "You'll see. Local boy makes good after eight years in jail. Mitrović is a Croat, and Yugoslavia's still six republics in search of a country."

"Isn't Tito a Croat too?"

"Sure, but he sits up there in Belgrade, and they have the feeling here in Croatia that he's too busy with the rest of the country and has sort of let them down. Monday, Wednesday, and Friday they're still at war with the Serbs. Mitrović is their white hope. The funny part of it is, from what Dad's man in Berlin told me, Mitrović is as much a nationalist as Tito himself."

"That would be Charlie Evans?"

"The name he gave me." Frazer grinned. "He holds down a desk in American International Tours. I'm beginning to think you people outnumber American Express."

"We're not first," Jane said, "but we try harder."

They said ouch together.

"Who's this Vogel?" Frazer asked. "The lawyer. I was impressed."

"We don't have diplomatic relations with East Germany, so it's people like Vogel who make contact possible. He's a loyal citizen of the German Democratic Republic, but he's valuable to both sides.. Except for our magicians behind the Iron Curtain, he's one of a very few people over there who know how to get in touch with Dad."

"You're telling me. He made a phone call and a kid who couldn't have been eighteen showed up and drove me out of East Berlin. An hour and a half after we left Vogel's office, a couple of Vopos took me out into no-man's-land, and half an hour after that Charlie Evans was shaking hands with me. Does that happen all the time?"

"Often enough. And then you called me."

"And then I called you."

"What will you do when you see her?"

"I don't know, Jane. Play it by ear, I guess."

"It isn't exactly like Severing and me, I know. There are no rules. She's not breaking any laws. And she's your daughter. Brad? I know it won't do any good saying this, but whatever happens, try not to let it hurt you too much. I'm worried about you. I . . . just for the record, I was scared every minute you were there. In Bautzen. Before that. From the time you left Hannover. I couldn't think straight. I could hardly even sleep, and if you knew me better I'm somebody who can sleep in the Place de la Concorde on Bastille Day. Mr. Gutenburg sent me home. I wasn't much good around the office."

"You can sleep all right," Frazer said, smiling.

"Stop it. Now you're making me blush. Don't you know I'm too old and too sophisticated to blush?"

One moment they were still above the red tile roofs of Cavtat and the next they had dropped down into the village. Frazer made a right turn along a big sweeping curve of bay. "Hotel's a kilometer up the road," he said.

Again there was the anomaly of concrete and glass architecture. "That's the Hotel Cavtat," Frazer said. "Where Severing and Cindy are staying, along with most of the press corps. The Epidaurus gets the overflow, us included."

They drove past the Hotel Cavtat. A few hardy types were swimming in the bay, moving fast, churning the blue water and then emerging to towel themselves briskly on the dock. Cars were parked along the waterfront, bearing license plates and nationality plaques from a dozen countries.

"Aren't you going to see if she's back yet?"

"It's too early. There's a dinner in town for Mitrović at eight, right after they get back from Montenegro."

"You almost sound relieved. Or shouldn't I have said that?"

"Hell, I don't know. I'm just not sure of myself, that's all. I don't know what I'm going to say to her, but whatever it is, if she says no the next move is hers. She's not a child."

"She's not a grown woman."

"Sure, but . . ."

"And you're her father. Though I can't see you playing the autocratic parent."

"Maybe," Frazer said, "that's the trouble."

They were seated on the terrace of the Hotel Epidaurus, watching the sun go down over the bay. A black fishing boat bobbed on the flame-colored water.

"Let me know if it's too cold for you," Frazer said.

"No, I wouldn't miss this for anything. I've never seen a more beautiful sunset." Jane turned up the collar of her trenchcoat. She said nothing else for awhile. Then she said: "Tell me how he died."

"It was fast, Jane. About as fast and as clean . . ."

"You said on the phone you were there. Tell me about it."

He told her. He told it straight, except for the matter of the facial tic, which was the one part he would never forget, the tic growing more and more pronounced as Bill Halladay realized he had fewer and fewer seconds to live.

Jane's face was averted. She was staring at the low Cavtat skyline that looked two-dimensional against the sunset, like the cutouts of a city on the horizon inside a planetarium.

"He always," she said, "thought of himself as a man of the world. It was an image he tried to live up to, and it was so pathetically wrong. He was a little boy all his life. A wife was just somebody to come home to from his escapades, like a mother, to pat his head and tell him what a big . . ." Her voice broke. She was crying.

"Hey," Frazer said gently. "Hey, now."

"I'm all right now."

"No, go ahead and cry."

"I wish I . . . was there anything I could have done? To make him feel more confidence in himself? Maybe if he needed mothering I should have . . ."

"Any man lucky enough to have you for a wife," Frazer began, and then he realized it was not a beginning but a complete statement.

Jane tried to laugh. "Mr. Frazer, sir, you have a way of saying exactly the right thing. A girl could get to depend on that," she said. "I know it was all over between Bill and me years ago, but we shared a lot of life together, even if it went sour, and I . . . I'm getting cold. I'd like to go inside now."

"How about some dinner?"

Jane managed a real smile. "I'm hungry enough to eat two horses, saddles included."

"Yugoslav cuisine being what it is, you're liable to do just that."

But the meal was delicious. The main dish was something called *čevapčići,* skewered and grilled patties of heavily peppered lamb and pork.

"When I'm old," Jane said, "I'll probably be as plump as a milkmaid. I love to eat."

"Well, at least I can't say I wasn't warned."

Jane looked up at him while he poured two glasses of the dark, almost sirupy red wine. Her face became animated, ready for speech, her mouth not quite forming the words.

"What is it?" he said.

"This is hard to say, Brad. I like you. A lot. I told you how it made me feel, knowing you were in Bautzen, and there wasn't a thing I could do except wait. But would you do us both a favor? I don't know about you, but this is a mixed up time for me. There's so much happening to both of us. Just go slowly, all right?"

Frazer looked at his watch. "All right," he said, feeling his cheeks grow warm. "Slow it is, but not right now. I've got to see the police before eight and register as a journalist."

"A journalist?"

He told her of his talk with Babunović at the airport. "Some people get involved with traffic cops everywhere they go," he said. "But not me. For me it's the secret police. I've been collecting alphabet-soup agencies."

"In this case the UBDA. If Dad were Dun and Bradstreet he'd give them an A rating. The Yugoslav State Security Police are a solid professional outfit. How did you get along with Mr. Babunović?"

"I don't think he believed me. He pretended to, though."

"Which means you'll be watched."

"I don't have anything to hide."

"Wouldn't that depend on Severing?" Jane suggested.

The Obala restaurant, except for the dining rooms of the hotels, was the only public eating place in the village of Cavtat. Obala meant waterfront, and that was where the restaurant was located. It stood behind a vine-covered terrace, the vines bare and withered now, a squat stone building from which emerged the sound of male voices singing. A faint greenish glow remained in the sky. The shops on either side of the Obala were shuttered for the night, but crowds were promenading on the broad quay.

"Do we just go inside?" Jane asked.

"No hurry. It looks like Mitrović hasn't showed up yet."

A deep voice behind them called: "Ah, Mr. Frazer. And the beautiful Mrs. Hayward, I believe?"

It was Babunović, the big bearlike UBDA agent. He was wearing a dark jacket, which looked at least one size too small for him, and a tie. He ran a big finger around under the buttoned collar of his shirt. His face was very red.

"You have seen police?"

"Yes," Frazer said.

"And all is in order?"

Frazer took out the press card.

"Splendid, splendid," Babunović said, not looking at it. "They say Ernest Mitrović had big welcome in Titograd. It will be more so here in Cavtat. Mitrović was born half kilometer from where we . . ."

"Here they come," Jane said.

Half a dozen cars came roaring along the quay. The sound of their engines brought a crowd piling out through the wide doorway of the Obala. They joined the mob already waiting outside. Lights strung on the overhead arbor suddenly blinked on, giving an indoor look to the restaurant terrace.

Even before the motorcade had come to a stop, figures leaped from the last two cars. There were three of them, trotting toward the lead car, two with press cameras and the third with a miniature. When the first car rolled to a stop, they scuttled away from it backwards, their cameras high. "Room," somebody said irritably in English. "Give us some room." A flashbulb popped prematurely, and the same voice said: "Damn."

A tall, lean man, who had to be Ernest Mitrović, was first out of the lead car. Under the overhead lights he had a craggy, handsome, hawklike profile. He came striding through the crowd quickly, as though he had no time for formalities but was still happy to be there. The crowd began to applaud spontaneously, and Mitrović stood still for an instant to applaud back at them before continuing across the terrace. Flashbulbs flared. The pictures would show, in tomorrow's newspapers, Mitrović's well-wishers turned out in jackets and ties and Ernest Mitrović himself wearing a pair of baggy gray trousers and a black turtleneck sweater.

"He doesn't miss a trick," Jane said. "Jean-Jacques Rousseau, two centuries later. That's the image he's always cultivated, according to our files. Yugoslavia has to go its own way. That's what he preaches. He doesn't approve the Russian emphasis on heavy industry and scorns the creature comforts of the West. Back to nature, where the Yugoslavs can find themselves on home ground. So he still dresses like a *partisan*—only he's a lot more attractive than Fidel Castro in dirty fatigues and a grubby beard, and I don't have to point out that it's worked for Castro. As for how well it's worked for Mitrović, these aren't just hometown boosters you see here. There's a lot of talk about Mitrović being the heir apparent."

The heir apparent, followed by his coterie of aging former *partisans,* made his way slowly through the crowd, pushing forward, but stopping frequently to clutch an outstretched hand and smile and say a few words. Members of the press corps, looking tired after the long motorcade to Titograd and back, trailed after him.

When all the cars were empty, Frazer said: "That's funny." The possibility that Severing and Cindy wouldn't be in the motorcade had never occurred to him.

"Could we have missed them in the crowd?"

"Not a chance. I was watching. I don't get it."

He saw the troubled look on Jane's face and heard the rasp of an outboard motor beyond the parked cars. Then there was a bright glow and sound—tremendous sound—shattering everything, and Jane, the troubled look still on her face, was in the air, hurtling at him. She struck him hard and they both tumbled to the ground, and although his ears were ringing after the enormous blast of sound, he could still hear the screaming.

NINETEEN

Ordinarily the hotels Cavtat and Epidaurus were open only six months of the year, when the Dalmatian coast swarmed with summer tourists. Both were modern, first-class hotels, built with state funds and staffed by state personnel. They had been opened in March, on special government order, to accommodate not only the press corps, but Yugoslavs who had streamed in from all over the country to welcome Ernest Mitrović after his release from eight years in Sremska Mitrovika prison.

Cavtat's third hotel, the Supetar, was in the center of town, on the waterfront, and only a hundred yards or so from the Obala restaurant. Open all year, it was an older hostelry that predated the Communist takeover during the Second World War. It was given a C rating by the government tourist bureau, which meant it had gloomy, sparsely-furnished rooms, capricious plumbing, and a staff that, unlike the staffs of the Cavtat and Epidaurus, hadn't been trained in the government hotel schools in Belgrade and Sarajevo. The Supetar was far from full, despite Ernest Mitrović's homecoming.

Accordingly, after the bombing, it became a makeshift hospital. A first-aid clinic had been set up in the dining room, with the more seriously injured treated in the guest rooms upstairs. By ten o'clock that night, two hours after the explosion, Bradley Pickett Frazer and Jane Halladay had received medical attention. The ugly gash in Frazer's arm had been swabbed with iodine and bandaged. The laceration on Jane's cheek had been cleaned with hydrogen peroxide.

"You have immunization against tetanus?" the doctor asked

Frazer in German. He was a short man with a big gray mustache and wild, stand-up gray hair. A huge black and brindle Alsatian squatted at his feet.

"Yes," Frazer said.

"Then only a booster will be necessary," said the doctor. "You are lucky." He prepared the syringe and injected the toxoid into Frazer's arm. "Now you will go into the bar," he said.

Frazer shook his head. "We need some rest. We're staying at the Epidaurus."

"Now you will go into the bar."

Frazer looked back across the dining room. The line of first-aid patients divided halfway down the length of the room. A woman in a white smock was attending to half the patients and the gray-haired doctor to the remainder. Across the room, two policemen were standing at the door.

"A matter of the security police," the doctor said. "It will not take long."

Two men were just leaving the bar by its street entrance as Jane and Frazer came in. The room, with its ungainly overstuffed chairs and small hardwood bar, was empty except for a single figure seated before a table with his back facing them.

"Mr. Frazer, Mrs. Hayward," said Babunović, rising to his feet. He shook hands with Jane first, then with Frazer, very formally, nodding his head in the suggestion of a bow with each handshake. "I regret necessity of this. But upstairs man from Kotor is losing leg, another man has possible skull fracture, and there are five serious injuries besides minor ones like your own. Please be seated."

They sat across the table from him. He sighed and offered a red pack of Kolo cigarettes. Frazer took one. Except for an ashtray and two narrow notebooks, both shut, the table was bare.

"Despite security precautions," Babunović said, "determined man or men can succeed in assassination of exposed hero. America unfortunately learned that lesson in Dallas, Texas. But Ernest Mitrović was lucky. You perhaps know why?"

Frazer shook his head.

"Arbor. For grapevine over terrace of Obala restaurant. Very nice in summer. Saving life of Ernest Mitrović in winter."

He waited for a comment and got none. "Assassins in motorboat," he said. "Homemade bomb, Molotov cocktail. Petrol in wine bottle, rag for wick. But bomb explodes overhead on wire of arbor. Duck wire, you call it?"

"Chicken wire," Frazer said.

"Exactly. Chicken wire. Saving lives of Ernest Mitrović and others. Does that not seem strange?"

"Strange?" Frazer repeated.

"If assassin knows Cavtat, Obala terrace is bad place for Molotov cocktail thrown from boat. But stranger does not know this."

Babunović stubbed his cigarette out in the overflowing ashtray. "We have called United States Information Agency in Beograd. Mr. Chambers in charge. You know him, Mr. Frazer?"

Frazer had heard of, but never met, Burton Chambers, the USIA chief in Belgrade. Here it comes, he thought. "No, we never met," he said.

"We ask Mr. Chambers obvious question. Did USIA send Spanish bureau chief Frazer, Bradley Pickett, to Yugoslavia as journalist to cover release from prison of Ernest Mitrović? You can guess his answer, Mr. Frazer?"

Frazer looked at Jane. "You tell me," he said.

Babunović said: "Affirmative. Chambers knows you are here."

While Babunović lit another cigarette, Jane's lips formed the name Charlie Evans. Apparently the CIA man in Berlin had had the foresight to phone Belgrade and provide Frazer with substantiation of his cover. The tension in Frazer began to ease, but then Babunović said:

"Here you see police records for hotels Cavtat and Epidaurus, month of March." He pivoted the two notebooks on the table. "Epidaurus on right, Cavtat on left. Look at Epidaurus, please."

Frazer opened the notebook. There were several pages of entries, handwritten in blue ink, each entry written across two pages in neat columns for name, nationality (or place of birth for Yugoslavs), date of arrrival, and home address. He found entries for himself and Jane, the information gleaned from their passports.

"Nothing strange?" asked Babunović with a lazy smile.

"Not that I can see."

"Good. I agree. Now other book, from Cavtat."

Frazer opened the other book. Again there were several double pages of entries, and he scanned them quickly, wondering what Babunović had up his sleeve and then realizing what it was before he saw the entry for Frazer, Cindy, U.S.A., Williamsburg, Virginia. Two hotels, perhaps a dozen American names in all, and two of them Frazer, not together. His eyes scanned the hand-written entries and found Cindy's name under that of Curtis Severing. There were a dozen more names on the page, many of them German. He read them automatically. Suddenly his grip tightened on the notebook.

"You look surprised," Babunović said, as though surprise were the last thing he had expected from Frazer. He went on talking, but for a few moments the words had no meaning for Frazer, nor the dull ache in his left arm, nor Jane sitting at his side, nor the fact that they were here, in the bar of the Hotel Supetar in Cavtat, two hours after an attempt had been made on the life of Ernest Mitrović. All he could think of was the other name he had seen in the routine police records kept for the Hotel Cavtat.

". . . crime of violence," Babunović was saying. "You look. You hope to find something. I ask myself, Mr. Frazer, why are two people, both named Frazer, both born in State of Virginia, here in Cavtat? In two different hotels. Now I ask you: is Frazer common American name?"

"Not particularly," Frazer admitted.

"And less so with zed, yes? Is English in origin?"

"Scottish."

"Scottish, yes. Who is Frazer, Cindy? Wait, please. United

States Information Agency journalist Frazer and friend Mrs. Hayward . . ." Babunović bowed his head in Jane's direction, not quite mockingly, "adjoining rooms in Hotel Epidaurus. Worldwide Press Association journalist Severing, Curtis, and friend Miss Frazer . . ." another bow of the head, in Frazer's direction, "adjoining rooms in Hotel Cavtat. This makes policeman wonder. But name of girl in book surprises you. Look at hands."

Frazer was still holding the notebook. His knuckles were white.

"Who is Frazer, Cindy?"

Frazer's mind was racing. He wished Charlie Evans hadn't been so efficient, calling Belgrade in case his identity was questioned. Now would have been a good time to tell Babunović the truth, or as much of the truth as he had to know. Cindy was a runaway daughter and Frazer wanted her back. But if Cindy were going to be contrary, and he had every reason to suspect she would be, a police pickup would only fan the flames of rebellion in her. Still, did he have any choice, now, with that other name in the book, routinely recorded as a guest of the Hotel Cavtat?

"Why does Frazer, Cindy, go on motorcade to Titograd," Babunović asked, "but not return to Cavtat?"

"She's not back here?"

"No, Mr. Frazer. On return journey Ernest Mitrović stops to make speech in Budva. American named Severing and young woman companion are not with motorcade when it leaves Budva. This also is strange."

Frazer took a deep breath. "I asked USIA for this assignment," he said. "Cindy's my daughter. She was in school in Switzerland and I got word that she'd run off, to Yugoslavia, with Curtis Severing. I came down here after her."

"Ahhh," sighed Babunović, as though letting out the breath Frazer had drawn. "Thank you for being honest. And Severing really is correspondent for Worldwide Press?"

"I know very little about Severing," Frazer hedged. "That's

why I'm here. I want to find my daughter. I hope you can help me."

"She is age . . . ?"

"Nineteen."

"Nineteen. Yes. A child. I will alert police in Budva. Have you photograph of daughter?"

Frazer removed a snapshot of Cindy from his wallet and handed it to Babunović.

"Is pretty thing," he said, and waited, as though expecting Frazer to tell him more. But Frazer said nothing. "You will remain at Hotel Epidaurus?"

"I won't leave Yugoslavia without Cindy."

"Age nineteen, a child," said Babunović. He stood up. "We will contact you." He shook hands, with Jane first, then with Frazer, and waved them toward the street door of the bar.

Outside the night was chill and overcast. A hundred yards along the quay, the Obala terrace had been roped off. A curious crowd still loitered there, but the cars of the motorcade had driven away.

"I hope that wasn't a mistake," Jane said. "Telling him as much of the truth as you did. Cindy won't like being picked up by the police. I hope you know what you're doing, Brad." She looked up at his face. "Is there something else? When Babunović showed you the second book you looked like you'd seen a ghost."

"The last entry in the book. Fritz Leser from Dresden. Alias Heinz Glaeske. He's here in Cavtat."

TWENTY

Colonel Glaeske's appearance in Yugoslavia surprised Frazer less than Severing's disappearance.

Glaeske was hardly an autonomous master spy with no one to answer to but himself. One moment he'd had Frazer and Cindy in his hands. The next, both were gone. Glaeske had botched the job. Not only couldn't he use Frazer's apparent defection for propaganda purposes, but Frazer was now free to air the whole dirty business to the world.

Put yourself in Glaeske's shoes, he thought. You've made a mess of it. You've kidnapped the daughter in a neutral country, spirited her off behind the Iron Curtain to force the father's defection, and now both daughter and father are out of your clutches. They can talk. They have nothing to lose by talking, and if they do talk, you have everything to lose. If you don't stop them, your usefulness to the East German Ministry for State Security is nil.

The only thing that could explain Glaeske's arrival in Yugoslavia was the absolute necessity of silencing Frazer, and Cindy too. Glaeske, Frazer realized by the time he returned with Jane to the Hotel Epidaurus, had flown to Yugoslavia to kill them.

Upstairs in her room, Frazer explained his line of reasoning to Jane. She listened silently, smoking, and then she nodded. "It makes sense. It makes frightening sense. What are you going to do?"

"I wait for him to make a move. And try to be ready for it."

"You could tell Babunović."

Frazer shook his head. "That's the one thing I can't do. How could I predict his reaction? They've already had an attempted assassination here. The last thing they want is more trouble. If I tell Babunović, he's liable to pick up my passport—for delivery at the border when I get there to claim it. Then what happens to Cindy? No, Babunović's out. I've got to find Cindy first."

"Every time you take a step outside the hotel, Glaeske may be waiting for you with a gun. Maybe he's outside right now."

Jane went to the window and drew the shutters closed. She smiled wanly. "And now I make sure the door's locked and we hide under the bed together, is that it? Brad, what *are* you going to do."

"I told you. Find Cindy."

Jane opened the closet door and pulled her suitcase out. She rummaged inside and turned to face Frazer with a small snub-nosed revolver in her hand. "It's a Colt Cobra," she said. "Lightweight aluminum frame, but as they say in the manual it packs a .38 caliber wallop." Her smile this time was more confident. "Don't look so surprised. After all I am a lady spy. This is my arsenal. Do you know how to use it?"

Frazer nodded. She gave him the revolver, and he hefted it on his palm, amazed that the cool smooth feel of less than a pound of aluminum alloy could make him feel so much less vulnerable.

"Okay," he said, "now let's worry about Severing. Did you ever read CIA's dossier on him?"

"Read it? I practically memorized it."

"He comes here as a phony journalist, allegedly to get a line on Ernest Mitrović for Colonel Denikin. But meanwhile, what's going through his mind? He's struck out in the West, so he defects. Then at Bautzen he begins to get the idea, maybe, that he's just being used. Glaeske isn't interested in him at all. Glaeske's interested in me. Which means he's struck out behind the Iron Curtain, too. Along comes a crack at Yugoslavia and he jumps at it because . . . sure. He speaks Serbo-Croat. Denikin told me that. And he . . . what did Tommy Grayling say? Didn't Severing spend a couple of years down here during the war?"

"With the Wehrmacht. He would have been about eighteen

then. He was badly wounded and apparently left for dead. A personable teen-ager, I guess, because he was taken in by a family in Montenegro. He didn't get back to Germany until two years after the war was over."

"Titograd's the capital of Montenegro," Frazer said. "Budva's on the Montenegran coast, and Budva's where he left the motorcade."

"His friends again?"

"That's what it looks like."

"He talked about those two years freely. That's how the information got into his dossier. It was one of the big experiences of his life. They were Montenegran nationalists, a family named . . . damn it, I can't think of their name. It's right on the tip of my tongue, but I can't think of it. You're right about Budva. I'm almost sure they lived in Budva. It's not much of a city, if we knew the name we could . . . Njegoš!" Jane cried. "A man named Borislav Njegoš."

"Budva and Borislav Njegoš, okay," Frazer said. He looked at his watch. It was five after eleven. "If I start now, I ought to make it by a little after one. Get some sleep, why don't you? We'll all be on a plane for Zürich in the morning."

"I'm going with you," Jane said.

"No you're not. Get some sleep."

"Just in case you forgot, I'm a working girl. Dad wants me to see Severing."

"I won't argue with you, but . . ."

"Then don't. What bothers me is we could be leading Glaeske to your daughter."

"I don't think so," Frazer said. "'Cavtat's swarming with police. Glaeske can't make any kind of a move here. But you've got to figure the MfS will have the same kind of dossier on Severing that Dad has. Sooner or later Glaeske will come to the same conclusion—Budva and Borislav Njegoš. The only question is who reached those conclusions first."

Frazer went to the door. For the first time since his arrival in

Yugoslavia he knew he was getting somewhere. He said no more to Jane about remaining in Cavtat.

"I'd put it away if I were you," she said with a smile.

"Put what away?"

"The gun."

He looked down at the little revolver in his hand and thrust it into his coat pocket.

It is no more than forty miles as the crow flies from Cavtat to Budva, but the road follows the twisting coastline most of the way and takes a wide, serpentine detour around the Bays of Kotor. By the time you reach Hercegnovi you are in Montenegro.

At night, in the darkness along the corniche drive, there is no way of telling you have all but crossed a frontier, except for the briefly seen roadsigns written in Cyrillic. Montenegro, Frazer knew, had always been the trouble spot of Yugoslavia. Fifty years ago, King Nicolas I had declared it an independent monarchy, despite the Hapsburg hold on the rest of the country. Then had come the creation of Yugoslavia shortly after the First World War, and Nicolas, first and last king of the abortive monarchy, had died in exile in Paris. Under Tito's Federal Socialist regime, Montenegro was one of the six autonomous republics, and the word *autonomous* was the key to the thinking of the people of that mountainous southern region of the country. If most Yugoslavs, following Tito's lead, had come to distrust Moscow, most Montenegrans, following their own impulses, distrusted Belgrade. They were, Frazer knew, as proudly independent as the Basques of Spain, and capable of giving Belgrade the same hard time that the Basques traditionally gave Madrid. But while the Basques had their confrères across the border in France, Montenegro, tucked into the southwest corner of Yugoslavia, was Tito's march against Albania, and nobody liked the Albanians.

"You don't happen to speak Serbo-Coat?" Frazer asked hopefully, as they drove south out of Hercegnovi toward the Bays of Kotor.

"Not a word."

"I can count to ten and say *dobar dan,* which is *hello,* and, uh, *do vidjenja,* which is *good-bye,* and *please* and *thank you* . . . and I guess that's about it."

"Let's hope Mr. Njegoš speaks some German."

"Could be. It's what passes for a second language in Yugoslavia. Look at that."

Far off ahead of them they could see the lights of Kotor at the head of the fjord. Before starting, they had studied the Putnik-supplied map. Budva was less than fifteen kilometers beyond Kotor.

Frazer's mouth was dry. He longed for a cup of coffee, even the thick, harsh Turkish coffee drunk all over Yugoslavia. He stepped on the gas in a straight-away. The little Zlastva surged reliably forward.

They parked outside the Hotel Avala in Budva. The streets were deserted, and only two cars were parked for the night in front of the hotel, both with the YU nationality plaque of Yugoslavia. The surf rushed and ebbed below the great stone ramparts of the sea wall. A stiff wind blew in off the water.

A single lamp on the concierge's desk cast a feeble light inside the musty lobby. The concierge, a big old man with an enormous mustache which quivered with his snoring, came awake noisily.

"*Jest?*" he said, peering short-sightedly at them.

"Have you a telephone book?" Frazer asked in German.

"A room? You wish a room?" The old man's German was barely comprehensible.

"No. A telephone book."

A large toothless smile preceded the old man's creaky disappearance under the counter. He reappeared with a slender, tattered phone book.

Frazer opened it. All the entries were written in Cyrillic.

"I can't read Cyrillic."

"Can't read?" chuckled the old man. He thought that was very funny.

"We want to find a man named Borislav Njegoš who lives here in Budva."

"Who?"

"Njegoš. Borislav."

"Ah, so," sighed the old man. He licked a thumb and began to turn pages. He kept licking his thumb and turning more pages. He closed the book and started all over again. "Here in Budva, you say?"

"Yes."

"Ahh. Njegoš, Borislav. Shall I telephone?"

"No thank you. We want to find his house. Can you help us?"

The old man peered short-sightedly at the page he had settled on, scratched his head, disappeared under the counter again, reappeared with a tourist map of the city and a pencil, licked the pencil point, scowled at the map, and drew a large X and a small x on it.

"Here is Hotel Avala," he said, indicating the X. "Here is house of Njegoš, Borislav," he said, indicating the x.

Frazer took out a few crumpled dinar notes.

"No charge," said the old man.

"Then thank you."

"Do vidjenja."

"Do vidjenja."

The old man was asleep again by the time they left the lobby.

The house was on a small square not far from the city walls. A single palm tree stood sentry duty in the dim light of a distant street lamp. The buildings were shabby but imposing, with pock-marked stone façades and ornate balconies. No other cars were parked in the square.

Frazer checked the city map under the Zlastva's dome light.

"That's the place, if the old man was right," he said, indicating a building beyond the palm tree.

They walked across the square, their footsteps very loud on the cobblestones. The building they approached was four stories high. No more than four apartments to the floor, Frazer estimated. At most, sixteen in all, but no guarantee that the old man had sent them to the right address. And no guarantee, come to think of it, that their guess about Borislav Njegoš had been right. It had seemed logical enough in the comfortable, modern hotel room in Cavtat, but now, on the streets of an unknown city, in the middle of the night, he wasn't so sure. There were so many frustrating imponderables—even a lock on the street door of the apartment house would be enough to stymie them.

The door was not locked. Large and heavy, it opened easily. Beyond it Frazer had expected to find himself indoors, but instead walked with Jane into a cobblestone courtyard, like a small reproduction of the square outside. There was even another palm tree, appropriately smaller. Dimly he could make out a doorway at each far corner of the courtyard.

They tried the left one first, entering a pitch-dark vestibule. Frazer lit a march, and Jane came against him suddenly. A cat, hissing, streaked past them and outside.

The match revealed a flight of stairs going up and, along the opposite wall, eight mail slots, each with a name under it.

Frazer swore softly. "Cyrillic," he said. The match went out. The darkness was absolute.

"I took a year of Greek in college," Jane told him as he struck another match. In its glow she studied the mail slots. "First one's, um, Efendić," she said. "Um, no, no . . . here it is: Njegoš! It's number four, but how do we know what order they're numbered in?"

"Work our way up," Frazer said. "If Efendić is the first apartment, we count three from there. Or we light a match at each door."

"If they have names on the doors."

Their urgent whispering sounded very loud in the small vestibule. They started up the narrow wooden stairs, Frazer first, Jane following. The smell of olive oil and peppers hung heavy in the stairwell. The steps creaked.

Frazer lit a match on the first floor. "Efendić," Jane said, reading the name under the wrought-iron knocker.

There was another door before the stairs began again in back. "Next floor up in the rear," Frazer said tensely, wondering if the long chase were nearing its end, and letting the wonder trigger hope. Maybe Cindy was there, one floor over his head, sleeping now, in an alien bed, tired of running with Severing, afraid perhaps, never dreaming her father was this close.

They went up the stairs and along the hall. They reached the door, where Frazer lit another match. It flared briefly and went out—just enough time for Jane to see the name and say: "Njegoš."

Frazer's heart was pounding. He lifted and let fall the door knocker.

TWENTY-ONE

The door did not open a few cautious middle-of-the-night inches. It was flung open suddenly, and a large woman stood in the doorway wearing a faded robe on her Junoesque body and an expectant look, not quite a smile, on her broad, handsome face. Her large dark eyes stared out at Frazer and Jane, and the expectant look gave way to one of wariness.

"Frau Njegoš?"

"What do you want at this hour?" she asked in a deep voice, her German fluent. "Who are you?" They were not the questions of a frightened housewife faced with an unknown caller at one-thirty in the morning. They were asked boldly and with an almost aggressive self-confidence.

"My name is Frazer. This is Mrs. Hayward. We're Americans. We're looking for Borislav Njegoš."

"He's not home. Why are you looking for him?"

The advantage, Frazer realized, was hers, while she stood barring the doorway and asking more questions than she was answering.

"May we come inside?"

"Why?"

Jane said: "It's very important, Frau Njegoš. We wouldn't bother you if it weren't."

"If it's important to you, you can come back in the morning."

"We wouldn't be here now," Jane said, "if it could wait until morning."

The woman kept looking at Jane, and the big dark eyes narrowed. Frazer realized then that she was older than she had at first seemed. Forty-five at least, or a well-preserved fifty.

"I'm sorry," she said. "My husband is not here."

"Can you tell us where he is?" Frazer asked, then was sorry he had spoken. The woman seemed to have more rapport with Jane.

"No," she said, and started to shut the door.

Jane spoke quickly. "It isn't your husband we want to find. It's an Amer . . . a German, a man named Severing."

"Well," Frau Njegoš said with a cold smile, "is he American or is he German?" Then the smile faded. "What name did you say?"

"Severing. Curtis Severing. He was born German, Frau Njegoš. He's been an American since about 1950."

"Curtis Severing," said Frau Njegoš softly. "He is here in Yugoslavia? You must be mistaken."

"No, he's here," Jane said.

Frau Njegoš considered that for a moment. "What are you to Curtis Severing?" she asked finally.

"It would take a while to tell you," Jane said.

The big woman stepped back. Her face had grown pale. "Come in, please," she said.

It was a large, square sitting room, the ceiling high, the walls covered with faded rose velvet, the windows hidden behind floor-to-ceiling shutters, all of it lighted by an elaborate crystal chandelier. In that *fin-de-siècle* setting the furniture seemed out of place, contemporary and mass-produced without style, all pale wood veneer and nubby upholstery, purchased from a people's factory in Belgrade or Zagreb.

Frau Njegoš had disappeared through a doorway. "I'll only be a moment," she called. They heard the sound of crockery rattling. "Would you like some Turkish coffee?"

"Don't bother," Frazer said, and Jane gave him an amused but warning look, which seemed to say: I can get through to this woman, so how about letting me do the talking?

"We'd love some, if it isn't too much trouble," she said, and Frau Njegoš' voice came back:

"No trouble at all."

She returned in a few minutes, bearing a tray that held a burnished copper coffeepot, small cups without saucers, a bottle of *šlivovica,* and three glasses. The coffee smelled very strong.

After pouring the coffee and *šlivovica,* Frau Njegoš sat down next to Jane on the sofa.

The coffee was hot, strong, and grainy. Frau Njegoš raised her glass of *šlivovica.* "To Curtis Severing," she said. She drank, downing a hefty ounce of the harsh, colorless *eau-de-vie.* She looked down at the remaining ounce and drank that too, putting the glass down with a sigh and a flash of even white teeth. She leaned forward to refill her glass, her straight, waist-length black hair cascading over her face. Brushing it aside, she said:

"The last time I saw Curtis Severing was here in Budva. The war had been over for two years. He was a boy hardly twenty years old. What is he like now? In his forties, yes, a few years younger than I. He is an American now, you say?"

"That's right," Jane said.

The white teeth flashed again. "I am glad. It was I who taught him to hate his own people. And if one has no homeland . . . He is well? What does he look like, now?"

"Handsome," Jane said promptly. "Distinguished looking."

"Handsome, of course. Yes, always that. The last day, at the railroad station. I went down with Curtis to see him off. Our families had arranged my marriage to Borislav Njegoš. We had no words. There was no future for him here. Is he married?"

"No," Jane said. "He's not married."

"All these years and never married?"

"He's a bachelor," Jane said.

"Then only out of choice," Frau Njegoš said with pride. "He could snap his fingers and get any woman he wished." She laughed, deep in her throat, remembering. "Any woman he wished." She sighed again and got up and went to the shutters, opening them and gazing out at the dark night. She was a big, strapping woman, lost in her memories of the irresistible Curtis Severing. She turned abruptly and was in the present again. "But how could he come here, after all this time, and not see me?"

"You met him through your husband?" Jane asked.

"Boro's family and mine were with the *partisans*. We lived on Sveti Stefan, on the old pirate island like pirates, raiding the enemy. We fought the Germans. They had come, an entire corps of them, because no Italian army is a match for the men of Montenegro. You would like more *šlivovica?* Or more coffee?"

They had more coffee. Frau Njegoš sipped at a third *šlivovica,* her dark eyes wistful. Frazer fought and curbed his impatience. If the woman didn't know where Severing was, maybe her husband did. But Jane seemed content, even determined, to let Frau Njegoš reminisce. Frazer said nothing.

"They came one day. Paratroopers landing on our island. They chose a bad day. There was wind, and many of them were trapped in their own shrouds. We routed them. One was Curtis Severing. He was hardly more than a boy. I found them, Boro standing over him with a knife. It was that close—that close. The German boy looked so innocent, with his blue eyes and wild dark hair, like a gypsy—as if he belonged in the mountains of Montenegro. Boro raised the knife. I pleaded with him. It was those eyes, so wondering and innocent. Boro handed the knife to me. We took the boy in with us and nursed him. He regained his health. He lived among us, an enemy soldier, and then no longer an enemy or a soldier. His war was over. All of us on the island liked him. I . . . Curtis and I . . . Borislav knew what was between us, but he was older and patient, and he knew it would end."

Frau Njegoš had gone to the window again, the glass in her hand, standing with her broad shoulders and the deep curves of her hips framed between the open shutters, remembering in the night.

"Forgive me," she said at last, facing them again, her big dark eyes gleaming. "But it comes as a shock to know he is here after all these years. Why did he come back?"

"He's running," Jane said. "He's in trouble."

"Trouble?" said Frau Njegoš vaguely, still all wrapped up in the past. "With the Germans? Because he deserted? After twenty years, and they still . . ."

"It's the Germans," Jane said. "But another matter."

"Then why didn't he come to me? I saved his life once."

"We think he came to your husband for help. We're almost sure of it."

Without warning Frau Njegoš began to laugh. It was a harsh sound, torn from her throat like a sob. "To Borislav for help . . . now? To Boro at a time like this?"

"Where is your husband?" Jane asked softly.

"You said trouble. What kind of trouble?"

Jane cast a quick glance across the room at Frazer, who nodded.

"Severing was working for the American Army," Jane said slowly. "Secret work. Then he did something foolish. He began to supply information to the East Germans. They wanted more. He became involved with their secret police, and then he escaped. He came here. They came after him. They're looking for him now."

"And you?" Frau Njegoš demanded suspiciously. "Who are you? You say you're Americans, but you speak German."

Jane took her passport from her handbag and showed the pale blue plastic-covered booklet to Frau Njegoš. "We're Americans. See for yourself. We've got to reach Curtis Severing before the Germans do. Before it's too late. Tell us where to find your husband."

Frau Njegoš shook her head.

"Why can't you tell us?" Jane asked reasonably. "What are you afraid of?"

Frau Njegoš shook her head again.

"Whatever it is, is it more important than Curtis Severing's life?"

Frau Njegoš collected the coffee cups and the glasses, replacing them on the tray. She would not meet Jane's gaze, but looked sullenly down at the floor. "Go away," she said. "I have nothing more to say."

"Even though you hold Curtis Severing's life in your hands?"

"Go now. You have no right to do this to me. Leave me in peace."

She went to the door and opened it, her broad shoulders slumped. She looked old.

"I hope you know what you're doing," Jane said.

She got no response. They were through the doorway. The door shut softly behind them. They were in the dark hallway, groping their way toward the stairs. Then a shaft of light fell across them.

"Wait," Frau Njegoš said.

TWENTY-TWO

There was no moon, no starlight, no other traffic on the pot-holed coast road, except for a pair of headlights that dropped behind them as they left the outskirts of Budva. Their own headlights picked out rows of cypress trees and an occasional umbrella pine. Sometimes, when the road turned to the right, they could see below them the black sheen of the sea.

"Slowly now," Frau Njegoš said. "We turn off soon."

Frazer missed the sign but saw the narrow side road to the right as soon as Frau Njegoš did. She was seated in front with him, her weight tensely forward, one arm resting on the dash-board, obviously unaccustomed to driving at night. Jane sat in the rear, silently smoking.

The side road was narrow and poorly paved. It was a contin-uous series of looping switchback turns that gave frequent glimpses of the sea. On the shining blackness Frazer saw some-thing darker, more solid. He decided it was an island just off the coast.

"Sveti Stefan," Frau Njegoš told him, speaking the name of the island in a bemused voice, as though it could conjure up images that only she could see. "We must stop here," she said.

Frazer braked and pulled off onto the shoulder of the road. "In summer," Frau Njegoš told him, "Sveti Stefan is a hotel. The entire island, every cottage on it. In winter it is deserted, except for a watchman. He is my husband's friend, but just now I fear he has reason to be afraid. He might do something fool-ish. We will walk."

It took them ten minutes to descend, on foot, to sea-level. The sound of the surf grew louder, hissing sibilantly on the massive, eroded rocks. Halfway down the steep road Frazer could see a narrow finger of land, a causeway, jutting out across the water to the small island. There were no lights. The island itself presented a low silhouette against the sea; there could have been no building more than two stories high. They set foot on the causeway.

A voice hailed them in Serbo-Croat, a man's voice, sounding nervous.

"Ivo, Ivo Džeba," Frau Njegoš said. "If you have a gun, old man, put it away. It is I, Borislav's wife."

"Ivanka? Why do you speak German?"

"Because the people with me speak German."

"Who are they?" the voice asked suspiciously, in German.

"Friends of Curtis'."

"Friends? Have you heard the radio? We need no more friends now."

A flashlight winked on suddenly. Its beam wavered at their feet, then higher.

"I heard the radio," Ivanka Njegoš said wearily, squinting in the glare of the flashlight. "Curtis went with them?"

"Yes."

"Have they returned?"

"Not yet."

"We'll wait—on the island."

"The others . . ."

"The others obey Borislav. So do you."

"Perhaps," the old man said, "obeying Borislav is a mistake."

But he lowered the light to the ground again, and they followed him across the causeway.

The old man was as nimble as a goat, as he led the way along the narrow paths of the island. Two or three times Ivanka Njegoš cautioned him to slow down, especially when he leaped sure-footedly up or down a short flight of unseen stairs. There were more stairs than level stretches on the island's pathways.

They stopped at last before a stone cottage. The surf was

loud. A hundred yards off, the Adriatic stretched flat and black with only faint phosphorescence where the surf broke.

For a moment the old man stood still, gazing out across the blackness as though watching for something. Whatever it was he didn't see it. He turned, took four long strides and knocked on the cottage door. The beam of his flashlight, which he held cupped in his hand, gave only a feeble red glow.

The door opened. The flashlight went out. Frazer heard voices, Ivanka Njegoš' and a man's, arguing.

"He doesn't like it, but he says it is all right," Ivanka told them finally. "We can wait inside."

The door banged shut behind them, and abruptly there was light, the glow of a kerosene lamp on a wood-plank table in the middle of the large room. Frazer saw three windows with heavy blankets hung across them, styleless peasant furniture, none of it upholstered, a telephone on an end table, and two men wearing sheepskin jackets and baggy trousers. Dirty dishes were stacked on the table, and the remains of a salami and a loaf of bread. A dozen empty wine bottles had been piled in one corner of the room. On the table, alongside the dishes, was an almost full bottle of wine and a chessboard, the pieces large and ornately carved in ivory. A third man was seated at the table, huddled over the board, deep in thought, studying the pieces through round, steel-rimmed glasses. He looked up once, saw Ivanka Njegoš, nodded absent-mindedly, and returned to pondering the chessboard.

Of the two men wearing sheepskin jackets, the older was the watchman. He went outside again without a word to anyone. The other man called after him angrily, something to do with the light of the kerosene lamp, Frazer guessed, but the old man had opened and shut the door quickly, and was gone. The other man shook his head and slumped heavily into a chair at the table. He was a very large man, big all over but not fat, with a heavy stubble of gray beard and bloodshot eyes. He might have been drunk. He scowled at the chessboard, lifted the wine bottle and drank, grunted once, banged the bottle down, and moved a knight.

It was so cold in the room that Frazer could see his own breath. Jane, her arms crossed over her breasts in an attempt to keep warm, was shivering slightly.

"When does Severing return?" she asked Ivanka.

"I don't know."

"Where is he?"

The smaller man seated at the table looked up from the chessboard. His glasses hung low on the bridge of his nose and slightly askew. He had a gaunt face and a furrowed forehead. Deep brackets outlined his thin lips. His hair was thinning on top but neatly combed. He was wearing shirt, tie, sweater, and tweed jacket. He had shaved recently. He might have been, Frazer decided, fifty-five or sixty years old.

"You speak German well," he said, "but with an accent. Is it British?"

"American," Jane said.

"American. Imagine that," the man said in English. "I don't have much chance to speak English here. Are you from New York? Or California? Most Americans who visit Montenegro seem to be from New York or California."

"I'm from Pennsylvania," Jane said.

"Pennsylvania, yes. I always wanted to visit the United States. Instead I spent ten years in Sremska Mitrovika prison, where I knew not only Djilas but Ernest Mitrović. Is your friend also from Pennsylvania?"

"Virginia," Frazer said.

"Virginia. The South. Here in Montenegro, the south of my country . . ." he began vaguely, then shrugged, as though he found it difficult to make whatever point he was going to make in English, and changed the subject: "I taught English and American literature in Ljubljana almost ten years, and I have never been to England or America. Foolish, isn't it? Tell me, what do you think of John Steinbeck?" He did not wait for an answer. "Dated, I suppose? He is a writer who never came to terms with America after your Great Depression. And Hemingway? For Hemingway the style of living is everything. Not what you do—that is of no importance—but how you do it. How delightfully different from the Communist orientation, in which the means are of no consequence, no consequences whatever, but only the ends."

He looked up defiantly. "Using Hemingway as a springboard —is that the right word?—I tried to teach my students in Ljubljana that you cannot live with the ends if the means disturb you morally. Would you say that is a fair statement of the Hemingway ethic?"

"I think so," Jane said, looking at Frazer.

"Unfortunately, I attempted to apply those ideas to the political life of Yugoslavia. Ernest Mitrović, then the Minister of the Interior, did not approve." He laughed nervously. "Ten years in Sremska Mitrovika prison. Bulat is my name. Ante Bulat. Tell me, what do you think of William Faulkner? I have always found Faulkner dull, but perhaps that is because I do not understand the South."

"I grew up there, but I'm not sure I understand it either," Frazer said.

"People say the same about this southern corner of my country," Ante Bulat said. "Montenegro as a consequence has suffered tragically in the twentieth century. In 1923 there was the massacre of the Moslems. My own father took part, riding down from the mountains and killing with the sword like a Cossack. Moslem blood flowed in the streets of Budva and Hercegnovi. Even women and children were slaughtered. I asked my father why, but he did not know why.

"Then during the Second World War there were more massacres. The Chetniks under Mijailović were Serbs, the Communists under the Marshal and Ernest Mitrović, Croats—but Montenegro is neither Serb nor Croat. What did their civil war mean to us? Now the Marshal and Ernest Mitrović say there is only one Yugoslavia, but the men of Montenegro remember.

How can we forget? Blood flowed in the streets of Budva and Hercegnovi again, and it was not only Moslem blood. You had to fight the Nazis Ernest Mitrović's way, or not at all. Anything else was treason. No, we remember."

Ante Bulat rubbed his pink, cleanly shaven face. "Now, with the Marshal in his seventies and the possibility of Mitrović taking over . . . That would be two generations of Croat power. Meanwhile they release Djilas from prison also, Djilas who is a man of Montenegro, but the day he opens his mouth politically is the day he returns to Sremska Mitrovika. The chain must be broken. We want no Croat dynasty and no more blood baths in Montenegro. But don't you see the tragedy of it? The only way to fight the anachronism of a dictatorship is to use the methods of the dictatorship. What is to be done?"

Again Ante Bulat rubbed his face. "You are a Hemingway man, then? Believing in action, with morality? I approve. I would like to hear you argue that point—Faulkner versus Hemingway—with the young lady inside."

Frazer was so intent on the strange literary and political monologue, on the old pirate island, at two o'clock in the morning, by the former professor of English and American literature at the University of Ljubljana, that it took a moment for the words to register.

"What did you say?"

"The young lady inside. Your countrywoman. She has a decided preference for Faulkner. She maintains that Hemingway . . ."

"Where is she?"

"Sleeping. How wonderfully well the young can sleep."

"I want to see her."

"Why not?" Ante Bulat said.

TWENTY-THREE

The room was dark. In the light of the candle that Bulat had given him, Frazer could see two beds, two chairs, a blanket-covered window, a sink, and a high, narrow wardrobe. From hooks above the sink two toothbrushes hung. One of the beds had been made up: the pillow puffed invitingly, the blanket stretched stiffly across the mattress with one corner folded back. Someone was asleep in the other bed.

Frazer shut the door softly. The candle flame flickered, then brightened. Standing there, just over the threshold, the candle in his hand, Frazer did not move. It was cold in the room and only the top of the sleeper's head and the dark hair spread on the pillow showed. Then an arm emerged from under the covers, a girl's arm, slender and delicate, wearing a baggy striped pajama sleeve, and then the face appeared, Cindy's face, child-like in the unconcern of healthy sleep. Frazer took a step toward the bed. In a moment he would wake her. He had the feeling that it would be a beginning, as if God or fate took two strangers, one a girl of nineteen, the other a man of forty-one, and said, you are the daughter, you are the father. It was a beginning, but he did not know how to begin.

He took another step, and she stirred again, the not-quite-awake lips moving and softening, almost in a smile, the eyelids fluttering, the face only slightly swollen now, the lashes soft and dark against the pale, smooth cheeks.

He wanted the moment to stretch and last, the father awake and alert and feeling capable because he had not been tested, the daughter asleep and defenseless and feeling a drowsy contentment because she had been asked neither to give anything she did not have—or having, did not want to part with—nor to accept anything she did not require.

Then Cindy was sitting up in bed suddenly, the ridiculously large striped pajamas shapeless on her body. She blinked at the candlelight and stretched her arms.

"Curtis? Is it all finished?"

"Man outside," Frazer said gently, "claims you like Faulkner better than Hemingway. I told him you were nuts."

"Daddy!"

She sprang from the bed and rushed into his arms. For an instant he felt her body against his, her complete, and because complete, temporary surrender. She was laughing or crying, probably both, and her hands were kneading his back while his were patting her shoulders awkwardly through the coarse pajama jacket.

"What are you doing here? How did you *get* here? I'm dreaming, I've got to be dreaming."

Then the moment was over. She sat on the edge of the bed. He sat next to her, warily, holding the candle. Hot wax dripped on his fingers.

"I'll get something," she said, and returned with a glass from the sink. She set it on the night table upside down, took the candle, let wax drip on the glass and attached the candle.

"Now then," she said with grave humor. They were his words, spoken many times—when she was a little girl, spoken severely because punishment or at least criticism was in the offing, when she was more mature, spoken with a certain wry humor because they both knew what was coming.

"Is Curtis back yet, Daddy? Have you met him?"

"No, not yet."

"What time is it?"

"Almost two-thirty."

"I'm worried. They should have been back."

"Where'd they go?"

"Up the coast. In a boat."

"Curtis and who else?"

"A man named Njegoš. Curtis knew him during the war."

"I know. Do you know what's going on?"

"Well, I'm not exactly fluent in Serbo-Croat," Cindy said with a forced laugh.

"Can you guess?"

"Something to do with a man named Mitrović. He just got out of jail. He's a politician."

"There was a dinner for Ernest Mitrović in Cavtat last night. That's his home town."

"I know. I was staying there."

"You and Severing joined Mitrović's motorcade to Titograd, Severing as a reporter, but you left the motorcade in Budva. How come?"

"Daddy, I wish you wouldn't throw questions at me like that. I'm not on trial."

He knew she was right. He knew he should have waited, but he also knew he couldn't wait. Severing would return—and then what?

"If only you knew Curtis the way I know him."

"I know a lot about him."

"That's not the same thing."

"All right. Tell me."

"He's gentle and . . ."

"Was he gentle when he did that to your eye?"

"I told you. I took a fall skiing," Cindy said with her earnest, wide-eyed expression. "What can I do if you don't believe me?"

"I want to believe you, Cindy. Show me I can."

"I . . . all right," she said defiantly. "You're right. Curtis did it. But it was my fault. He had to do it. He loves me. Honestly he does." Cindy looked up at him. "Daddy? Aren't you going to say anything?"

"What am I supposed to say? That I'm glad he loves you enough to give you a black eye and break your rib?"

"You don't understand. It wasn't the way you think it was at all."

"Then how was it?"

"The German, Colonel Glaeske. It was because of him. Curtis wanted me to go with him, but Colonel Glaeske said no."

"Said no? It was what he wanted all along. He wanted Severing to defect so he could get his hands on you. Severing was nothing. Nothing."

"He was sent on an important job down here," Cindy said with stubborn pride.

"Not by Glaeske he wasn't. Colonel Denikin sent him."

Cindy's laughter was less forced this time. "Oh Lord," she said, "I guess it shouldn't surprise me. Nothing you do, once you set out to do it, ever surprises me, Daddy. You followed us to Bautzen, didn't you?"

"I followed you to Bautzen."

"You would be," Cindy said with wry nineteen-year-old wisdom, "hell on wheels to be married to. You know why?"

"Uh-uh. Tell me."

"Because you're the most absolutely capable man in the history of the known universe, that's why. You want to do something, no matter what it is, and somehow you get it done. It's frightening. I won't even ask you how you got to Bautzen. Knowing you, you probably got personal permission, in writing, from Walter Ulbricht."

Suddenly some of the tension had left Frazer, and he was smiling. How a child sees her father, he thought.

"What's so funny?"

"If you only knew,"

"Tell me."

"No, it's not important. What was Severing trying to prove to Glaeske?" But it was important, and part of its importance was that he could not, or would not, tell her. She thought of him as capable, as implacable, and he supposed that in many ways, and from her point of view, he was. But the one area in which he lacked confidence, and thus capability, was the area that ought to have concerned her most. He lacked it as a father.

"They had an argument. It was the night of the fondue party on Wasserngrat. Curtis said he'd go with Colonel Glaeske only if

I came too. I said I wasn't sure I wanted either one of us to go."

"You did?"

"Curtis told me to, before. It was his way of proving things to Colonel Glaeske. He said he had to show Glaeske he had me wrapped around his little finger. We argued. It must have been pretty convincing to Glaeske because he let me come."

"I told you Severing had Glaeske figured all wrong. He wanted you to come. Severing was the means of getting you to Bautzen."

"I can't believe that."

"Is that when Severing beat you?"

Was he harping on it needlessly, the outraged father? Or did he want to drive the point home because there would be a showdown with Severing when he returned to Sveti Stefan? Frazer wasn't sure himself.

Cindy looked away from him. "I wish I didn't have to tell you," she said. "You'd never understand in a million years."

"Why don't you try me?"

"He didn't really mean to hurt me. Not like that. He just slapped me. I knew he was going to do it, but still. I was supposed to stand there and take it. One or two slaps, you know? But . . . I don't know, nobody ever hit me like that before. I saw red. I hit him back. Then he started in punching me. It was all my fault," Cindy finished lamely.

Of course, Frazer thought, and it was also the fault of the woman who had lived with Severing in Saanen before Cindy came along. Women apparently goaded Curtis Severing to violence. God, he thought what's she gotten into? And how can I get her out of it without making her hate me?

"What happens when he comes back?" he asked.

"What happens? I don't understand."

"There's a woman with me. A Mrs. Hayward. You met her in Gstaad, I think. She works for the CIA. A man in Curtis Severing's position can't just defect and expect a few pairs of shoulders to shrug in Washington. They could make a pretty good case against him for treason."

"Because he looked into his own heart and decided what he had to do?"

"Severing's decision to defect was a pragmatic one," Frazer said, more sharply than he had intended. "Make no mistake about that. A lot of Germans working for American intelligence are double agents. We know it, and the Reds know it. There comes a time when their usefulness to both sides drops to about zero. That's what happened to your friend Curtis Severing."

"He's not German, he's American," Cindy said with childish, stubborn logic. "And anyway he's more than a friend."

"Has he asked you to marry him?"

Cindy managed a wan smile. "Oh, Daddy, if you could see your face! The American father, afraid his daughter's been compromised. It's so Victorian."

"Has he?"

"We haven't actually spoken about marriage."

"Do you want to spend the rest of your life behind the Iron Curtain?"

"Yugoslavia isn't behind the Iron Curtain."

"Does Severing plan on staying here?"

"I'm not sure. I guess so."

"Because there's no more future for him in East Germany than there'd be in the States?"

"You keep throwing questions at me."

"All right," he said after a while. "All right. I'll try not to. Cindy, listen to me. I'm flying back to Switzerland tomorrow, with Mrs. Hayward. I want you to come with us. I want you to go back to Geneva, back to school, back to the life you have to lead before you're ready to decide what kind of life you want to lead."

"What if I said no?"

"I guess I'm saying you can't say no."

"It's not that simple, Daddy. Look at me. Do you see the

nineteen-year-old co-ed spending her junior year abroad? Somebody who would enjoy being flirted with by . . . by a kid like
Tommy Grayling?"

"Grayling's all right," Frazer said. "Maybe you think he's a
kid, but he's doing a man-sized job for the CIC."

"Tommy Grayling?"

"Tommy Grayling."

"You mean all the time in Gstaad he was . . . spying on
me?"

"Keeping Curtis Severing under surveillance, yes."

"*Gray*ling? I thought he liked me."

"He does like you."

"I can't go back to Switzerland," Cindy said dramatically.
"I've changed. I'm not a child any more. These pajamas—whose
do you think they are?"

He knew what was coming. It had been there all along, from
his first conversation in Gstaad with the Küblis. It had been
there in Saanen, outside the chalet, when Cindy had looked up
at Severing and kissed him. It had been there again in Bautzen,
with Cindy and Severing living in the married quarters, and
with Mrs. Marvin Rice saying little Cinderella was happy. It
was there now, in the shared bedroom, with a bed turned back
for Curtis Severing and Cindy dressed in his baggy pajamas,
with the two toothbrushes hanging together on their hooks over
the sink. But all along he had tried to put it out of his mind.
She was Cindy, she was his daughter, she was a child.

"I . . . I don't have to put it into words for you, Daddy," she
said. "Do I?"

He wished he knew what the right words were. There were
words, if he could find them, that would ease her pain at having
caused him pain and disappointment. There were words, if he
could find them, that would get her over the notion that she was
now a grown woman because she was a fallen woman, and that
there was no going back.

"There's a whole lot of co-eds in the States," he said gently,
aware that the South was creeping into his voice "who have a

casual affair with their professor. They get over it, Cindy. Lots
of girls go through a phase of finding older men attractive. It
doesn't change their whole life."

"A casual affair?" Cindy said. "You think it's like that?
Daddy, if you could only understand."

"I'm trying to understand," he said, a little stiffly. He touched
her shoulder tentatively. She drew away.

"Curtis is about your age," she said. "He even looks a little
like you, Daddy. That wouldn't surprise Mr. Freud very much,
would it? If you only knew how much I admired you, all my
life. From the time I was a little girl and even . . . well, despite your politics? But that's the whole point. Your politics are
exactly one hundred percent correct, and it comes natural to
you. It's one of the reasons you're the most capable man in the
whole known universe. It's one of the reasons, maybe, why I
joined AFID. Remember that dapper little hypocrite in Caine,
Alabama? What was his name?"

"Mr. Breeze. I remember. And dapper little hypocrite de-
scribes him perfectly."

"I was so proud of you then, and I couldn't say it. I just
couldn't. You're so hard to . . . to live up to. You're awesome."
She smiled at him, finally, a real smile. "There, I said it."

"It's nice to know I'm awesome. I will study my awesome face
with considerable interest from now on every time I shave."

"Daddy, you're making fun of me."

"No I'm not. I'm trying to understand the same things you're
trying to understand. Awesome. And pretty hard to get close
to?"

"Putting it mildly. You have this wall. The sign says no trespassing."

"What about you?"

"I want people to get close to me."

"Severing?"

"Sure, but other people too."

"No, I mean is he hard to get close to."

"Curtis? Oh, no. That's the whole difference. He's not capable like you. He's just the opposite. In one way or another he's been running all his life. He needs me. He needed me almost from the first minute we met. I feel so sorry for him. I feel so . . . important, knowing how much he needs me. Can you understand that? I can't leave him. I could never leave him in a million years."

Now what do I say? Frazer wondered. Do I tell her that to mistake pity for love is foolish and dangerous? Do I offer some pompous parental platitude on the improbability of a nineteen-year-old girl mothering a man twice her age? Do I tell her that cholera needs a host organism too?

He said none of those things. There was a light tapping on the door and Jane called softly:

"Brad? A boat. They're coming."

TWENTY-FOUR

A cold wind blew in gusts across the island, carrying salt spray like a fine, driving rain. It was totally dark except for the glow of Curtis Severing's cigarette. He dragged deeply on it and in that moment his face came out of the darkness, gaunt and haggard, but handsome.

"Look," he said. "What's the point of this? I'm beat. I want to curl up somewhere and sleep for about a year." He had a deep voice and a faintly wheedling manner of speaking, as though he expected objections to every phrase he uttered.

"This won't take long," Frazer said. They stood in the lee of one of Sveti Stefan's ancient buildings, but the wind had a way of coming around corners to seek them out. Frazer turned up the collar of the topcoat Charlie Evans had supplied him with in Berlin.

"Okay, just make it fast, will you? Old Ivo's prowling around out here somewhere, and he's scared. He's liable to shoot first and ask questions afterwards."

"As soon as it's light," Frazer said, "I'm driving up to Čilipi with Cindy. We're flying out of here. What about you?"

"That's a laugh. You think they'll just let you waltz off this island?"

"Why shouldn't they?"

"You've got to be kidding," Severing said. "Don't you know what you walked into?"

"No. Tell me."

"They're a bunch of wild-eyed fanatics. Bulat, the disillusioned intellectual. Potučnik who sits around playing chess all the time and remembering how his father was executed as a

Chetnik spy, thanks to Ernest Mitrovič. My old buddy Boro Njegoš. Montenegro *über alles,* and the crazy notion that he can get a revolution going by . . . I'm talking too much."

"By assassinating Ernest Mitrović?"

"All right," Severing said slowly. "By assassinating Mitrović. Look how far that got. On the radio they said Mitrović was hardly scratched. They call themselves the Committee for Montenegran Autonomy," he went on in his complaining tone of voice. "They're the ring-leaders. They have maybe fifty members, all mildly nuts or worse, full of paranoid ideas that Belgrade's bleeding this part of the country dry and . . ."

"And you went along for the ride," Frazer said.

"Well what the hell else could I do? I looked up Njegoš in Budva, while Mitrović was making his speech. I have a few hundred marks, and after they're gone what am I supposed to do, starve to death? The man they had to pilot the boat chickened out, and I'm a pretty good guy with an outboard motor. Njegoš paid me good money to take him up to Cavtat."

"Did you know what he had in mind?"

"I knew it would be something cockeyed. I didn't know how cockeyed until he pulled the bomb out from under a tarp. You can forget about taking off. They'll never let you."

"Frau Njegoš might."

Severing considered that. "I never thought of Ivanka," he said. "She still has a soft spot in her heart for a Kraut kid who dropped onto this island once upon a time. You really think she can talk them into letting us go?"

"What would you do if she did?"

"You mean, would I come with you? Christ, yes."

"And then what?"

Severing tossed his cigarette into a puddle, and the darkness was absolute again. "Yeah, I see what you mean. I'm kind of in a jam. Money. It's always money. Things just got out of hand, that's all. I was in debt. A little bit of gambling, nothing I couldn't handle, and then a whole hell of a lot of gambling, and before I knew it I owed a pile. The MfS paid me pretty good money, just when I needed it. Not that that's an excuse," Severing added quickly. "I did a stupid thing. I regret it."

"The MfS paid you good money," Frazer said dryly. "Njegoš paid you good money. Ivanka has a soft spot in her heart for you, and so does Cindy. A bit of an opportunist, aren't you, Mr. Severing?"

"What's that supposed to mean?"

"I thought it was pretty clear."

"Okay, you're a flag-waver, you don't understand how a guy can get in a bind, you don't like me. So what?"

"Cindy," Frazer said. "She likes you."

"She's a good kid," Severing said.

"She thinks she's in love with you."

"We've been through a lot together. She's young. You know how it is."

"No. How is it?"

Severing laughed anxiously. "What do you want me to say?"

It was not, Frazer realized, a rhetorical question. Curtis Severing, opportunist, was willing to bend whichever way the wind blew. If Frazer played the aggrieved father, insisting that Severing make an honest woman of Cindy, Severing would go along with that for a day, or a week, or however long it was necessary to get out of what he called the bind he was in. If Frazer told him to keep away from Cindy, he would do that as willingly. He had charm, as proven by Ivanka Njegoš or Cindy herself. What he did not have, what he totally lacked, was substance. Like so much of the human flotsam cast up on the beaches of Europe by two world wars and the threat of atomic destruction, he was a hollow man.

Or maybe, Frazer thought, he was being unfair to Severing because Cindy was involved. He said, "Say we all get out of here. Then what?"

"You mean what about Cindy?"

"Yes. Cindy."

"I'm a wrong guy, I'm no good for her. You'd want me to keep my distance . . . is that what you're trying to say?"

"I'm not trying to say anything. I'm asking you."

Severing laughed anxiously again. "I can't read you," he said. "Give me a clue, Mr. Frazer, will you?"

"Cindy thinks she's in love with you. I want whatever she wants. What if I asked you to marry her?"

"Are you serious? I'm twice her age. I . . ."

"I'm serious," Frazer said, and Severing answered gravely, "I think I could make Cindy happy."

"What if I asked you to keep away from her? Permanently."

"Hey, what is this?" Severing said. "I don't get you at all."

"I asked you a simple question. Answer it."

"If that's what you thought best for Cindy . . ."

"You'd agree to keep away from her, if we all got out of here?"

"We both want what's best for Cindy, Mr. Frazer. We see eye to eye on that," Severing said earnestly.

"You'd marry her?" Frazer asked.

"But you just now said . . ."

"Would you?"

"If that's what . . . yes. Yes, I would."

"You'd keep away from her?"

"Listen, what is this? You keep putting words into my mouth. I don't know what you want me to say."

"You've already said it," Frazer told him. "Now I'm going to make a small speech. For your sake I hope you didn't open up to Colonel Glaeske in Bautzen, because the next person you get to use your charm on is a CIA agent, and she could be willing to make a deal with you. After that you're on your own. Come within shouting distance of Cindy and I'll break your goddamn neck."

Severing said nothing for a while. Then he said: "Why didn't you say that in the first place? For a while there I thought you wanted me to make an honest woman of her. Christ, you had me worried. I mean, Cindy's a good kid. I like her. But do I look like the kind of guy who wants to settle down? A wife would only cramp my style. I've got plans for myself, big plans."

"You've made a great success of them so far," Frazer said.

The big man named Potučnik and little Ante Bulat were still playing chess. Borislav Njegoš and his wife were in a corner of the room, arguing. Ivanka Njegoš towered over her husband, who was a flabby moon-faced man with a befuddled expression on his face and a large, unkempt mustache. He looked a tired and disillusioned sixty. Ivanka was doing most of the talking. He would nod, he would shake his head, he would get a word or two in edgewise, until Ivanka's throaty voice, hardly more than a whisper, silenced him.

"They've been inside a long time, Daddy," Cindy said. She was wearing parka and ski-pants. Her dark hair was tied back in a pony-tail. "Can Mrs. Hayward really help Curtis?"

"Maybe. It's up to him."

"She's nice. I really like her. What did you and Curtis talk about outside?"

"How we're going to get out of here, mostly."

"That's all? I thought . . ."

"Severing's got a lot on his mind."

"The way they like him here," Cindy said proudly. "Did you notice? That's the way he is. He's got friends all over. I know he's had a rotten deal, but once he . . ."

Her voice broke off as Ivanka Njegoš approached them, her husband trailing two steps behind.

"Tell them, Boro," Ivanka said firmly.

Njegoš looked at them. He looked up at his strapping handsome wife. He cleared his throat. "If you agree to leave Yugoslavia absolutely as soon as possible," he began.

"They agree," Ivanka told him. "Of course they agree."

"Then the Committee for Montenegran Autonomy," Njegoš continued, clearing his throat again, "will not object to your leaving Sveti Stefan."

"The Committee," Ivanka said bitterly. "After last night there is no Committee. Just you, Ante, and Potučnik."

"The Committee," Njegoš said, "has met with a setback. Revolutionary movements have survived such setbacks before." His eyes were wide, showing white all around the irises. "It is the cause that determines the fate of men, not the reverse. We proved that here on Sveti Stefan once before. Can you deny that?"

"No, Borislav," Ivanka said.

"The Committee must awaken the people of Montenegro."

"We'll talk about it later, Borislav," Ivanka said gently.

"One small setback merely increases my determination . . . The men of Montenegro must rise . . . A small determined group, totally committed . . ."

His voice had risen. It was high and strident at the end of his barely coherent speech. Potučnik's head turned slowly. The big man got up from the table. In the light of the kerosene lamp his face was a ruddy mask. He spoke slowly and haltingly for some time, his voice a monotone. He kept shaking his head. Borislav kept staring at him, disbelief in the wide eyes. After a while Potučnik turned to Ivanka and showed her the palms of his big hands. He said something contritely, and Ivanka nodded. A slow smile of relief spread on the big man's face. He went back to the table and spoke to Ante Bulat.

"They're quitting," Ivanka said in German, not looking at her husband.

"A small, determined group, totally committed," Borislav Njegoš said. Despite the cold, he was sweating. Droplets had collected in his mustache. He brushed at them irritably. "Naturally, they are quitting," he went on. "It does not surprise me. They knew. They both knew. They would not tell me. The arbor in Cavtat. The wire. They knew all about the wire. They knew the bomb could not reach its target. What a trusting fool I've been! The government. Yes, naturally. They were in the pay of the government all this time. Why don't you leave me also, Ivanka? He's back. Your lover is back. You don't need me now. Go with the German. The war will end soon, he will return to his own country, they will forget that he deserted. Go with him. Don't you think I know what's been going on behind my back? What sort of fool do you take me for?"

He did not wait for an answer. He stalked to the door and yanked it open.

"Borislav," Ivanka called. There were tears of pity in her eyes. She started after him.

Her husband ducked his head into the high sheepskin collar of his jacket and plunged outside, into the wind and darkness. "Germans!" he screamed. "Parachutists! Nazis! He's here, the deserter Curtis Severing is here! Severing . . ."

A volley of shots rang out.

Potučnik, moving very quickly, reached the door before Ivanka. A gun had materialized in his hand. He stood to one side, waiting. A second passed. Another. Then there were slow footsteps.

Borislav Njegoš appeared at the doorway. He came inside, past Potučnik, walking slowly. He reached the center of the room. Potučnik shut and bolted the door. Ivanka Njegoš went to her husband. He tried to say something. He smiled a tired, shy smile and said, "Yes, naturally," and then the blood welled up suddenly past his lips and he fell.

TWENTY-FIVE

Ante Bulat came out of the bedroom. He spoke to Potučnik for a while in Serbo-Croat. He said in English: "A grave wound, but he is still alive. There is internal bleeding."

Fifteen minutes had passed since the shooting. Frazer and Potučnik had carried the wounded man into the bedroom. His wife and Jane were still with him.

"He is ranting," Ante Bulat said. "It is 1944 all over again. The Nazis, he says. The Germans are here. It is the Germans who shot him."

Frazer didn't say anything. Severing licked his lips and stared at the door. Cindy was seated at the table, her face pale and set.

"You should have known that man before," Ante Bulat said. "He was . . . how can I explain it? . . . a driving force. He spoke, and you listened. If he said you could walk from here to the Albanian border on your bare feet, you would be proud to do it. He had a tremendous will, a single purpose. Montenegro. What does Montenegro matter to him now? Even if he lives . . ."

Ante Bulat sighed. "We were friends from the time we were children," he said. "Tell me, do I surrender to the police, now, so that he can have a doctor? He may die anyway. He may not even wish to live."

"That's not the police out there," Frazer told him.

Ante Bulat stared at him blankly.

"Would the police just start shooting? They'd use a loud-speaker, wouldn't they, try to get you out of here with your hands up?"

"Not the police? I don't understand."

"They're Germans. After me and Severing. We could use the phone to call the police, and get that doctor."

"The phone? It is not an outside line. It connects with a phone in the main building. That's the only outside telephone on the island."

Jane came into the room. There was a dark stain on the collar of her trenchcoat. "He's unconscious," she said. "Every time he breathes, there's blood. We've got to get a doctor for him."

Potučnik, who had been prowling the room restlessly, went to the window. Gingerly he lifted a corner of the heavy blanket hanging over it. Glass shattered, and there was the sound of a single shot. Potučnik let the blanket fall. He nodded solemnly, poking a large finger at the hole in the blanket.

The telephone rang.

They all looked at it. It rang again. Potučnik chuckled, shaking his head in disbelief, as though gunfire and a ringing telephone were incompatible. Ante Bulat picked up the receiver, listened for a moment and said: "They want Severing."

"Me?" Severing said.

"A man's voice. He spoke German." Bulat handed the phone to Severing, who stood there dumbly with the old-fashioned standard in one hand and the receiver in the other.

"It's Glaeske," Frazer told him.

Severing cupped his hand over the mouthpiece. "You've got to be kidding."

"No, it's Glaeske all right."

Severing took his hand off the mouthpiece. "Yes?" he said, clearing his throat. "This is Severing."

He listened. He said yes once and no twice. He listened some more. "Then I guess you do," he said, and took the receiver slowly from his ear. Frazer could hear the click as Glaeske hung up.

"Just what kind of bastard does he think I am?" Severing said slowly.

Cindy went to him. He put the phone down and took her hand. Frazer turned away from the look in her eyes.

"He said it's not me he's after. He wants you and your father. If I deliver you I get to walk out of here. That's what he said. He's got three men outside. They come in after us as soon as it's light. They come in shooting. There's no hurry, he said. We're not going anywhere. We saw what happened when somebody tried. When they can see, they come in and get us. Unless I deliver you first. What does he think I am?"

Cindy turned into his arms. "I know what you are," she said, holding him tight. "You're the man I love."

The man she loved, responding stiffly to her embrace, stared over her head at the bolted door.

Half an hour had passed. It was almost four-thirty. In less than two hours, dawn.

Potučnik had opened another bottle of wine. He was sitting at the table, drinking steadily, staring morosely at the walls. Jane had gone into the bedroom and returned. There was no change in Borislav Njegoš' condition. Cindy and Severing sat close together, talking. Severing was chain-smoking.

It had been a slow, blank half hour for Frazer. As long as they kept away from the windows, there was no gunfire. As long as they sat there, waiting for Glaeske to come in after them, there was no danger. That would change at dawn.

"We were like brothers," Ante Bulat told Frazer. "I want you to understand. I am not a violent man. The inclination to violence was all Borislav's, the ideas mine. You put two chemicals together, each one harmless in itself, and you get an explosion. That was Borislav and me. This Mitrović business . . . I wanted to say no. I thought I would say no. I waited for the moment, but the moment did not come. Look at me. I was a teacher. All I ever wanted was to be a teacher. Do I look like a wild-eyed revolutionary? Tell me, perhaps a man does not understand himself at all. And now Borislav is inside, dying. And if your Germans don't get us, the police will. What is to be done now, can you tell me that?"

A man resorts to violence, Frazer thought, when his back is to the wall. For Ante Bulat, former teacher, jailed for his ideas, free now but barred from his profession, violence was the answer to intellectual frustration. For Colonel Glaeske, now, violence was a means of protecting himself. And for me? Frazer wondered. My back is sure as hell to the wall. What do I do about it, Ante Bulat, for whom violence was never a way of life? What do I do about it, Colonel Glaeske, for whom violence was always so much a way of life that you could hope to enlist Severing's aid merely by announcing your intentions on the telephone?

What is to be done, Ante Bulat? I'm a product of the twentieth century, the most dangerous but the most sheltering of all centuries, reasonably intelligent, reasonably fit, reasonably sure that Glaeske is going to come in here shooting in another hour and a half. And I sit here, Ante Bulat, listening to your hair-shirted confession and waiting, as Glaeske wants me to wait, while he himself waits in the darkness out there somewhere . . .

The telephone.

Glaeske wasn't outside. Why should he be? He had gunmen for that. All he had to do was wait, out of danger, beside the telephone. That was where he was now. He had to be.

". . . bleeding to death, and I cannot lift a finger to help him," Ante Bulat was saying.

"Maybe you can," Frazer said.

"How? There is nothing. Nothing."

"If we could get to the phone, we could call the police. They'd send a doctor."

"The police? The police would love to get their hands on us now. What good would the police do Boro?"

"They could save his life," Frazer said flatly.

"And afterwards?"

"He's mentally disturbed. They'd take that into consideration."

"What about me? Or Potučnik?"

"His life," Frazer said, "or your freedom. It's up to you."

Ante Bulat just looked at him.

"Where's that phone?"

Bulat rubbed his pink, clean-shaven face. "Let me think. I don't know, let me think."

From the bedroom doorway a woman's voice said: "There is no time to think. I want my husband to live." It was Ivanka, her face pale, her dark eyes fixed accusingly on Bulat. "Any time until now was the time to think. Now is the time to act."

"If Boro could only tell us what he wishes for himself."

"I am telling you."

Bulat stared at her over the rims of his glasses. "Ask Potučnik," he said. "Let Potučnik decide."

But Potučnik's big head was down on the table alongside an empty wine bottle.

"An intellectual who cannot make up his mind," Ivanka said bitterly, "and a drunkard. These are my husband's friends, and he is in there, on his back, bleeding to death."

"The sea wall," Bulat said at last. "Walk to the sea wall and turn left. Follow the wall for two hundred meters. You will reach a staircase going up and a big building. In summer, it is the dining room and the casino. You will find your telephone there."

Frazer looked at the snub-nosed, aluminum alloy revolver. He broke the cylinder open—a bullet in each of five chambers and the sixth, which would fall under the hammer when he swung the cylinder shut again, empty. The revolver smelled of oil and was cold and slightly slippery to the touch. He clicked the cylinder into place, shoved the revolver back into his topcoat pocket. He looked at the bolted door. In a moment he would go through it, gun in hand, into the darkness, where three men, also holding guns, were waiting to kill him. He felt remote, as though watching a character in a play prepare for the inevitability of violence, the possibility of sudden death.

"We'll go out the bedroom window," Severing said. "They won't expect that."

"What?" The gun was in his hand again. He hadn't been aware of removing it from his pocket a second time.

"The bedroom window. With luck they'll never see us leave."

"You're staying here," Frazer said. "Someone's got to."

"I don't see it that way. The important thing's getting to that phone. They won't move in on us till it's light. Glaeske said so."

"The bedroom window," Frazer said. He felt a wild impulse to laugh. "They could have walked in on us. Just like that."

Ivanka shook her head. "They would have found me waiting for them." She showed him a long-barreled gun, an automatic. "A German Luger, from the war. I am a good shot."

"I'll bet you are. That makes two of us," Jane said. "Brad, if I had a gun I'd say Severing's right. He ought to go with you."

"What is she saying?" Ivanka asked in German.

Frazer told her.

Ivanka smiled faintly. "I don't believe Potučnik will miss his." She went to the table and returned with another Luger. Expertly she pulled the butt-plate and slammed it back into place with the palm of her hand.

Frazer took the Luger from her and gave the little revolver to Jane. He waited for some sign of fear in himself. There was none. He had to walk out of there, and find his way to Glaeske, and shoot to kill if necessary. His legs would do the walking, his eyes would see what had to be seen, his right hand would hold the Luger. He still felt that odd remoteness, but impatience too. He wanted to get it over with.

Cindy was talking to him, her eyes big. She kissed him. She was talking to Severing. She was trying her hardest not to cry. Severing said something that made her smile, and she held him with the trusting vulnerability of a child.

The door. The hallway. The dark bedroom. The wounded man's gasping fight for air and life. Jane's hand in his, and her voice a soft whisper: "There are two dames in here who think the world of you, Bradley Frazer. As we say in southern Pennsylvania, y'all come back, heah?"

"I'll come back," Frazer said.

Jane opened the casement windows to the sound of wind and surf. He was on the sill and over it, waiting for gunfire. There was none. He felt Severing's leg swing against his back. They were standing on the wet, slippery cobblestones. They could see nothing.

Glaeske's three gunmen could see nothing.

He groped for and found the cold stone wall of the cottage with his left hand. The Luger was in his right.

He started walking. The wind howled, the surf roared. He could not hear Severing's footsteps or his own.

TWENTY-SIX

There was very little wasted space on the island of Sveti Stefan. Pirate's lair, fishing village, hotel—whatever its function, all its small area had to be utilized. You could walk from one end of the island to the other, in the maze of crooked narrow paths and staircases, on the slick, worn cobblestones and, except for an occasional crosspath, always have solid stone walls on both sides. If you stood in the middle of a path and stretched your arms, you touched stone with either hand. If you held a gun in one hand and made your way through the darkness, there was still the comforting feel of one wall. No one was going to take a shot at you from any distance, even assuming he could see you.

But the architecture of the island made the possibility of an ambush more acute. Glaeske's men could have been waiting anywhere, behind any corner, provided they could see. But they can't see any better than we can, Frazer thought. And they can't hear us any more than we can hear our own footsteps.

The pounding, sucking sound of the surf under the sea wall grew louder. With each step they took they were drenched with spray. Frazer could taste the salt on his lips. Another step and he encountered something solid. The surf thundered directly below. It was the sea wall.

They walked along it, faster now, sure of their way. Two hundred meters more, all of it along the wall, a staircase going up, then the watchman's quarters, the casino, and Glaeske.

The spray was continuous, like a driving rain, one wave smashing itself to spume even while another was ebbing back. They were almost ankle deep in icy water. Once, suddenly, Severing was down. Frazer helped him to his feet.

"All right?"

"Hurt my knee. I'll live. Come on."

They went slowly after that, Severing in obvious pain. Maybe I misjudged him, Frazer thought. He didn't have to volunteer for this. Maybe I was just being the protective parent, ready to condemn before I understood, ready to insist that no man is good enough for my daughter. He's made mistakes, sure, and he's had to live with them, but who hasn't?

They reached the staircase, water streaming down the steps like a spillway. When they started climbing, for the first time Frazer could feel the fear. His mouth was dry. It was difficult for him to swallow. There was a tightness in his legs. He felt awkward. His finger on the trigger of the Luger, the safety catch still in place, was stiff with cold.

There was a small stone landing, the upper sea wall, and a door set in a stone recess. There might have been windows too, but Frazer couldn't see them.

Now what? he thought. Do we try the door? If it opens, do we just walk in?

He ran his free hand across the door. The wet smooth wood was studded with metal. A small diamond-shaped window with bars across it was cut into the middle of the door. He could see nothing through the glass. It was as dark inside as out. The fear, which had been so long in coming, grew. Maybe Glaeske was on the other side of the door, six inches away, smiling, waiting to shoot.

Maybe Glaeske wasn't in there at all.

He walked as far as he could on the small landing and reached another wall. There was no break in the façade of the building, no window he could touch except the small window on the door itself. The only way in was through the door.

He stood in front of it again, not knowing what to do. He felt Severing touch him, and Severing was talking against his ear: "Try the door. If it opens we go inside running. If it's locked he might hear you. Shoot the lock out, and we still go inside running. He doesn't know we're here. We'll have a few seconds before he can think straight. Okay?"

"Okay," Frazer said. "Ready?"

"Now."

Frazer felt for and found the door latch. It was locked. He thumbed the Luger off safety, the fear gone now, except for the dryness in his mouth, and pulled the trigger. Flame spouted from his hand and the Luger slapped back against his palm three times. The sound deafened him. The acrid smell of cordite was in his nostrils as he hit the latch with his free hand and the door with his shoulder.

The door held for one terrible moment, and then it gave.

They were inside and running even before the door banged against a wall.

Three seconds of darkness and then, abruptly, light from an ornate chandelier overhead. Frazer stood there, blinking, the Luger hanging from his hand. A gun roared twice and a bullet ricocheted somewhere close by, whining.

Severing threw himself down behind a tarp-covered chair, crouching there, breathing hard. Frazer dropped to his knees alongside.

They were in a large lobby, the walls rough-hewn, the almost threadbare Persian carpets and ornate chandelier out of place, the high-backed chairs all covered with canvas, a long stone counter running the length of the lobby, keys hanging in neat rows behind it on a wall of empty pigeonholes.

The chair that was their protection was heavy and over-stuffed. Frazer wondered, almost calmly, if it could stop a bullet.

Severing touched his shoulder and pointed. The stone counter. If Glaeske had thrown the light switch and fired almost in the same instant, he had to be behind it. Twenty feet away, perhaps twenty-five. Another chair, halfway, the only cover. Frazer heard the wind behind him, through the open door. No other sound. At the far end of the counter he saw a stone archway with a door set in it. On the counter, a dozen feet this side of the archway, stood the telephone.

He leaped, keeping low, for the second chair. A single shot

crashed. He could hear it thud into the upholstery. The chair tilted back on its rear legs and then settled as he reached it. On his knees he pushed it with his shoulder toward the counter, using it as a shield. The Persian carpet bunched and the chair almost went over again. He shouldered it closer to the counter. Less than ten feet now.

If Severing were armed, covering him with fire as he approached, it would have been simple. But Severing wasn't armed.

Glaeske didn't know that. If Glaeske thought Severing could pin him down, behind the counter, giving Frazer a chance to reach him, the German might panic. Panicking, he might empty his gun at them.

"Cover me," Frazer shouted. "I'm going in on him."

Glaeske's response was instantaneous. Three shots rang out in quick succession, one of them thudding into Frazer's chair, driving it back against his shoulder, the other two for Severing.

That made six shots. If Glaeske had a revolver, he was all through. If he had a Luger, which was more likely, that left him one bullet. And even if he had fresh cartridges, it would take him time to reload.

"The door!" Severing cried. "Behind you."

Frazer's chair nudged the counter. He pivoted and started to rise. A man he had never seen before, tall, blond hair plastered wetly to his head, raincoat drenched, came running through the doorway. He had a gun and fired it once, the bullet striking the side of the counter and sending splinters of stone stinging against Frazer's face. Frazer fired twice. The blond man screamed and buckled at the waist, slamming back into the doorway and down.

Then something heavy smashed with shocking force against Frazer's left shoulder. He heard the shot as though it were far away. He clung to the top of the chair and looked up and saw Glaeske, rising now, above the counter, the bald head gleaming under the light of the chandelier, the rectangular face expressionless, the gun, an automatic, a Luger as he had thought, pointing at him, not three feet away, and suddenly there were two Lugers, two Glaeskes, and the numbness in his shoulder, no pain as yet, sapped the strength from him. He thought he was going to faint the instant before Glaeske shot at point-blank range and killed him, and then his vision steadied on one Luger and one Glaeske and he raised his own gun, it wavering all over, and fired, missing, not even close, unable to hold his hand steady.

Glaeske squeezed the trigger. The Luger made a clicking sound.

He saw Glaeske running along his side of the counter, one hand at his pocket, fumbling there, then the hand free of the pocket with a fresh clip for the Luger, and by then Glaeske was at the archway and through the door and running with Severing right behind him.

Frazer, on his feet, was lurching after them. His knees felt weak and oddly uncoordinated, as though the mechanism of ball and socket no longer fit properly. His left arm, completely numb, hung straight down at his side, flapping uselessly against his hip. He reached the archway and went through it without waiting to find out if Glaeske had reloaded yet. There was tardy fire, two shots, almost as an afterthought, and then he was down on his knees, feeling the warm wetness on his shoulder and chest, behind something large and bulky, kneeling next to Severing.

He had expected the casino, but the room, dimly lit by the light streaming in behind him, was too small for that. He saw a rack on the wall, with billiard cues standing in a neat row. They were down behind a billiard table. Beyond it, on the far wall, was a bar, the back-bar shelf empty, the mirror reflecting the table and doorway.

"He's back there," Severing said. Then he looked at Frazer. "You're hit."

"No, I'm okay."

Silence for half a minute. They could hear the wind only faintly.

Then Glaeske's voice: "Mr. Frazer, can you hear me?" Calmly, almost in a conversational tone.

Frazer said nothing. Severing fidgeted and coughed nervously.

"Mr. Frazer, I believe you fired three times at the door. Is that correct? Three times. And three more times inside, I believe? A fine German weapon, the Luger, seven shots in all. That leaves you one bullet, unless of course you had the forethought to come equipped with fresh cartridges, as I did. Did you have the forethought, Mr. Frazer? No? A pity. What are you going to do with your one bullet?"

Frazer did not speak. The pain was beginning in his shoulder now. He clenched his fist experimentally on the Luger. His hand was steadier. He could fire, and fire accurately, if Glaeske exposed himself.

One shot. And if he missed?

Something crashed in a corner of the room. Silence again, then Glaeske:

"You impress me. That was a bottle. I was hoping to draw your fire. Is this a bottle also, Mr. Frazer?"

Another crash. "If I raised my head, quickly, once, would you shoot? One chance, Mr. Frazer, that's all you'd have. And if you missed?"

Something moved behind the bar. For a split-second Glaeske's face appeared. He ducked out of sight again. "What? Can't I draw your fire at all?" he taunted. "Are you afraid, Mr. Frazer?"

Severing, crouching near Frazer, changed his position. He coughed nervously again.

"I am prepared to make a deal with you," Glaeske said. "You have only one bullet, Mr. Frazer. You are not going to leave this room alive. But what about your daughter? Would you like her to live? Nineteen years old, isn't she, with her whole life ahead of her? Throw your gun on the floor. Surrender to the inevitable, and the child goes free."

It wasn't, Frazer knew, a serious offer. It was ridiculous, and Glaeske must have known it was ridiculous even as he made it. He had to kill Cindy, just as he had to kill Frazer. Then why bother making the offer at all? Surely he doesn't think I'm fool enough . . .

Not me, Frazer thought suddenly, shockingly. He's really talking to Severing.

"My men have their instructions, Mr. Frazer. You understand, unless I stop them, they will kill the girl. Are you going to be pig-headed?" Glaeske called across the room. "Can't you convince him for me, Curtis?"

Severing crouched there, studying Frazer as though he had never seen him before.

"The phone," Frazer said in a tight whisper. "I can cover him here. Can you get back to the phone?"

Severing looked over his shoulder. There was twenty feet of bare stone floor between the end of the billiard table and the doorway. The last half of it was exposed to fire from the bar.

"Cover him? With one bullet?" Severing licked his lips. In the dim light Frazer could see the sheen of sweat on his face. "He'd shoot me dead before I reached the doorway. He'd kill us both. He's going to kill us both anyway. We're dead," Severing shouted. "We're as good as dead."

His words echoed from across the room: "As good as dead. Precisely, Curtis. Unless . . ."

Frazer looked at Severing. His eyes had narrowed, his mouth was open, silently repeating the word unless.

"Why should I kill you, Curtis? The Ministry for State Security can use your services. That was our mutual plan all along, wasn't it?

"Wasn't it, Curtis Severing?

"Wasn't it?

"Otherwise, why did you defect?"

"Stop it!" Severing cried. "I don't want to hear any more, stop it, make him stop!"

He crouched forward and came up with a billiard ball from the tray under the table. He hurled it. The back-bar mirror shattered. The ball bounced and rolled across the floor.

After that Glaeske was silent, waiting.

It had to be the phone or nothing. They had to reach it, and reach it within the next few minutes. Had to call the police, mention Babunović and the UBDA if necessary, get the police to Sveti Stefan, in force, before dawn.

Ten minutes had passed without Glaeske saying anything else. The phone, and one bullet in the Luger. Someone had to crawl back across the floor and out to the lobby. Severing had refused to try it. Someone, with that single bullet, had to cover Glaeske. How can I trust Severing? Frazer thought. He wants to live. I can't blame him for wanting to live. Suppose I give him the gun. Suppose I try getting back to the lobby. One bullet, to keep Glaeske from taking a potshot at me, and then nothing. He's afraid. He's switched sides before.

I could take the gun with me. No I can't. It would be impossible to crawl back to the lobby and cover Glaeske at the same time. It would be suicide.

Give the gun to Severing, and hope. That or nothing.

He tried to move his shoulder. It was stiff and painful. He didn't think it was bleeding now.

"I'm going to make a try for the phone," he whispered.

"He'd kill you before you reached the door."

"I've got to try it."

"He'd kill us both."

"You already said that," Frazer told him savagely. "You want to sit there and let them kill Cindy?"

"I don't want to die."

"Okay, wait. What happens if we wait?"

"I don't know. I don't know anything now." Severing was almost sobbing. "Tell me what to do."

"If we wait, they finish what they have to do at the cottage and come up here after us."

"Tell me what . . . to do."

"I'm going to give you the gun," Frazer said.

"I can't cover you with one bullet. Don't ask me to. It's impossible."

"All right. No covering fire. I know that. Glaeske may get a shot at me. He may not. Don't shoot unless you get a good shot at him. You shoot to kill, or you don't shoot at all."

Severing looked at him. He shook his head. "Don't make me do it."

"I've got to," Frazer said.

He held out the gun.

"It won't work," Severing said.

"Take it."

"You don't know what you're doing. Don't make me."

"It's the only chance we have."

Severing shook his head.

Frazer put the gun in his hand. Severing stared down at it. His hand was trembling.

Easing himself around slowly, Frazer began to crawl toward the door.

For the first ten feet there was no danger. He wouldn't come within Glaeske's range of vision until he was halfway to the door. The light was brighter there ahead of him, but still not good. In bad light, at a distance of thirty feet or more, a handgun was only a moderately reliable weapon. He did not know what kind of shot Glaeske was. If Glaeske missed, he might expose himself for a better shot. That would give Severing his chance.

On his right elbow and his knees, Frazer paused. It was hard work without the use of his left arm. He was sweating. As nearly as he could judge, he was just short of the point of no return. Another foot or two at the most, and Glaeske would see him. One tremendous effort, he thought. Get up, maybe, and run. Cover those last ten feet as quickly as possible, even if that meant presenting a standing target. He looked back over his shoulder. A corner of the billiard table still hid the bar. He craned his neck further and saw Severing.

Severing had turned to watch him. He was sitting cross-legged on the floor, right elbow on his knee, the Luger in his hand pointing at Frazer. He saw Frazer looking at him.

I gave him the gun, Frazer thought. He warned me. He knew what was going through his own mind. I didn't listen.

He's going to shoot me.

"Damn you," Severing said.

Frazer waited for the shot.

"Why'd you have to turn around?"

Frazer waited to die.

"I can't," Severing said. "I can't."

He looked at Frazer a moment longer, on the floor, at point-blank range, and then he was on his feet, the gun still in his hand, swinging around to face Glaeske and shouting:

"I've got it, I've got Frazer's gun. Come and get him."

Glaeske's head appeared behind the bar, and the Luger. "You made one mistake, Curtis," he said gently. "I wanted both of you."

He fired twice, and Severing was hit, jerking back but clinging to the edge of the billiard table with his left hand. His torso slumped across the green felt. He raised his head and his right arm. There was another shot. Glaeske's head snapped back. His jaw was no longer there. He fell behind the bar.

Frazer went to Severing first. He was still slumped across the billiard table, the Luger, empty now, still clutched in his hand. He was dead. Glaeske next, behind the bar, sprawled grotesquely in the narrow space, head against the bottom of the back-bar shelving, legs jackknifed against the bar, jaw gone, eyes wide and sightless, the Luger on the floor. Frazer retrieved it and stumbled toward the lobby.

He was going to kill me, he thought. If I hadn't turned around. But I did turn and then . . . what? He couldn't do it.

He was going to let Glaeske do it. Or was he? He exposed himself to Glaeske's fire. He didn't have to do that.

It was one way to get a shot at Glaeske. Maybe the only way.

Did Severing know that, in the last moment of his life?

What do I tell Cindy?

He lurched past the billiard table where Severing lay, and
went out to the telephone.

TWENTY-SEVEN

Tommy Grayling, boyishly enthusiastic under the neat crewcut, his eyes smiling behind the shell-rimmed glasses, came into the room. It was a large, airy room, the big french windows thrown open to the morning sun, the furniture authentic French regency, the view from the windows showing an ornamental garden, a grove of olive trees, and beyond that the sea.

"Quite a pile," Grayling said. "I sort of expected a dungeon, or a good old-fashioned Balkan jail anyway. Who do *you* know?"

"He doesn't like hospitals," Jane Halladay said. "You should have seen him when they tried to keep him in one."

"But a palace?" Grayling said. "At least it looks like a palace."

"That's exactly what it is," Jane said. "Miločer. It was the summer residence of the royal family, when Yugoslavia had a royal family. It's a hotel now. I guess the Security Police figured our Mr. Frazer needed a vacation. Seriously, Tommy . . ."

"Did you call me Tommy? What happened to Mr. Graph?"

"We've got to humor the patient. He doesn't like Mr. Graph. Or Mrs. Hayward. Or Mrs. Halladay, for that matter. He also says he doesn't like creamed spinach or steak, unless it's rare, and, let me see, what else don't you like, darling?"

"What's going on here?" Grayling said.

"We wish we could say you were the first to know, Tommy, but there's Cindy, and a UBDA agent named Babunović and . . . oh heck, Tommy, congratulate us, will you?"

"The name's going to be Mrs. Frazer as soon as we can arrange it," Frazer said.

Grayling ran a hand, back to front, through his crewcut. "Pinch me before I kiss the bride," he said. "I didn't even know you *liked* each other."

He kissed the bride-to-be. He shook Frazer's hand. He looked at the cast on Frazer's shoulder and left arm. "Nobody told me about that either," he said.

"Nobody told you about a million things," Jane said. "Want to get started? It'll only take about a year."

"That's why I'm here," Grayling said.

He sat down, and Jane started talking.

An hour later, Frazer was saying: "Babunović and the UBDA played it cagey. They saw someone from the East German embassy in Belgrade yesterday, and they decided to let the East Germans carry the ball. If they wanted to own up to an MfS colonel coming down here to commit murder, that was all right with Babunović. At least that's what he said. He was bluffing, of course. He knew they never would. Glaeske was just Fritz Leser, camera dealer from Dresden, who somehow got involved with Njegoš' Committee for Montenegran Autonomy. Same for his henchmen. Two of them are still alive, and they get to be tried by the Yugoslavs for complicity in the attempt on Mitrović's life."

"They had a whole hell of a lot to do with that, didn't they?" Grayling said dryly.

"Man from the East German embassy had a little talk with them, Babunović said. They'll get a jail sentence, but it won't be stiff. They'll keep their mouths shut."

"What about this Njegoš guy? He'll have to cooperate too, won't he?"

"They still don't know if he'll live," Jane said. "His wife will do the cooperating. So will a funny little man named Bulat, who's the least likely terrorist I ever saw."

"He's lucky," Frazer said. "They could have thrown the book at him, and he knows it. They're not going to. Instead he testifies the way they want him to testify about Fritz Leser, and he'll wind up with the minimum sentence. Leser was just a soldier of fortune. That's the way it will come out at the trial."

"What about you?" Grayling said.

"Us?" Jane asked innocently.

"We never set foot on Sveti Stefan at all," Frazer said.

"This Babunović I've got to see," Grayling said. "He could teach CIC a thing or two." He lit a cigarette. "I'll probably have a million other questions, but I can't think of a thing now." He was smiling, and then he stopped smiling. "How's Cindy?" he asked.

"It's been pretty rough on her."

"If there's anything I can do," Grayling said. "You know how I feel about her."

"Give her time, Tommy. She has to find out who she is all over again. She's been sleeping a lot and taking long walks on the beach and . . ."

"And," Jane said, "if I ever saw trust in a girl's eyes, it's when she looks at her father. She's going to be all right."

"Where is she?"

"Asleep," Frazer told him. "She'll join us for lunch."

"Tommy," Jane said, "maybe you ought to have that talk with Babunović. To see how it's done. Can you learn to say Curtis Severing went to Bautzen as a CIA plant to warn Major Halladay that he'd been blown?"

"Hey, what is this?" Grayling demanded.

"Curtis Severing was sent to Bautzen as a CIA plant to warn Major Halladay that he'd been blown. His way of getting out of Bautzen was to come here. He knew Boro Njegoš and his wife during the war, and three days ago he saw Mrs. Njegoš in Budva. He went to Sveti Stefan for her, to try to convince her husband to surrender himself to the police. He would have succeeded, except for Fritz Leser, who refused to surrender. Leser drew a gun. He shot Severing, and Severing shot him."

"Jesus," Tommy Grayling said.

"That's what my report to Dad is going to say."

"How will you make it stick? Who sent Severing to Bautzen as a plant, for crying out loud?"

"Why, that part of it's simple, Tommy. I did."

"Jesus," Grayling said again. "I can't do it. How can I do it?"

"You're going to," Jane told him. "For Cindy."

For Cindy, Frazer thought, and he heard their voices, arguing, and he knew Jane would have her way, but he was back on the island again, having called the police, waiting in the lobby, Glaeske's Luger in his hand, the seconds dragging, the minutes crawling, and suddenly he remembered that they were waiting too, in the cottage, not knowing, and he did not know how to call them.

Glaeske, he had thought desperately, Glaeske had done it, hadn't he? He searched the shelf under the counter. There had to be something, some way of reaching them. He found maps, tourist brochures, an old newspaper. Nothing.

Then he saw the empty pigeon-holes behind the counter, the keys hanging neatly on their hooks, each key with a little brass plaque and on each plaque a number.

He started at the beginning, dialing, letting each number ring just three times before trying the next. He did not know how long it took, but finally he heard Jane's voice: "Hello? Brad? Brad?" He hardly knew what he was going to say. He sat there, looking at the phone, saying nothing. "Brad?"

Then the words just came out and what he said was: "You're going to marry me."

"Brad, Brad, you're all right, thank God."

He felt drunk. "Did you hear what I said?"

"You said I'm going to marry you."

"I'm going to marry you. Is that what I said?"

"That's what you said."

"I'm going to marry you," he said. He thought she was crying.

He told her what had happened. He thought he was going to

tell it straight about Severing, but he was no longer sure what the truth was. "I was shot," he said. "Glaeske shot me. Wait. In the shoulder. I'm all right. Severing got the gun from me. Glaeske and Severing shot each other. They're both dead."

They talked some more. He didn't remember about what, except that she wouldn't tell Cindy. He wanted to tell Cindy himself. He hung up finally. The wind had died down. He heard the sound of a car, of more than one car. Somehow he found the strength to drag himself outside. There were headlights on the causeway. Three cars. He heard a quick volley of gunfire, saw the spurts of orange flame. A pale gray dawn stood in the eastern sky. He went, one slow step at a time, down the stairs.

Cindy and Jane came running toward him. Cindy's long dark hair was flying. She reached him first. He leaned against the sea wall. He could hardly stand.

He took Cindy's arm, high up near the shoulder. He squeezed it hard. She was laughing and crying at the same time.

"Listen to me," he said. "You were right about Severing. I was wrong. He didn't have to come up here with me. He did. I never would have made it without him. He saved my life."

"I knew it, I knew if you just . . . Daddy? Where is he? Daddy?"

"He saved my life. He got Glaeske before Glaeske could finish me. He's dead, Cindy. He died saving my life."

Cindy was against his shoulder, crying. He looked over her head at Jane, straight into Jane's steady gaze, and he thought: She knows, she knows.

But how could she know? He didn't even know himself.